SWANNA
IN
LOVE

dead ink

First published in the US in 2024 by Akashic Books.
First published in Great Britain in 2024 by Dead Ink,
an imprint of Cinder House Publishing Limited.

Print ISBN 9781915368584
eBook ISBN 9781915368591

Cover design by Emma Ewbank / emmaewbank.com
Typeset by Laura Jones-Rivera / lauraflojo.com

Printed in Great Britain by CPI Group (UK) Ltd, Croydon

www.deadinkbooks.com

Supported using public funding by
ARTS COUNCIL ENGLAND

Funded by UK Government

MIX
Paper | Supporting
responsible forestry
FSC® C171272
www.fsc.org

SWANNA IN LOVE

JENNIFER BELLE

dead ink

For my brother, Matthew

People do not give it credence that a fourteen-year-old girl could leave home and go off in the wintertime to avenge her father's blood but it did not seem so strange then, although I will say it did not happen every day.

—Charles Portis, *True Grit*

We fell in love, I knew it had to end.

—Bruce Springsteen, "Hungry Heart"

1

There were two buses—one to New York and one to Boston. I got on the New York bus and sat next to Jacquie Beller.

She pointed out the window to someone's older brother. "I just had S.E.C.," she said. "With that boy. It was so great."

S.E.C. was short for serious eye contact. It was one of our main goals all summer. He turned and caught us staring at him. "I'm putting that on my list," she said. "I don't ever want to forget it."

The worst thing about being on this bus was that Labor Day was in eight days and then school would start, which was unimaginable but that wasn't going to ruin the two and a half hours that lay ahead of us. We had plans to take the love quiz in *Seventeen*, make lists of things that happened at camp, and pass around our address books to get everyone's phone number. She had forced her mother to mail her the *Weekly Wag*, which was a New York City newspaper that had personal ads in the back, like if a man saw a woman at a concert or on a street corner, but was too shy to ask her out, or couldn't because she was with another man at the time, but he was sure she was the love of his life, he could put an ad searching for her in the back of the *Wag*. We loved reading those.

One of the male counselors got on with a clipboard and read off everyone's name who was supposed to be on the bus to New York.

"Jacqueline Beller?"

"Here."

"Nedim Adem?"

"Here." He was from Istanbul, Turkey, and someone was going to pick him up at the bus stop and bring him straight to JFK.

"Janie Rand?"

"Here."

"Swanna Swain?"

"Here," I said.

Then another counselor got on the bus and said something to him.

"Oh, Swanna, you have to get off the bus actually. Your parents are picking you up. Your mother called the office."

"Not *my* mother," I said, confused, and a few people laughed even though I hadn't meant to be funny. I'm one of those people who always gets a laugh for absolutely no reason.

"Really, you have to get off the bus," the counselor said.

My father had moved out before camp started, actually last Christmas, which was one of the reasons I got to go to camp in the first place, so I knew there was no way they were picking me up together, unless—I actually wasted my own time thinking—they weren't going to go through with the divorce.

"I don't think my parents would do that," I said. "They're separated." Even though my voice accidentally caught on the word *separated*, a few more people laughed.

"Well, I guess it's just your mother coming. But you have to get off the bus."

"My mother doesn't even know how to drive," I said.

I hadn't heard from her the whole time I was there although I'd written to her once a week at the address she'd given me for the artist colony where she was spending the summer. The other reason I got to go to camp.

I started to panic a little. My father would be at the bus stop waiting for me in New York. I didn't know what to do. I got up and walked to the front of the bus, intending to explain to the guy more privately that I would have to call my father first to check that I really was supposed to not come home.

When I got to the front of the bus, I saw my bags had been removed from the luggage compartment underneath and placed on the grass.

"I'm really sure I'm supposed to be on this bus," I said.

He showed me the little piece of scrap paper with someone's scrawled handwriting. *Swanna Swain—mother will pick up!*

"Mother? Or *father*?" I said.

"The bus has to go, Swanna."

I tried to think if there was anything I especially needed in my duffel bags. My contact lens kit was in there, the saline solution, enzyme tablets, and the machine I needed to disinfect them. But maybe I could just leave them there and stay on the bus and drive off without them.

"This sucks," I said. Again people laughed as if I had my own personal live studio audience. Something told me I should stay on the bus. Just sit back in my seat next to Jacquie and pretend I had narcolepsy or something. In two and a half hours I would be back in New York City. My father would be at the stop waiting for me.

We would have dinner someplace great. Shakespeare's for a burger or McBell's for a chicken pot pie. I liked McBell's even though their salad dressing was a clear thick mucusy sauce with little red dots strangely suspended in it and their bread had raisins in it.

"I wouldn't tell you to get off the bus if you weren't supposed to get off," the guy said.

"I'm going to stay on the bus because my mother doesn't know that my dad made special plans to pick me up, and when she comes someone in the office can just tell her."

"She is supposed to be on the bus," Jacquie said. She was standing in the aisle.

"I'm sure your parents communicated with each other," the man said.

"I'm sure they didn't," I said.

I started to head back to my seat but the man literally grabbed my arm. He actually blocked my way and sort of forced me off the bus like an SS officer in Nazi Germany, and the doors closed in front of me. I just stood there holding Jacquie's copy of the *Weekly Wag*.

I watched the bus drive down the dirt road, past the infirmary and the tennis courts, until it was out of sight.

I went to the office cabin to call my father, but the door was locked. I went to the phone booth on the porch of the canteen and dialed my father's number with a 0 in front of it. "Collect call from Swanna," I told the operator.

But the phone rang and he didn't pick up. "The party you are trying to reach is unavailable," the operator said after I forced her to try three times. He was probably out buying some snacks for me to eat when I got home. I couldn't wait to pop open a Tab.

I never saw a place empty out so fast. Over the next three hours, the counselors, music and dance teachers, the entire staff hot-tailed it out of there. It was sad, like when you see a clown smoking a cigarette before the circus. Seeing camp empty kind of ruined it. There was not a scrap of food left on the entire campus.

There had been one car in the parking lot, but when I came back from trying my father again, I was startled to see it gone.

I sat on the grassy hill with a scowl on my face.

I took off my high heels and laid them on the grass next to me. The leather on the heels was worn down. I'd worn them every day the whole time I was there. I took my diary out of one of my duffel bags and tried to write but the sentences came out too short and fast like trying to talk between sobs.

I looked at the *Weekly Wag*. Jacquie and I had called one of the ads in the back. It was visiting day and her parents took us both to dinner at the Red Lion Inn in Stockbridge, Mass. They had a room there because they were making a weekend out of it, and while they were at the bar we went up to the room and called the number in the ad from the hotel phone. A man answered. "Hi," I said, "I'm calling about the ad you placed in the *Wag*. I think I might be the woman you're looking for."

"You're kidding," he said, sounding incredibly hopeful.

"Well I was in row C, seat 11, and I was wearing a brown suede jacket and I have long blond hair and aviator glasses and I was with someone," I said, reading the details he had put in the ad. "But I did definitely notice you."

"I can't believe it," he said.

Jacquie had her face plastered next to mine, trying to hear him.

We talked for a while about how great the concert was, and then I could tell Jacquie was starting to get nervous that the phone bill would be too big. And then I blew it. I pronounced John Prine like *Preen*, and the man said, "What?"

And I said it again, "I just love John Preen."

And the man said, "I think it's Prine. I've never heard anyone pronounce his name like Preen." And then I hung up and Jacquie and I laughed hysterically for about an hour.

I couldn't wait to be in my own bed without the bottom of the upper bunk twelve inches above my face, coffin style. I wanted a forty-five-minute shower.

When I first laid eyes on the bunks I didn't think I could take it. I'd never been claustrophobic, but the idea of us sleeping on top of each other like that reminded me of photos I'd seen of the Holocaust. I had a split second to claim one, top or bottom. Both seemed bad but top seemed unimaginable, sleeping up there like a doll on a shelf. On the bottom, I imagined some girl's long hair hanging down ghoulishly as she peered over the edge of the top bunk. I took bottom because hoisting myself up there seemed impossible.

Just the day before, our towels had been merrily hanging over the wooden porch railing trying to dry. I couldn't even remember it now.

I sat on the hill and flipped through the *Wag*. It came out every Wednesday and cost seventy-five cents. This one was dated August 11. I had never paid any attention to the *Wag* but Jacquie said it was essential to get it, along with *Backstage*, every week in case there were any auditions for kids. It also had something Jacquie said was called a "Sex Column." We didn't know why it was called that since it just seemed to be by a sociology major and the weird dates she went on with a man she called "PhD," which stood for pretty hot dad. Jacquie and I couldn't believe how idiotic that sounded. I flipped through until I found her column.

Ten Great Things about Dating a Man Who's
Twenty Years Older Than You
By Mistress Amber

"The heart wants what it wants—or else it does not care" is a famous quote from Emily Dickinson. Your boyfriend might not know who Emily Dickinson is, but I can assure you mine does, and that's refreshing. Daisy and Rhonda and I were sitting around talking about men yesterday and they couldn't understand why I'd want to fall in love with a man twice my age. While they admit the boys they've been seeing are hopelessly immature, they still wonder what I could possibly see in my salt-and-pepper-haired scientist. I assure them he's not that old, but no matter what I do to convince them otherwise, they still see him as a cane-wielding, toothless elder. They don't know about his gorgeous eyes and magic tongue and great apartment, and of course I'm the one using the cane. While Rhonda was buying her guy a subway token because he lost his waiter job and Daisy was on another Staten Island Ferry

date, PhD and I were dining at Café des Artistes and planning a jaunt to the Cape. No, Rhonda, he is not "all wrinkly." He's forty-two, not one hundred and two. He might moan and groan once in a while, but only for the right reasons. And no, Daisy, I'm not worried if I marry him he'll die and leave me a grieving widow. No one knows the future after all, and I look great in black. So, I have compiled a list to help you understand the many pros of dating my prof:

1. *He has some money in his pocket.*
2. *His parents are dead.*
3. *He's busy with his children every other weekend.*
4. *You will always be so much sexier than his ex-wife.*
5. *He's an amazing lover, afraid of nothing, experienced, and unendingly grateful.*
6. *He can teach you how to do things like sail a yacht and play tennis, or identify all the constellations in the sky.*
7. *He has read the classics.*
8. *He knows what he wants and he won't waste your time.*
9. *He knows how to do his own laundry.*
10. *You don't have to worry he'll have a midlife crisis because you are his midlife crisis.*

I put the paper down because I didn't want to read any more, even though it was pretty interesting. I couldn't help thinking about my father because he was forty-two, the same age as PhD. Also, my father was an astronomer and was constantly pointing out the constellations. I couldn't believe they would publish something like this in the newspaper, and I felt kind of sorry for Daisy and Rhonda, although those probably weren't their real names.

To kill time I went over to my cabin. The bare mattresses were particularly depressing. I felt like I was trespassing even though I had spent the last six weeks there. For a minute I even wondered if I was in the wrong bunk. I went to the bathroom and drank some water from the sink using the last Dixie cup in the dispenser because I was dying of thirst.

Then I walked over to the adjoining boys' ice hockey camp to see if the rink was open, but the doors were locked. It had never been locked before, but their buses home were even earlier than ours. Once I had skated with Nestor Perez at night. He had borrowed hockey skates for me and laced them with my foot between his knees. I wasn't very good but I just had to hold onto his arm and I was skating.

I had been hoping I could buy some chips or Ring Dings from the machines they had.

I could see the machines through the glass doors, and also the big clock. It was after two. The bus had left over four hours ago, and my mother still wasn't here. I had to make a plan because I was sure she wasn't coming.

Using the laminated Red Cross Level 6 advanced swimming card I had gotten for being able to swim all the way to the dock and back, I jimmied open the heavy glass door of the ice rink. I couldn't believe it worked. I bought a Coke and a bag of Fritos from the machines in the lobby and sat in the bleachers gulping them down. We had a vending machine in my ballet school but they only had Tropicana orange, apple, and grapefruit juice.

Once I was drinking a grapefruit juice while I was putting on my toe shoes and my teacher said, "Need a little sugar before class, Swanna?" in a very snide way. I always thought of that every time I saw a concession machine.

I went to the pay phone and dialed a 0 before the 212 and my father's number.

"Operator. May I help you?" a woman said into the phone.

"Collect from Swanna," I said.

My dad didn't answer. After the phone rang seven times she said, "I'm not getting an answer, honey."

I hung up and put my original dime back in my pocket. I decided to try again in a few minutes so I went back into the rink and sat in the bleachers.

It was quiet. I expected the boys to rush onto the ice at any moment like a raft of penguins, but I was alone. I had sat there a good part of the summer watching Nestor Perez, wearing his jersey for extra warmth with *PEREZ* in black letters on my back. It was freezing in there.

Watching ice hockey always made me feel like I was at the penguin house at the Central Park Zoo or at the Coney Island aquarium, watching fish in a tank. It was quite aquatic. The boys tumbled and crashed and dodged each other but very gracefully, like they were moving through water. And then the Zamboni would emerge like a blue whale from behind these car-wash strips of clear plastic, causing the boys to dart and scatter like minnows.

Everyone was very somber when the Zamboni surfaced. It was blue and had the name *Olympia* written on its side, and it felt like an appearance from a Greek god.

I went back to the machine and put another quarter and

a dime in the slot and got another bag of Fritos, making sure I still had a dime left to try calling my dad collect again. I sucked the salt off of each Frito and finished them with the last of my Coke. There was a table covered with lost-and-found items and I went to see if any of them might be Nestor's but they all smelled pretty bad, so I didn't spend too much time looking for name tags. I took a puck and picked up a pair of skates, went back to the bleachers, and slid them onto my bare feet. There were a lot of socks on the table but there was no way I was going to touch them. I laced the skates as tightly as I could, took the yellow terry-cloth tea cozies off the blades, and stepped onto the ice.

I knew this was stupid. If I broke my leg no one would find me. These were hockey skates, which were almost impossible to skate in. I bent my knees and leaned forward and started by marching the way Nestor had shown me. Then I began to glide. I skated all the way around the rink sticking pretty closely to the wall. My ankles ached. I skated to the exact center and stood there for a few minutes looking over to where I would normally be sitting top row center. If I hadn't been kicked off the bus and been abandoned here, I never would have gotten to know this feeling of standing all alone in the middle of the rink with my arms spread out and my head thrown back. That's how life always was. Something good could happen. I skated cautiously back to the rink door and stepped onto solid ground.

I returned the skates to the table and tried calling collect one more time, but my dad wasn't home. He was probably frantically trying to figure out what to do or maybe even driving up to get me.

The bus I should have stayed on was already there, the kids on it already lying on their own beds watching their own TVs. Nedim Adem had already boarded his flight to Istanbul.

I went down to the lake because the lifeguards kept flavored ices that came in long plastic tubes in a big Styrofoam cooler in the boathouse, but the cooler was empty. I would have killed for one of those ices.

I went back to the hill where I had left my bags and sat down next to them. I had to decide what to do. I could wait to see if my father came to get me. The rule if you were lost was "stay put." But if he thought my mother was coming, he wouldn't know anything was wrong. I could hitchhike to the Red Lion Inn or all the way to New York. I had never hitchhiked before and I knew it was dangerous. I would have to leave my duffel bags because there was no way I could carry them. I had to make a decision before it got dark.

I lay back on the grassy hill and closed my eyes. I opened them to find my mother standing over me. Her hair was longer and blonder and she looked very thin and good. Her legs were tanned and her top was see-through of course.

"Come on," she said. "Get in the truck. I can't wait for you to meet Borislav."

I didn't know which was more horrifying, the word *truck* or the word *Borislav*.

"Do you want to see my bunk and the mainstage theater?" I asked. "And the lake?" My mother inexplicably loved lakes. As soon as I said it I regretted it, because my mother was probably going to attempt to skinny-dip. "Actually, I just remembered we're not allowed in the lake," I said.

"We really have to get on the road," she said.

2

My mother sat between me and the driver in the cab of the mint-green truck. Being from New York, I didn't drive in cars that much, but whenever I did I had a strange vision. I imagined ghosts lined up on both sides of the road clutching each other's wrists, making a human chain welcoming me to my death. It was terrifying but comforting too, like a Coca-Cola commercial—*I'd like to teach the world to sing*. That was seriously the thing I saw every time I got into a car in the country for some reason.

I had no idea who the driver was. My mother didn't drive so I figured she'd just hired the guy. The truck must be the country version of a taxi and he was going to take us to the train. Or maybe take us all the way back to the city.

"Borislav is an artist," my mother said. "He's Russian."

"Interesting," I said. Our family believed in always being nice to cabdrivers. I felt sorry for her that she had to be the one to sit next to him. "Where in Russia?"

"I was born here," he said. He didn't sound Russian at all.

"So when did you move to Russia?"

"He's from New Jersey," my mother said—could it be?— proudly. She put her hand on his jeans.

"So he's not from Russia," I said.

"This is what it's like having a daughter on the debate team," my mother said. She thought being on the debate team was one of the least attractive things about me. "Boys don't date girls who debate," she said.

He was wearing white sweat socks with flip-flops. He had plumber's crack. I'd seen it when he lifted my duffels into the back of the truck, and I'd made a mental note not to look at him again. My mother was grinning. She was dressed in clothes I had never seen. Her top had bell bottoms for sleeves. It was 1982 but she had gotten dressed in the seventies.

"Where are we going?" I asked.

"We're going to pick up your brother."

"Now?" I said. "How far is that? We're not going straight home?" I knew I sounded upset. I realized I hadn't really thought about my brother, although I had written him a lot of letters. I felt terrible that I didn't know how far apart our camps were.

Suddenly the man from New Jersey pulled over to the side of the road.

"Um," he said. He spoke quietly and I thought maybe he had said more and I'd somehow missed it. "Um. Swanna?" he said. I didn't even know he knew my name.

"Yeah?" I said, really starting to panic now.

"I just want you to know something."

"What?" I said.

"I just want you to know that I'm not trying to replace your father or anything like that."

"I know," I said. I had never been more horrified in my entire life. I didn't even know who this person was. I couldn't even remember his name. I had no idea what he was talking about. "Why are you telling me this?"

I looked to my mother for some kind of help, but she was still just grinning appreciatively at this moron.

He finally started driving again and I leaned against the door of the truck as hard as I could, hoping it would open and I would fall out. Then I would hitchhike to Camp Woods Lake and rescue my brother before he had to get the "I'm not trying to replace your father" speech and get us back to New York. I felt so sorry for my brother that he was going to have to get this speech and ride in this truck.

"I'm starving," I said. "I didn't eat all day. There was no food."

"For all that money you'd think they'd feed you."

"You were five hours late! Everyone had to be picked up by nine."

"I started writing a new poem," my mother said.

"There's a gas station," the man said.

"I have to call Dad," I said to my mother.

As soon as the truck stopped, I got out and walked into the store. I had seven dollars. I bought a large bag of Wise potato chips, Ring Dings, and a Tab. I opened the Ring Dings and ate them both while I was still at the counter. My mother was the most selfish person on the face of the earth. I was supposed to already be home watching TV.

"Is there a phone?" I asked the man behind the counter.

"It's out of order," he said.

I got back in the truck.

"What's that?" my mother asked.

"What?" I said.

"That poison junk."

"This is called food," I said, opening the bag of chips.

"You can't eat that."

"Yes I can." I put as big a handful of them as I could into my mouth.

"Swanna, you're really going to get fat."

I kept shoving handfuls of chips into my mouth until the man from New Jersey got back into the car. "I bought us lotto tickets," he said.

"That's exciting," my mother said, even though we didn't believe in lotto tickets in our family.

"I got three tickets and I got them all with the same number so if we win we can share the prize."

"That's fantastic," my mother said.

"You got three tickets with the same number?" I asked.

"Um. Yes," he said.

I could barely contain myself. "But you know that doesn't make sense."

"Swanna," my mother said, "it makes perfect sense."

"Mom, he bought three tickets with the same number. If he'd picked three different numbers we'd have three times the chance of winning."

"But this way it's fair," the man said.

"But we could have agreed to split all three tickets!" I said.

"I don't see what's wrong with what Borislav did," my mother said. "You're not being very gracious."

"I'm just saying it makes no sense!"

"Why not?" the man asked.

"Because we'd have three chances instead of one," I said to my mother instead of him.

He didn't say anything, just started the truck up again and stared straight ahead at the road.

There was a girl in my building named Indi who I idolized. She had a difficult stepfather. She went to the High School for Performing Arts for ballet. She was friends with me even though I was younger than she was. Once she came to my house and moved her nose all around like Samantha in *Bewitched*. Then she laughed. "Okay," she said.

"Okay what?" I said.

"Your mom."

"What?"

She laughed again. "It's just funny that they don't hide it."

"Hide what?" I said, having no idea what she was talking about.

"Marijuana."

"What?"

"Pot," she said. "Weed."

I didn't know what it was.

"That smell," she said. "This." She walked over to our plants on the dining room windowsill. "These are marijuana plants," she said, laughing.

"I don't think so," I said, furious.

"Maybe I wasn't supposed to say anything."

"No, you were," I had said.

The cab of the truck reeked of it now, and so did my mother. The man from New Jersey was drinking a beer, which he held between his thighs like a dick.

I drank the Tab, which I had done without for almost

the whole time I was away at camp except when Jacquie's parents took us to the Red Lion Inn and when my dad had come to see me in the play.

I thought about him waiting for me at the bus stop. I just had to get through this drive and then I would be home. At this rate, we'd get home after midnight but at least we'd get home. I couldn't wait to lie in my bed, even if it was at my mother's house, even if this man was there. My mother's bedroom was at the opposite end of the apartment from mine.

I felt so sorry for my brother that he was going to have to leave camp and get into this truck.

"Um. Your mother's told me a lot about you," the man said. He mumbled his words. He sounded like he was talking into a handkerchief. He sounded like a masked bank robber.

"I wish I could say the same," I said.

"This is the happiest day of my life," my mother announced. "Introducing the two of you."

Not the day I was born or my brother was born. Not the day I starred as Katisha in *The Mikado* or won the short story competition or the day she married my father. This day.

"Mom, why didn't you write to me all summer? I was supposed to go home on the bus."

"Your father didn't want you," my mother said.

"What!" I said, outraged. "Yes he did."

"No, he didn't. He has a new girlfriend. I think it's one of his students."

"How do you know that?"

"I asked him if I could have you and your brother and he said yes, he was seeing someone. This is very important to me."

"Well, going home was very important to me," I said.

"When you were a child and we took you to London, you sat on the plane next to your brother and you said, 'I hope Madding and I won't ruin your trip.' You used to be a very considerate child."

"Usually the parents are concerned if the kids are having a good time," I said.

"Um, Val," the driver said, "can I talk to you alone for a minute?" He pulled the car over to the side of the road again.

"Why are you stopping?" I said. "Most people don't have to pull over to talk. Most people can actually drive and talk at the same time." It was going to be a very long trip if he pulled over every time he wanted to say anything.

"Swanna, don't be rude," my mother said.

"Um, Val, do you mind if I talk to you over there?" He pointed to a tree and opened his door and got out.

I had to get out to let my mother out on my side. She tried to gracefully hop out of the truck and I watched her tiny veined fingers grip onto the seat. She pranced over to the tree with her sleeves billowing around her.

When they got back in, my mother said, "I would like very much for us not to quarrel and to try to get along. We're going to have a wonderful time."

3

We saw a diner and miraculously my mother said we should stop. She and I sat across from each other in a booth by the window which looked out at the truck. Whatever his name was had decided to stay in the truck and shut his eyes for a few minutes. I could have done with a different view.

"What can I get for you?" the waitress said. She was like Vera on the TV show *Alice*.

"There's stuffed cabbage," I told my mother. She couldn't ever order without me reminding her of what she would like. A chalkboard behind the counter said *stuffed cabbage* in appealing handwriting.

"Where do you see that?" my mother asked, helplessly holding the huge menu.

"There," I said, pointing to the sign. "Stuffed cabbage, meat loaf, roast beef."

"What's good?" my mother asked, looking pleadingly up at the waitress.

"The meat loaf is good," the waitress said.

I sat back against the ripped vinyl booth and shook my head. My mother always asked waitresses' and salesgirls' opinions, which was one of the things I hated most about her. There was no way my mother was going to order the meat loaf. She would never order anything with *meat* in the title. Or *loaf* for that matter. It could contain meat but not be called meat. She would definitely order anything with cabbage, but we'd have to go through this whole song and dance with the waitress.

"I don't eat meat," my mother said. "I'll have the stuffed cabbage."

"The stuffed cabbage has meat in it," the waitress said.

"Yes, but I like that. Stuffed cabbage, please."

"You get two sides. Salad, soup, peas, carrots, creamed corn, sauerkraut, red cabbage, French fries, mashed, baked," the waitress said.

I closed my eyes because this was going to be excruciating.

"Sides?" my mother said.

"Yes. Sides," I said. "Just choose two."

"Well, not mashed potatoes," my mother said. "That's much too fattening." She looked pointedly at me. "I love carrots," my mother said to the waitress.

The waitress wrote down carrots.

"But I don't think I want carrots. I certainly don't want peas."

I knew my mother wanted the red cabbage. "Why don't you just order the red cabbage and the sauerkraut now because that's what you're going to end up getting. She'll have red cabbage and the sauerkraut and the stuffed cabbage. All cabbage," I told the waitress.

"That's crazy," my mother said. "I'll have a baked potato and carrots."

The waitress wrote it down.

"No," my mother said. "I'll have the red cabbage and the sauerkraut and the mashed potatoes."

"That's three sides," the waitress and I both said at the same time. "And two of them are cabbage," I added.

"Oh, okay, no potatoes," my mother said. "I have a new boyfriend."

I cringed in my seat.

"I hear that," the waitress said. "Mushroom or tomato sauce on the stuffed cabbage?"

"She'll have tomato," I said.

"No," my mother said. "Mushr . . . tomato."

"My mother wants tomato sauce," I interpreted.

"Mother?" the waitress said. I braced myself for the usual *You look like sisters*. Every single person said we looked like sisters. "I thought *you* were the mother and *she* was *your* daughter."

"What?" I said. This was worse than I had expected.

"You could be her daughter," she said to my mother.

I looked at the waitress in disbelief. "She's thirty years older than I am. I'm fourteen."

"You look great," she said to my mother.

"Thank you," my mother said, nodding.

I ordered a chicken cutlet with mashed potatoes and peas.

"Don't scold me for asking this, but isn't that fattening?" my mother said.

"It's not more fattening than the stuffed cabbage." There was nothing I hated more in this world than being told my mother looked like my sister, or now, my daughter, except for when my mother told me not to scold her. When she told

23

me not to scold her, I wanted to take my knife and stab her to death in the diner booth.

The two things she said that I hated the most were *scold* and *quarrel*, and if I told her not to scold me, she would say she didn't want to quarrel. I tried to tell her that no one in 1982 used the word *quarrel*, but she didn't believe me. I knew *quarrel* was coming.

"Well, let's not quarrel," she said. "You would look younger if you lost a few pounds and didn't wear that eyeliner."

The man with the fake Russian name walked into the diner. "Um, hello," he said. He smiled and did a little clownish bow and then ducked into the booth next to my mother. So I had to sit and face the two of them. This was worse than being in the truck.

I wondered if someone watching us would think he was my brother. We already knew the waitress thought my mother was my daughter. But he really did look like her son.

The waitress came and put the plates of food in front of us.

"Um. That looks tasty," the man said. He reached behind him and grabbed a fork from the next table and held it in his fist like a bear. For the first time, I looked directly at his entire face instead of just his profile. He looked very familiar, like I had known him my whole life, but I couldn't put my finger on who he reminded me of. Maybe he was just from the neighborhood.

"Do you live on the Upper West Side?" I asked.

"Um. No." He looked like he had never heard of it.

"You look familiar to me," I said.

He was too busy eating my mother's stuffed cabbage to

answer me. Then he stopped eating and said, "Um. Would you please excuse me for a moment?" I just gave him a look telling him I would excuse him for my entire lifetime. "I have to, um, use the facilities."

He got up but walked in the opposite direction of the bathrooms. Then he walked right out the door.

"Where's he going?" I asked my mother.

"I think he's going to the bathroom," she said defensively.

"What bathroom?"

"He doesn't like to go in public."

I looked out the window, trying to see what bathroom he was going to use. "He's just walking into the woods," I said.

"He probably wants to go in the woods where it's more private."

"Um," I said. Now I had started doing it. "The woods is a public place. The restroom is private. He's going to poop in the woods instead of the bathroom?" I was practically yelling.

"Don't say *poop*. He does what he wants. I like that," my mother said. "If he wants to make a doo in the woods, that's his business. I think it's cool."

"You don't like it when I do what I want. Let me get this straight. The man just walked away from the men's room because he wants to shit in the woods. What is he going to use for toilet paper, a leaf?"

"I don't know," my mother said. "You're not being very nice. You're a very angry person."

When my mother said I was a very angry person, which she did constantly, I wanted to kill her all day long.

"Is he claustrophobic?" I asked, thinking maybe he didn't want to lock himself into the privacy of a bathroom stall.

"Why should he go into a smelly bathroom when he can be outdoors?" my mother actually said. She had never said a word like *smelly* in her entire life.

"*Be* outdoors? He's going to take a shit in the woods! Like a homeless person?"

"Well, he is homeless," my mother said.

"What!"

"He doesn't want to live with his parents in New Jersey anymore because they're too Catholic, so after we leave ArtCom—"

"What's ArtCom? What do you mean after *we* leave Art-Com? We're going home, aren't we?"

"It's the artist colony we're going to. We're staying there for two weeks."

"I'm not staying there," I said, choking on my chicken. "I'm going home."

"It's a wonderful place. For artists."

"You said you just came from an artist colony," I said.

"Yes, we were at Bread Loaf in Vermont. That's where I was. Borislav was a visiting artist. Now we're going to ArtCom."

"So you're going to two different artist colonies back-to-back? And the second one is in Vermont too?"

"Yes."

"Vermont sounds like the most horrible place on earth, filled with freeloading starving artists. That's probably why they call it Bread Loaf. All the artists think they'll get a sandwich."

"ArtCom is very prestigious. It's important. Borislav is nice enough to take us along! It's going to be like camp."

"Two weeks! Mom," I said, "that's impossible. School starts soon. What do you mean *like camp*? Are there kids?"

"I'm trying to give you interesting experiences. We're going to be together."

"What's he going to do at this ArtCamp?"

"ArtCom. He's going to make a very exciting sculpture out of hot tar."

"Tar, like they use for roads?"

"Yes."

"What's he making a sculpture of?" I asked.

"A road," she said. "And he's doing a series of Elvis Presley paintings."

That's when I realized who he looked like. Those square hurt lips and flat open cheeks. "Is he coming back in here?"

"Probably not for a long time. He might meet us at the truck. I should order something for him to go."

"Are you going to pay for him?" This went against everything my mother had ever taught me.

"He's going to be a famous artist one day," she said.

4

After the diner, my mother said that we were going to make a quick stop at Herman Melville's house. His name sounded familiar and I was worried it was one of her boring poet friends. But then I realized I was thinking of Herman Bachman who she taught with at Columbia. Then I realized that Herman Melville was the person who wrote *Moby-Dick*. My mother knew a lot of famous authors but I hadn't met Herman Melville yet. I was interested in meeting him mostly because my teachers were always very impressed when I mentioned that I knew the author of whatever book they were talking about. In fourth grade I forced Arnold Lobel to come talk to my class. He wrote all the *Frog and Toad* books.

"I think we should go straight to Madding," I said. It was getting late and no one had given me an answer on how long a drive it was to his camp.

"It's a very small museum," my mother said.

That's when I knew Herman Melville was dead. I was very relieved I hadn't said anything about meeting him or asked if he had any kids.

"I actually told Borislav we should stop there because I thought you would like it," my mother said.

"I wouldn't," I said.

When we pulled into Herman Melville's driveway, a few people were gathered outside the door of a big house painted mustard yellow. I had to open the truck door to let my mother out but I had no intention of going in.

"Tour's starting," an old woman called over to us.

I started to get back in the truck.

"What are you doing?" my mother said.

"I'm not going in."

"We came here for you," my mother said.

"We have to get Madding."

"You love whales!" my mother said.

"Are you joining us?" the old lady called out.

"Yes," my mother called back. "The view from his office is a mountain that looks exactly like a sperm whale. That's how he had the idea to write *Moby-Dick*. It was his inspiration."

"If you know everything about it, then why are we here?"

"You have to pay homage, Swanna. For a writer, you're being disrespectful."

"Actress," I corrected. "Who do I have to be respectful of? Do you really think Herman Melville cares if I see his house?"

"Yes, I do," my mother said. "I think he cares a great deal."

This was very typical of the kinds of arguments I had with her. They didn't make any sense.

The old lady went inside, trailed by the tourists. My mother rushed in and the man from New Jersey squished after her in his flip-flops.

I got back in the truck and cranked down the window. I watched a tall blond couple leave the gift shop, holding hands. They looked very romantic. He seemed grateful it was over, and she seemed grateful he had tolerated it. Maybe they were staying at the Red Lion Inn. I imagined them having sex in their room. Maybe they were on their honeymoon.

I smiled, thinking that Madding would have really gotten a kick out of the word *Dick*. I got out of the truck and walked around the house. I looked around hoping to see the mountain my mother had told me about. Then there it was—looming in the distance above the trees. It really did look like a whale—a big blue whale hanging low in the sky. Melville's whale. A mountain that inspired him to write a book that made him famous. God had given him that mountain.

Then I walked back to what God had given me, but all He had given me was Spermislav's truck.

Yeah, call me Ishmael. The truck was mint green with splotches of rust. All the other cars around it looked normal. It was badly proportioned with a very long tail and a small body. The cab had a back window with three chrome bars across it. If you were in the cab, you couldn't see out the back because there was too much stuff blocking the window. On its side, the word *Custom* was written in chrome script, surrounded by dots of rust as if someone had tried to kill it by tossing a pot of tomato sauce on it. Inside, the seat was covered in ripped material with an Aztec print on it. Of course, the worst thing about it was the New Jersey plates.

I thought about getting my Vivitar camera out of my duffel bag and taking a picture of it. But then I thought that was the kind of picture you looked at years later and had no idea why you had taken it. I had taken quite a few pictures like that.

I was starting to get very curious about the inside of that house because I actually did like places like that. There was nothing for me to do. I was embarrassed being anywhere near the truck and there was nowhere to sit. They were taking a really long time and I was starting to get more and more worried about my brother. What if he was alone at his camp the way I was at mine? He was only eight.

I went toward Melville's house and saw that you entered into a small gift shop. An old woman sat behind a desk. It wasn't the same old woman who was giving the tour.

"There's a tour starting in thirty minutes," she said.

I looked at the clock behind her, pretending to be interested. "I would like that," I said. "But is there a pay phone I could use?"

"No, I'm sorry, we don't have one."

"Oh, that's okay," I said. I picked up a kids version of *Moby-Dick* and pretended to look at it.

"That's an abridged edition," the woman said.

"I can see that," I said, putting it down. "Is there any way I could use your phone? I left something at a diner near here and I want to make sure they hold it for me."

"I'm sorry, we don't have a phone for visitors."

I was pretty sure Melville would want me to use his phone. "It's kind of an emergency. It's a local call and it won't take long," I said.

The woman looked nervous. "What did you leave?"

"My glasses," I said. "They were very expensive. They're tinted."

The woman looked like this was the most agonizing decision of her life, and I was about to say thanks anyway and leave when she stood up and had me follow her to a small office and handed me a Yellow Pages. I thanked her and she left me alone in the room.

I picked up the phone and dialed information, and when the operator answered, I said, "In Tolland, Mass., Camp Woods Lake," and she connected me. The phone rang a few times and a man picked up. I was relieved someone was still there.

"Hi," I said. I was trying to talk as softly as possible. "I'm Madding Swain's sister."

"Oh. Hi," he said. "Is everything all right?"

"I'm sorry we're so late picking him up. Please tell him we'll get there as soon as possible."

"You're picking him up?" the man said. "Today? Not Friday?"

"Isn't this the last day of camp?"

"No," the man said. "Camp ends on Friday."

"Oh," I said.

"I think he's on the bus list. Isn't he? Hold on . . . Yes, he's on the bus to New York. Do you want me to take him off the list? Are you picking him up instead?"

"No, keep him on the bus list," I said. "To New York."

"Do you want me to give him a message? He's at choice right now. It might take me a few minutes to track him down."

"No, that's okay," I said. "Thank you."

When I got back out to the parking area, my mother was talking very excitedly. "Borislav, Melville and Hawthorne were definitely lovers."

"She didn't say that," he said.

"Of course she didn't say that, but it was clear."

"You think everyone's lovers." He was actually right about that. My mother always thought people were having an affair. Probably because she was always having one.

"He had a close friendship with Hawthorne. Moves to the farm next door even though the house is too small for him and his wife and four children and mother-in-law. And he hates the house. *Dedicates Moby-Dick* to Hawthorne. You have to love someone to dedicate a book to them. His wife despises their friendship. Then one day he goes to visit Hawthorne's farm and Hawthorne has moved out in the dark of night and not left any word of where he's moved to. They were homosexuals together. I'm sure Hawthorne's wife found out and put a stop to it."

"I'm not sure you had to tell the whole group they were fucking," the man said.

I waited for my mother to tell him not to use that word, but she didn't. "Yes, I did," my mother said.

"We can't pick up Madding," I said.

"Why not?" my mother said.

"Because his camp's still going. It goes for almost another week."

"Why can't we pick him up?"

It was like talking to Miss Emily Litella on *Saturday Night Live*. "He has almost a whole other week of camp. He's not going to want to leave."

"Of course he is," my mother said. "He's my child. I'll pick him up whenever I like. This camp was your father's idea. I'm sure it's horrible. Sports. *Ew.*" She pretended to shudder.

"You have to tell them you're coming," I said. "You can't just flounce in whenever you feel like it. He has to pack and get everyone's phone numbers and wrap his pottery in newspaper and say goodbye to people. Does Dad know you're picking him up?"

"Why are you always taking your father's side and accusing me of kidnapping? Do you really think your father is thinking about you every minute?"

"Camp is very expensive," I said. "Dad is paying for it." I knew I was yelling. "Madding is happy there. He's at choice time right now." My voice caught on the words *choice time*. None of this was my choice.

"Um, you pay for these camps?" New Jersislav said.

I looked at him in disbelief, which I was starting to realize was how I always looked at him. I wished I had a mirror so I could memorize this look for my acting. If I was ever in a play or a movie and I had to look at someone in disbelief, all I would have to do is pretend I was talking to him.

"You don't just go and live there and eat and take classes and go on field trips for free," I said. "We saw a Barry Manilow concert at Tanglewood."

"Um, I'd pay to *not* see Barry Manilow."

"That would involve having money. Didn't your parents ever send you to camp?"

"Um, I think that's more of a Jewish thing."

I looked at my mother to see if she was registering any of this anti-Semitism, but she was just smiling at him.

"You mean Jews like to be put in camps?" I said. "You know we're Jewish, right?"

"That's not what he was saying," my mother said.

"I'm saying culturally it's a New York Jewish thing to send kids to summer camp."

"Well, tell that to Nestor Perez," I said, instantly wishing I hadn't mentioned his name.

"Who's Nestor Perez?" my mother said.

"There practically wasn't anyone Jewish at my camp," I said, but thinking through all the kids, I realized they mostly were. "This is the United States, not Russia. We don't expect to get things for free here. We're a capitalist society. You would die if you knew how much my brother's school cost."

"I'm sure I would," he said.

"He goes to Dalton. Have you ever even heard of Dalton?"

"Borislav has a good point," my mother said. "Camp is excessive. Madding's school is excessive. I didn't go to camp. My mother was afraid of germs."

"You went to the most expensive and excessive schools in the country! And you also went to camp," I reminded her.

"Maybe we should take Madding out of Dalton and put him in public school," my mother said.

I couldn't even speak. Changing schools was the worst thing that could happen to a person, and if she tried to do that, I would find a way to stop it.

5

We pulled into Camp Woods Lake and my mother went into the office to explain that we were taking Madding out of camp early. They went to go pack his things and I went to look for him. He was playing basketball. He ran over to me and said, "What the hell?" He gave me a big hug and I felt emotional all of a sudden.

"Are those your shorts?" I asked. They were way too short for him. He was wearing his Dalton T-shirt and flip-flops.

"I don't know," he said. His bangs were covering his eyes. He was too young to be at sleepaway camp.

"You shouldn't play basketball in flip-flops," I said.

"What are you doing here?" he asked.

"We're taking you home. She came to get me first," I said. "With a man."

"What man?"

"I don't know."

"A taxi driver?"

"No. It's a truck."

"A Mack truck?"

"No, a Ford truck. A pickup truck."

"Fords are good."

"It's not about the truck," I said.

37

He made me watch him play basketball for a long time and then we sat and he talked all about how terrible the scrambled eggs were and he acted out eating one bite and throwing up.

"Where's the truck?" he asked. "I want to see it."

I walked back toward the lot with him and he saw it. His things were next to it—two duffels, a Morris Bros. shopping bag, a tennis racket, the teddy bear I had gotten him last Christmas, and a birdhouse, with a slanted roof covered in green sod, a hole, and a dowel sticking out for a perch.

"Those are Jersey plates," Madding said. "Embarrassing."

"That's where he's from."

"Who? That man with Mom?"

I pointed over to where he was standing. "That's the man who drove us here. I think he's supposedly Mom's boyfriend."

Madding got a very angry look on his face. "Is that the artist?"

"Not the famous artist. This is a different one. He's really, really horrible."

Madding understood and shook his head in agreement. "Does Dad know?"

"I don't think so or he wouldn't have let Mom pick us up."

"Is he missing any fingers?"

"No. The famous one has missing fingers, not this bum."

"Madding!" my mother yelled.

He left me standing there and ran over to hug her. Then he showed her the birdhouse. My mother's whatever-he-was came over to Madding and I could see he was pretending to be very interested and asking some idiotic questions about it, and Madding was just standing there earnestly answering him.

The guy put the birdhouse and Madding's duffels in the back of the truck. Then Madding climbed into the back. I walked toward them and stood next to the truck.

"Mom, Madding can't ride like that," I said.

"Why not?" she said.

"It's dangerous!"

"I don't want to have a big quarrel," my mother said.

"It's like a hay ride," Madding said. "It's like a covered wagon."

"Covered wagons didn't go sixty miles an hour," I said.

"They could go fairly fast," Madding said.

"Um, we better get going. They won't let us in after a certain time," Boro-the-Clown said.

"We're not going home?" Madding said.

"We're going to an artist colony," I said. "I think it's safer if he sits on my lap inside."

"He'll have more fun back here," my mother said.

"He can't ride back here alone," I said. "I'll have to ride with him."

The man put his hand out to help me climb up but I didn't take it.

"What if we have to go to the bathroom? How will we tell you?" I asked. There was no way they could see us or hear us from inside the cab. The window was blocked by a mattress and a lot of army bags and rolled-up tarps, my duffel bags, and now Madding's duffel bags and birdhouse. "We'd be right at the edge," I said.

"It's called the tailgate," Madding said.

I climbed up into the back of the truck after Madding. There was so much stuff, I had to sit wedged in, cross-legged.

"Goodbye, camp," he said.

Without warning, we pulled out of the driveway. Madding and I looked at each other. My long hair was blowing everywhere. I held onto my hair with one hand and Madding with the other. I didn't feel like talking and we couldn't have heard each other anyway. We turned off a long tree-lined road onto a highway. Every time we hit a bump we screamed and held on to each other. If one of us fell out of the truck, it would just keep driving and my mother would never know. If my brother fell out, I would jump out too. Cars passed us and the drivers and passengers looked at us. My hair must look really crazy, I thought.

Cars were honking at us. They were driving past and honking at the man from New Jersey and my mother and shouting at them.

"Why are they honking?" Madding shouted. "We might have a flat tire."

"I think that's what they do here. Like if you're on a boat and another boat passes by, everyone waves."

We slowed in some traffic and a man in a black car pulled up right next to us. "You're not safe!" he yelled.

I pretended I couldn't hear him.

"Hold on, be careful!" the man yelled.

"We're fine!" I yelled back. I hated when strangers talked to me like I was a child. I was fourteen. I was from New York. I took the subway every day with lunatics. I rode between cars. I hated when people told me what to do.

He moved up to my mom's side of the truck and started honking. I heard him screaming something and my mother screaming back. He kept honking and tailing us. Maybe he was Ishmael and he'd follow us for the rest of the trip. Madding sat up on his knees and I grabbed his wrist. "Sit down!" I shouted.

"We're famous," he said. He leaned over the side of the truck and waved at the man in the car. "I'm going to stand up." He stood up and put his arms out like he was surfing.

"Stop!" I screamed. I grabbed his wrist hard and pulled him down.

Every single person in every single car stared at us. A few honked and screamed things.

"Just ignore them," I told Madding.

He scrunched down and put his head in my lap. We drove that way for a while and I closed my eyes against the wind. It was dark now.

Finally we pulled off on an exit ramp. When I opened my eyes we were on a country road. The other cars were gone.

6

"**M**y children are not like other children," my mother said.

My brother and I stood on the square piece of stone outside the door trying not to look like other children.

"I'm sorry, Val. There's no children allowed in the house. It's clearly stated in the letter. No visitors."

"Yes," my mother said. "They're not visitors, they're my children. We are one person." She put her arms around me and my brother, pressing us all together like conjoined triplets.

My brother was holding his penis through his pants.

"Mom," I said.

My mother didn't acknowledge me. I thought maybe saying the word *Mom* made me seem like other children.

"Val," I said, "I think Madding has to use the bathroom."

"Nadine, may my son use the ladies' room?" my mother asked the woman. The woman ran her fingers through her short black hair.

"Men's," my brother said.

"Okay," the woman said, moving her short square body out

of the doorway. My doctor had told me I was going to be short when I grew up, but if I grew up that short, I would kill myself.

"And if I could just give them a small meal." Madding hadn't had anything to eat since we'd picked him up, but he'd had dinner at camp.

"Dinner was over three hours ago," the woman said.

"I didn't realize this was a zoo with feeding times," my mother said.

"Dinner is served in the dining room from seven to nine. You're welcome to eat at any other time but you have to provide your own food. People have things in the kitchen labeled with their names and the date. Every Thursday we throw out anything that isn't dated."

My brother yawned and squeezed his penis. When he yawned he looked exactly the way he did when he was a baby. His mouth formed a slanted *O*.

"I'm sure no one will mind if we borrow some food. We can go to the Key Food in the morning."

Key Food was our supermarket on Broadway and 91st Street in Manhattan. I was pretty sure they didn't have Key Foods here.

She shoved us slightly so that we entered the house, and the woman pointed to a door with peeling light-blue paint and a long black latch. She lifted the latch and my brother went into the bathroom and I guarded the door.

"What do you think is going to happen?" he asked when he came out.

"I think we'll leave this hellhole," I said. "We'll go to a motel with a soda machine and then tomorrow we'll drive back to the city."

"It's not that bad here though," Madding said.

"I think it is. Kids aren't allowed."

"But no one's sick or anything with big bumps on their skin."

"Did you think we were going to a lepers' colony?" I asked. "This is an *artists'* colony."

"Oh," he said.

The woman with the short hair—Nadine—was still arguing with our mother. "Where is Borislav?" she asked. "He's the primary grantee. When he called and asked if he could have you share his studio as collaborator, we agreed, but technically you are his guest."

"I'm a poet. Published."

"Yes, you said that. But my point is, we're already accommodating his out-of-the-ordinary request to have you here. There's no way we can also accommodate your children. Or *any* children."

"Oh, they're no trouble. They'll stay in the room."

"They aren't allowed on the second floor. Where is Bor?" the woman asked.

"He's in the truck. He'll be here in a minute."

We all turned and looked out the dark window behind us toward the truck but saw nothing but ourselves.

Finally we went out to the truck.

"That horrible woman says the children aren't permitted," my mother told him.

"That's not very welcoming," he said.

"Yeah, we have to drive back to New York tonight," I said.

"We're hungry," my brother said.

"Do you have any money?" the man asked my mother.

"Just what I gave you," she said. "I can get more in the morning if we can find a bank. I have my checkbook."

"We don't have any money?" I said.

"I'll just get us settled in our room," the man said. He hoisted a huge duffel bag from the back of the truck over his shoulder and walked his baggy-jeaned walk to the door. A few minutes later a light went on in a room on the second floor of the three-story house. Then he came out again carrying the same duffel bag which was now empty. "Get in," he told me.

"What?" I said.

"Get in." It was unzipped. My mother was smiling in total approval.

"No," I said.

The inside smelled like an old fishy lake. He zipped it up around me like a sleeping bag with my head sticking out. Then he hoisted me over his shoulder facedown. I heard him breathing up the stairs. I didn't know if the woman was watching him carry me up, but if she was, she would have heard him say, "You're not light," to the bag.

I am luggage, I thought, now I am luggage. He put me down, unzipped me, and I squirmed out on a bed. I was in a room with just a twin bed and a small desk.

I started to say something and he put his hand over my mouth. I put my hand on his hairy, clammy one and pulled it off me like a leech. If he touched me again, I would call the police.

"If you touch me again, I'll call the cops on you," I said.

He put his hands up over his head like he was under arrest and grinned at me. Then he went back downstairs with the empty duffel bag to carry my brother up.

My brother loved riding in the duffel bag. The four of us stood in the small bedroom not sure what to do next.

"There's only one bed," I said. "Shhhh," the man said.

"No, I will not *shhh*," I said, louder. "We can't all sleep in here."

"I can sleep on the floor," my brother said. "Me and Swan can both sleep on the floor."

"Swan and I," my mother said. It was important to have good grammar when you were bums illegally sleeping on the floor of a tiny room.

The floor wasn't even big enough. I wasn't going to sleep in that room while my mother slept in the bed with that man.

Someone knocked on the door.

The man walked over to it and said, "Um. Who is it?"

"I know the kids are in there," the woman from downstairs said. She opened the door and my brother dove under the bed. "Hi, Nadine, I didn't know Val's kids couldn't be here.

Could they just sleep in the screened-in porch tonight? It's too late to find anything else now."

There was no way I was going to sleep in a screened-in porch.

"No," Nadine said. "I'm sorry. They can't."

"What about your studio?" my mother said.

"Studios become available tomorrow morning," Nadine said. "And I already made an exception to have all that tar delivered there."

My brother's stomach made a loud gurgling sound under the bed and he started to giggle.

"Please figure something out and leave the house," Nadine said, and shut the door behind her.

7

I lay on the mattress in the back of the truck next to my brother.

"This sucks," I said.

"It's fun," he said. "Do you think this works? We could watch *Saturday Night Live*." He was pointing to a small TV in the truck with us.

"There's nowhere to plug it in, and it's Sunday."

"Jane, you inseparable slut," he said.

"Inseparable slut?" I said. "That doesn't even make sense. It's 'Jane, you ignorant slut.'"

"I don't know what that is."

"Dan Aykroyd says it to Jane Curtin during *Weekend Update*. It's hilarious. Since when do you watch *Saturday Night Live*?" I asked.

"My counselor at camp told us about it." Madding actually had a very good vocabulary, but he got a lot of words wrong. I always loved when he did that. Once he had all his stuffed animals lined up and he was performing a wedding ceremony and he said, "Speak now or forever hold your penis."

At his Dalton interview they asked him what he wanted to be when he grew up, and he said, "I want to be a French photographer of naked ladies."

I felt very guilty for not writing those things down.

"What's his name again?"

"Whose?"

"The guy? Mom's uh . . ." I heard his voice crack. He knew the man was our mother's new boyfriend. They were up in that room sleeping in a single bed. I looked over at Madding and saw he was in full chin tremble. It looked like a baby chick hatching from an egg when his chin shook like that. He couldn't even remember the guy's name. Then I realized I couldn't remember it either. My mind was completely blank.

Please don't cry, I thought, please don't cry. Not about myself but about him.

"I have to pee again," he said.

"I do too," I said.

"What are we supposed to do?"

"I don't know," I said, panicking. I hadn't thought of that. We would have to walk all the way to the house.

I sat up and looked over at it. There were a few lights on inside but there were no outside lights and no concrete path that I could remember. We were parked pretty far away. And the whole way we'd be on grass. Even if we put our shoes on, there'd still be bugs and snakes. Then I realized nothing was stopping the snakes from coming into the truck.

"They don't allow children," my brother said.

"She said we couldn't sleep in there, but I'm sure we could go into the bathroom again. Why don't you just go and I'll watch you from here? If the door is locked you can knock. The lights are on so I'm sure some people are up."

My brother sat up and looked out at the house. "Will you come with me?"

I did not want to walk in the grass. "Mom!" I screamed, as loud as I could. "Moooommmmmm!"

I screamed "Mom!" for a few minutes. Then Madding screamed it too at the same time. Then we alternated screaming it.

"I just peed," Madding said, sounding scared.

I felt the wet spot on the mattress next to me with my fingertips. And then the pee gushed out of me too, soaking my nightgown and the sheet and mattress.

"Look what you did! Why'd you do that?" I said. "Now what are we supposed to do? Why'd you have to pee like a baby? Now I'm the one who has to clean up everything."

"I'm sorry," Madding said. "I was too scared."

I sat up and rifled around in my duffel bag for some shorts and a towel. I peeled off my wet underpants and put on the shorts and stuffed my nightgown into a plastic bag. I made Madding give me his wet pajama bottoms and I gave him the shorts he had worn that day that weren't even his.

"Help me," I said. We took the wet foam mattress and threw it into the grass. Then we put down all our towels from camp. The floor of the truck had ridges so it wasn't comfortable, but Madding was falling asleep.

"Borislav," I whispered. "I think that's his name."

"Yeah, Boring Slut," he said. "Boring Slob." He put his hand on my arm.

Boring Slob. That was a good one, I thought.

When I was eight and my brother was two, my parents sent us to Grasse in the south of France, with our nanny Pierrette. We were living in London for a year in a beautiful town house in Chelsea. My mother had won a Guggenheim and my father had taken a sabbatical.

I complained that I didn't like Pierrette. Once a week she made us accompany her to her diet doctor. She took a laxative before the long double-decker bus ride, and when we got to the doctor's office she would go to the bathroom to lose as much weight as possible before she got on the scale.

"Merde," she'd say while she struggled with the side zipper on her trousers. We had to go in the bathroom with her because she didn't want us sitting alone in the waiting room. We had to listen to her shitting.

Afterward we'd go to a bakery and eat sweets, but she'd say that Madding could have more than me because he was naturally thin and I was naturally fat.

When I complained about going to the doctor, my parents suggested she could take us to France to see her mother and her brothers. She had only been our nanny for a short time, but my parents liked that she was teaching us French, and the delicious cannelloni she served at their dinner parties.

I didn't think it was a good idea to go to another country with her, but my parents insisted. "You will take care of your brother," my parents said. I held my brother's hand when the plane landed in Nice. We were going to spend one night there in the apartment of one of her five brothers, and then go to her mother's farmhouse in Grasse.

When we got to the brother's apartment, all the brothers were there to greet us. They all had shaggy blond hair like Pierrette and they seemed to think my brother was cute. "Je m'appelle Alain," one said to me, and I said, "Je m'appelle Swanna," and that was the extent of the conversation.

I had to pee very badly and I told Pierrette that, but she was laughing and talking to her brothers who she hadn't seen in years. She hadn't been able to afford it until my parents paid for her trip.

"I have to pee," I told her repeatedly. "I don't know where the loo is."

We all sat on a long sectional, the brothers laughing and slapping their hands on the cushions. I tried to hold it in. I saw a door that I thought might be the bathroom, but I didn't think I could stand without peeing. Finally, unable to take it anymore, I stood and the pee poured out of me onto the wood floor. There was silence. Pierrette made the clucking *tsk tsk* sound I despised. The brothers laughed and talked very fast in French. She yanked my wet underpants down and I stepped out of them. Then she threw them at Alain and he threw them at someone else and they went flying from one to the other while I stood seething with anger. I hated France and I hated Pierrette.

"What are they saying?" I asked.

"They are deciding which one of them is going to give you a spanking for pissing on the floor like a cow," she said.

The next day, at the farmhouse in Grasse, my brother and I played outside in the dusty garden. I hated this place but I was happy to be away from Pierrette's brothers. Two-year-old Madding was digging up a rock from the dirt, using another rock as a shovel. The family dog came to see what he was doing. It had shaggy blond hair like the brothers and a long nose like a wolf. "Le chien," I told my brother. "Dog."

Then he tried to give the rock to the dog, but the dog wouldn't take it. He hit the dog with the rock.

"No," I said. "Be gentle."

He hit the dog again. Then the dog snapped his jaws at Madding's face. For a moment my brother was shocked and didn't say anything. Then he started to scream and cry. There was blood everywhere. I couldn't see his face, only blood. There was blood all over the dog's face too.

"Pierrette!" I screamed. I ran toward the house yelling for help.

Someone scooped him up and put him in a car. "You stay here," Pierrette told me.

I was locked inside the house, alone with the dog. I didn't know where they had taken him. There was a telephone and I tried to call my parents, but a woman kept coming on and talking in French and I kept giving up. I turned on the television and watched a man dressed like Elvis Presley.

I kept one eye on the dog the whole time.

Sometime after dark, the phone rang and I answered it.

"Swanna," Pierrette said, "we are still at the hospital. The news, it is bad. He lost his eye. You will see his face is bandaged up."

I sat there wondering how I was going to explain this to my parents. How was I going to tell them that Madding had lost his eye? I had promised them that I would take care of him. I was so frozen with fear, I wished the dog would just go ahead and kill me.

"Look what you did!" I screamed at him. "Bad dog!"

When we got back to our parents in London, we went to the doctor to remove the bandage covering his missing eye. I held my breath as the bandage was lifted, expecting a hole where the eye had been, or a gash instead of an eye.

My brother would have to wear a pirate patch, I supposed. But what I saw, to my amazement, was his eye, whole and unharmed, with just a tiny scar from stitches on his cheek beneath it.

Then my parents had a very important dinner party. The publisher Christopher MacLehose came and he was very tall and elegant. Pierrette served her special homemade cannelloni. After dinner, my father threw something out in the garbage can, and right there in plain sight were six empty cans. That night, Christopher MacLehose had eaten the English version of Chef Boyardee. For that, they fired her on the spot.

In the morning we got up and hauled the mattress back onto the truck with the wet side down.

There were three main buildings—the house where people slept, the dining hall which was locked between meals, and the barn, which was a big open space for readings or music performances. Then there were small cabins all around called "the studios." All the freaks in the house had breakfast that they actually had to take turns cooking, and then everyone got a lunch in a brown bag and went to his or her private studio to create. Because my mother wasn't officially an artist there, she didn't get a lunch and neither did we. She brought us buttered toast she had nabbed from the dining room, and tea for me and milk and a banana for my brother. My brother couldn't survive if he didn't have at least one banana twenty times a day. She was holding a big book by Dostoyevsky. She probably thought she was a Russian now too.

"We're not going to sleep out here again," I said.

"Oh, Swanna."

"I'm deathly serious. We want to go home to New York."
Suddenly the words *New York* sounded foreign and impossible, like *Narnia* or *Never-Never Land*.

"What are we doing today?" my brother asked.

"We're going bowling tonight," my mother said.

"Yay!" Madding said.

"Bowling?" I scoffed. My mother had never done anything
like bowling in her entire life. My father took us places every
weekend and she stayed home with a terrible headache. Once
she had come with us to Coney Island and spent an hour
saying that Nathan's hot dogs were too fattening and criticizing every single french fry I put in my mouth, and then
she simply sat down on the steps leading to the boardwalk
and refused to stand up because she had a terrible headache
that day too. People had to wind around her on the steps and
she just sat there with her head in her hands no matter how
much we begged for her to please stand up. A small part of
me admired the absolute femininity of it, the way she wept
and said she could not bear to take another step, the way she
finally rose shakily on her platform velvet shoes, reluctantly
ate a hot dog only because she was near the starvation point,
and had a few sips of root beer, announcing she'd never had a
soda in her life, and my father had to practically carry her to
our car. She was all womanly humorlessness, something I was
sure I would never quite achieve. I could never sit on the steps
like that. On the way home she had lain down in the backseat
of the car, moaning with the cup of ice on her head, and I sat
up front next to my dad with Madding on my lap, and my dad
tried to cheer her up by singing the Hoffman's root beer jingle:

The prettiest girl
I ever saw
was drinking Hoffman's
right through a straw.
The prettiest girl I ev-er saw
was drinking Hoff-man's through a straw . . .

To my mother, Coney Island was like the man who had once flashed us on the subway. The look of horror on her face was the same.

And that was the look we were definitely going to see at the bowling alley.

"Isn't that nice? It was Borislav's idea."

She pronounced each syllable of *Borislav* very distinctly, with a slight fake accent of some kind. *Bor-is-slav*, pronounced like three compliments.

"Are you going bowling with us?" Madding asked my mother.

"Of course!" she said.

"I'll teach you," Madding said.

"Are we going to get any breakfast besides this?" I asked.

"What else are we going to do today besides bowling?" my brother said.

"You're going to play. We're going to read. Swanna, you're not going to believe who is a fellow here."

"Who?" I said.

"Dorie Korn."

"No idea who that is."

"Dorie Korn. Ms. Korn. Your guidance counselor."

"What? Did Dad send her here?"

"What?"

"Did Dad call her because I wasn't on the bus? Is she bringing us home?" He knew we were here. He had sent help.

"What are you talking about? She's a painter. She's here for the whole summer."

"Is she a man?" Madding asked.

"No, she's just an extremely unattractive woman," my mother said.

"That's why they call her a fellow?"

"No, the artists here are all called fellows. Like I am a Guggenheim fellow. A fellow is a distinguished colleague. This is cozy." My mother had climbed into the truck, leaving her Dr. Scholl's on the grass. She crawled to the top of the thin foam mattress and moved her butt all around like a hen. She leaned against the tattered cardboard boxes, old red plaid suitcase, dusty slide projector, and Pearl Paint bag that were our headboard. "It's heavenly up here."

"When is Ms. Korn going back to New York?"

"I don't know. You can ask her yourself. She's going bowling with us. There's a whole group going."

I hadn't been doing well in American government, Latin, or science since my father moved out, and I hadn't been doing well in math since the day I was born, so I had to go to Ms. Korn quite a bit to discuss it. She was literally the stupidest woman I had ever met. She had *New Yorker* cartoons on her stupid bulletin board and I told her I had won the contest in the back where you write your own caption for a cartoon when I was nine, and she believed me. She believed absolutely everything I said. She loved me. I told her how much pot my parents smoked and that my father was an alcoholic and I was pretty sure they were both going to commit suicide, which was true. I told her I was a latchkey kid and when I got home, the first place I looked was the kitchen to see if anyone's head was in the oven. One time when I had gotten a zero out of a hundred on a Latin test and I'd had to talk to her about it, she actually cried. She said my parents sounded severely depressed and that I was one of the smartest girls she had ever met. The more I failed, the smarter she thought I was.

She wore flowered blouses tucked into black skirts and the worst boots imaginable, puffy like little down jackets on her feet. There was no way she was a painter. My mother must be wrong. My mother was terrible at knowing who anyone was and she'd never set foot inside my school, so I didn't know how she'd even know who Ms. Korn was.

"Are you sure it's Ms. Korn?" I said.

"Yes, she said she worked at your school and I asked her if she knew you and she said you were her favorite student. She told me you said your father is going to commit suicide."

This is great, I thought. As soon as Ms. Korn saw me and my brother and this truck, she would take us home.

"What are her paintings like?" I asked. I would have to make a point of complimenting them, so it was better for me to be prepared.

"She paints green peppers coupled together like they are making love. Very sensual. And pears."

Nothing could have prepared me for that.

"Making love," Madding said, and snickered.

"I think she's in love with Borislav," my mother said. "I think she came on to him at breakfast. She didn't know we were together."

"Maybe she thinks he's a vegetable," I said, trying not to throw up.

"She was kind enough to cash a check for me. So I don't have to find a bank today."

Suddenly I saw a snake. I screamed. It was slithering in the grass right near the truck.

"Kill it! Kill it!" Madding and I screamed. We stood on the mattress and jumped up and down. "Kill it! Kill it!"

I didn't really think she would kill it. We could never count on her for something like that. She would just say we were being ridiculous and quote a Shakespeare sonnet about nature or something like that. We were trapped there. If it slithered up the side of the truck, I would die.

Her Dr. Scholl's were lying useless in the grass. Madding and I were holding each other.

She started to quote Shakespeare as I predicted, something about an innocent flower having a serpent under it, but then suddenly, she picked up the Dostoyevsky and hurled it at the snake, like Wonder Woman whipping her lasso of truth. The book crashed down on it. It lay lifeless in the grass, killed by the Russian missile.

I had to admit I was impressed. In that one moment she was different. She wasn't fragile. She wasn't a beautiful blonde. She wasn't glamorous. She wasn't stoned. She was a mother.

8

As soon as we walked in, I realized we'd been tricked. The only other kids were a boy and a girl with their dad. They were much younger than us. They were the only ones bowling. There was art all over the walls.

"Why isn't anyone bowling?" I said.

"They've turned the bowling alley into an art gallery!" my mother said. "It's a group show."

"Rip-off," my brother said.

"It's not a rip-off. You and Swanna can bowl," my mother said. "You can bowl next to those people." She pointed to the dad and the tiny kids.

"This isn't even real bowling," Madding said. "Those pins are skinny." He sounded really disappointed. He hadn't learned how to not get his hopes up yet.

"Yes it is," my mother said angrily, as if she had any idea what bowling even was.

"I think it's called candlepin bowling," I said. I had read it on the sign when we came in. Another big strike against Vermont. This was truly the most horrible state in the union.

"What do we have to do?" my mother said to Bowlmoronislav. "I want you to mingle. Don't worry about us."

"Um, I think we get them bowling shoes."

My mother took her wallet out of her pocketbook and gave me a ten-dollar bill. "Get shoes for you and your brother and tell them you're going to do bowling. But make sure to look at the art."

"I'll get us some drinks," Candlepinhead said.

My mother handed him money too. I couldn't believe she was paying for this guy. I could believe everything else, but not that.

"So we're supposed to bowl alone," I said.

"You're not alone. Let me show you Bor-i-slav's work." She was still pronouncing his name like it was in a rare foreign language. I didn't want to tell her she sounded like a lunatic and to stop doing that because I figured he would get really sick of hearing his name butchered and would break up with her.

I secretly liked art but I would never tell my mother that. She'd had an affair with a very famous artist the whole time she was married to my father, so we had quite a bit of his art in our apartment. I always wondered why my father didn't mind having the famous artist's art all over the walls—one wall of our living room was literally covered with a giant three-dimensional zigzag thing—but I guess if it was worth hundreds of thousands of dollars, he could look the other way.

My mother was wearing a dress I had never seen before, sheer and paisley with golden strands of thread in it, and a necklace the famous artist had given her which she thought was great but I was never too impressed with. She looked really good as usual. She was wearing her leather sandals that were custom-made with thousands of straps. She had very high arches and perfect legs like a dancer's.

She must really like this guy to even step foot in a place like this.

I got us shoes and they told us to go to lane number two, which was next to the other kids.

"Go get started," I told Madding. "I'll be right back."

I walked away from him toward the pay phone sign. It looked like it was from the fifties. The whole place had a great feel, like the drive-in movie scene in *Grease* with the dancing hot dogs. But it was also very dark.

I put a dime in the pay phone and said, "Collect from Swanna," when the operator came on.

The phone rang and rang and rang and then my father picked up.

"I have a collect call from Donna," the operator said.

"Who?" my father said.

"Swanna!" I yelled into the phone. "Dad, it's me."

"Collect from Donna, do you accept the charges?" the operator said.

"Donna Murphy?" my father said. She was a family friend who was also their pot dealer. "Okay."

I let out this gasping sound of relief. "Hi, Dad."

"Oh, Swanzy, how are ya?" He sounded very thrown off, like he was expecting to have to go bail Donna Murphy out of jail or something. There was so much I wanted to tell him.

"I'm fine," I said. "Did you go to the bus stop?"

"What? What bus stop?"

"To pick me up." My voice was breaking.

"No. Was I supposed to go to the bus stop to pick you up?"

"No, Mom picked me up. And Madding. She said she told you."

"Yes, your mother was supposed to get you. Are you at the bus stop now? Did she pick you up? That was a few days ago, wasn't it?" My eyes welled with tears and I tried to shake them off. He didn't even know we were okay. For all he knew, I could still be sitting on that hill at camp. He was always saying we were the most important things in the world to him, but the truth was, we were in the horrible state of Vermont, sleeping outside in a truck, and he didn't care at all.

"Do you even know where we are?" I said, trying to sound like I was kidding. "Like even what state we're in?"

"Uh, no," he said with a sort of laugh. "What state are you in? Is everything all right?"

"Everything's fine." Something squeezed hard in my chest and I had a painful feeling in my stomach and lower, in between my legs. There was no reason for me to cry, I told myself.

"Swan, are you okay?"

"Yeah, I'm in a bowling alley." I sounded like I was choking.

"That sounds fun!" my father said.

I heard someone in the background saying something—"Sloan, the game's on." It was a woman.

"Vermont is beautiful," my father said.

"Who's that?" I asked.

He paused. "A friend of mine," he said. "We're watching the Red Sox game."

"Madding and I have to sleep outside in a truck."

"What?"

"They don't allow kids in the house. We have no money for food. It's very dangerous here."

"Sloan," I heard the woman say.

"What do you mean it's dangerous? Put your mother on the phone."

"No," I said. "I'm not with my mother. I'm actually here with some camp friends. It's a big coincidence. I ran into this guy from camp, Nestor Perez, and his friends from the boys' hockey camp. I better go."

"That's nice," my father said.

"Yeah, I met some nice kids out here."

"All right, well, call me tomorrow. Is there a number there where I can reach you?"

"No, we're not in the house. We're in a truck." I was crying hard now so there were silences between my words.

"All right, call me tomorrow, will ya? Let me know when you're coming home. What day does school start?"

"Okay, bye," I whispered, and hung up. I pushed my back into the Formica wall of the phone booth and cried very hard and completely silently. My dad didn't want us. My ex-dad.

"Groovy shirt," a man's voice said behind me. "*WNEW-FM 102.7.*" He said it in a radio deejay voice like *This is WKRP in Cincinnati.*

"What?" I said, without turning around.

"On the back of your shirt."

I looked down and saw I was wearing my Elton John T-shirt from when I went to his concert in Central Park. It said, *Elton John, NYC Parks, keep them green*, with a picture of trees parted by a winding road that was like the keys on a piano. A counselor in the costume department at camp had cut it up for me, giving it a wide scoop neck and letting a tiny bit of my stomach show.

"Sorry, I'm using the phone," I said, and picked up the receiver. I didn't want to turn around because my face was covered in tears.

"Sorry," he said.

I waited a few seconds and wiped my face on my T-shirt, and then hung up the phone and turned around. He was still standing there staring at me.

"You done?" he said.

"Oh, sure," I said.

"You okay?"

"I'm fine," I said, trying to get past him.

"Wait. You're crying."

"I'm fine," I said. "My contacts were bothering me."

"Do you want me to take a look? I'm a doctor." He was smiling down at me. He had feathered hair that was mostly light brown with some darker streaks in it, and a pretty handsome face with stubble. He matched the foliage outside that was starting to turn. He looked like Vermont.

"You're an eye doctor?"

"Obstetrician."

"You don't look like a doctor," I said.

"You can ask my kids what I do. They can vouch for me." He pointed to the two little kids who were bowling in the lane next to the one I had set Madding up in.

Madding was talking to them. He could make friends with anyone. When we went to Cape Cod, Madding would just go up to a family on the beach and spend the whole day with them, eating their sandwiches and peaches and everything. You'd look over and see some other mom putting suntan lotion on him.

"How old?" I asked.

"Thirty-seven."

"I meant how old are your kids?"

"Oh! Four and six."

"Where's your stethoscope?" I said it in a very challenging and suspicious way.

"Car," he said, looking right at me. "What do you think I do if I don't look like a doctor?"

"I don't know," I said. "Maybe a garage guy."

"A garage guy?" He let out a very big laugh. "You mean a car mechanic? A grease monkey? I think I'm going to decide to take that as a compliment."

I shrugged and smiled. "Maybe a lumberjack." I was really starting to amuse myself.

"A lumberjack? Now you're just being flattering. Hey, we're both wearing shirts from concerts," he said. "Boston Garden on my birthday two years ago. December fifteenth."

"*Bruce Springsteen and the E Street Band*," I read on his chest.

"If you're done with the phone, I have to call my wife and tell her I haven't damaged the children."

"She should trust you if you're really a doctor."

"You would think. Maybe she doesn't believe I'm a doctor either. I just brought them here to get out of her hair for a couple of hours, but it's a strange crowd tonight. Art show of some kind. Hey, listen to that. It's Springsteen." A song had just started. "'Hungry Heart.' This song makes me so happy."

We both listened for a minute. I did like it but I couldn't help thinking about the wife and kids in Baltimore, Jack. And I couldn't help wondering if I was more like the man in the song when I should feel like the kids. Maybe that was why people liked it, because everyone wanted to feel like the man. Talking about music made me very tense. I didn't feel confident in that area. "He uses some bad grammar," I said.

"What?"

"You heard me."

"Are you serious?"

"Kind of," I said.

"Bad grammar?"

"*Don't make no difference what nobody says*," I said, pointing my finger up as if the words were written over my head. "Double negative."

"You're criticizing the Boss's grammar? That's tremendous. Incredible. Let me make this call and then maybe I could buy you a beer and you can correct some of the greatest songs ever recorded."

I saw Ms. Korn standing in front of a painting of green peppers. I waved at her but she didn't see me.

"Oh, you're with this group. You're an artist," he said.

"Writer," I said. It was strange that I said writer when I really should have said actress. I had no idea why *writer* came out of my mouth.

"Ah, right, grammar. But you're with the art group."

"Not really. But I have to go over there." I smiled at him.

"I'm glad you're feeling better," he said. "Maybe sometime you could tell me why you were crying."

"Bye," I said, and walked toward Ms. Korn, past about a dozen lanes. I didn't feel like telling him that I was too young to drink beer and explain to him what I was doing there with these crazy people and that my ex-father couldn't care less where I was. This guy seemed so happy with his kids and his normal life. He was a normal dad.

It must have been a pretty short call with his wife because when I glanced back, he was already with his kids and Madding, bowling again.

"Swanna!" Ms. Korn said. She seemed even more excited to see me than when I came to her office at school because I was failing something. "Your mother told me you were here!"

"I didn't know you were a painter. I *love* your work." I said it in as enthusiastic a way as possible without sounding sarcastic at all. I looked at the peppers with a very impressed expression on my face. "These would look very nice in a kitchen," I said.

"Thank you!" She most likely didn't get too many compliments, so the kitchen comment had probably given me enough bang for my buck.

My mother was very perverted to think they were "making love." They were just sitting in a bowl, although in one of the paintings one pepper had the words *I'm sick of being celibate* painted over it. I knew what celibate meant and it wasn't good.

"Just because I paint doesn't mean I don't love being a guidance counselor," she said.

I couldn't imagine how anyone could love being a guidance counselor and get lied to by people like me all day long. What a waste of time. She probably got lied to by at least twenty-five kids a day.

"I'm trying to get back to—" I stopped myself before I said New York because I thought of my father with that woman. I didn't know what I was supposed to do now. Madding and I could go to my mother's apartment and stay there by ourselves. I didn't have a key although there was a room in the basement with everyone's key on its own tiny hook. There were probably plenty of cans of Progresso soup and I was very good friends with the man who owned the bread store, so I could probably borrow some loaves of bread and eat mayonnaise sandwiches. Or Madding and I could sell books and toys on the street. Once we had sold a first-edition copy of *Tarzan* for fifty cents and my father was furious.

"To ArtCom?" Ms. Korn said.

"To New York," I said.

"Why? It's so wonderful here."

People traveled from all over the world to come to New York, I wanted to point out.

"I'm actually here against my father's wishes. My mother has kidnapped me technically. If I call the police she could get arrested. My father wants me to come home. They're putting me in the middle of their divorce."

Ms. Korn made a sad face that I had seen before. Nobody was more upset about my parents' divorce than Ms. Korn.

"Why don't you just enjoy your time here? Have you finished your summer reading?"

I couldn't believe she had the nerve to talk to me about summer reading when I was telling her I was in the middle of a custody battle. I had probably already read more books than she would ever read in her lifetime.

"How long are you staying here?" I asked.

"I have to leave tomorrow. We're expected back at school on Wednesday. We have to get there before you guys."

"Can you take my brother and me back with you tomorrow? I'd be happy to reimburse you for all the gas and tolls."

"I don't think that's a good idea, I'm sorry."

"I don't think you understand the danger I'm in here."

"You don't look like you're in danger, Swanna. Your mother is not that bad, you know. Don't you think you're being a little uptight? You really have to get serious this year at school. I would love to see you at an excellent college. Every grade will count from now on."

She looked so pathetic standing in front of her paintings with her wrinkly green pepper tits.

"That's okay, we'll just hitchhike," I said.

"Swanna, that would be much too dangerous."

"Don't worry about it," I said, and turned and walked away. I heard her call my name but I just kept going.

I saw the nice dad leaving with his kids. "Bye, Elton John," he said, but I just walked right past him.

Madding had left the lane. His sneakers were abandoned on the floor so I picked them up and went to the little arcade looking for him, but he wasn't there. He wasn't at the concession stand. Then I saw him with my mother and Dorkislav and someone else I knew from the city—a horrible man named Richard Henri, which was a totally fake name you were supposed to pronounce in a French accent but absolutely no one did. I had met him when my mother dragged me to a poetry reading at a gallery in SoHo.

"Swanna," my mother called, "you have to see Borislav's work."

I walked over there, ignoring Richard Henri, and looked at the painting which was unfortunately very clearly my mother, naked, sitting on Elvis Presley's lap.

"Hello, Swanna," Richard Henri said. He put his hand out for me to shake so I quickly put my hand in Madding's shoe like a glove and extended the shoe for him to shake. "Your raven hair's gotten so long."

"Are you done bowling?" I asked Madding.

"I'd be happy to bowl with you kids," Richard Henri said. "Swanna, you're so tan and lovely. Can I have a hug? I haven't seen you in ages."

I looked at him in disbelief, then I looked at my mother who didn't seem to care at all that this disgusting man wanted to hug me.

"I'm the only one who can hug her," Madding said. He took his sneakers and went to a plastic bench to put them on.

"I have never understood how your mother can be so blond and your tresses so black." He said it like he wanted an answer to a question he had given so much thought to over the years. "And both Jewesses. Who was that man you were speaking with?"

"I have no idea what you're talking about," I said.

"Isn't this painting extraordinary?" my mother said, looking at the one of herself.

"The tall man in the dungarees. You know who I'm talking about," Richard Henri said.

"Ree-shaar is an old friend of Bor-i-slav," my mother said. She pronounced both names so ridiculously I almost laughed out loud.

"Drinking buddies," he said. "Mostly at Puffy's. You know Puffy's, right, Swanna?"

"No," I said.

"Puffy's?" he said again.

"What the hell is Puffy's?" I said.

"Swanna," my mother said, "you're being very rude!"

"*I'm* being rude?" I wasn't the one looking at my chest. "I've just never heard of a place called Puffy's."

"It's a bar in Tribeca," Richard Henri said. "And I think we both know you have heard of it."

"No, I haven't."

"Yes, you have."

"That's pretty nuts," I said.

"Really, it doesn't ring a bell? Tile floor. Hot sake machine. The corner of Hudson and Harrison. I think when I saw you there you were having hot sake."

"I don't know what that is."

"I believe you know it quite well," he said.

My mother put her hands out like one of the models on *Let's Make a Deal.* "Richard Henri is a great writer. He just finished a new novel. It's so exciting."

"He's accusing me of being somewhere I never was," I said to my mother. Tile floors, green peppers, hot sake. All these people were insane.

"He's not accusing you of anything. You probably were there and you don't remember. Maybe you were there with your father. He likes bars."

"I wasn't there," I said.

"Yes you were. You took off your shirt to show everyone, quite a spectacle to behold," Richard Henri said.

"What?" I said.

My mother laughed.

"This is libel, Mom."

"She's on the debate team," my mother said. She gave me an angry look. "Swanna took off all her clothes in Janet Fish's art class when she was two. Janet Fish had to call me and say, 'Swanna will not keep her clothes on.' So I would not be surprised."

Richard Henri smiled. "It was fine. I didn't mind."

I could feel my face burning. I was angrier than I had ever been in my entire life. If I had a gun I would have used it. I wished so much Ms. Korn could have heard this.

9

That night, we lay in the back of the truck looking up at the stars.

"Tell me about Bronwyn and Jonwyn," Madding said.

Bronwyn and Jonwyn were a brother and sister I made up and Madding loved them, but I was terrible at coming up with stories on the spot. I lived in fear of him saying, "Tell me about Bronwyn and Jonwyn," which he did constantly.

"Okay," I said. "Where did we last leave them?"

"Cape Cod," Madding said. "They were playing on the beach in North Truro."

"Okay. So it's high tide and a whale swims over and offers them a ride on his back. And Bronwyn and Jonwyn are lying on his back and looking up at the stars. The whale is swimming very carefully so they won't—"

Suddenly I froze. I heard a rustling sound. Madding heard it too and put his hand in mine. I slowly sat up and saw something coming toward us. It was a bear. A big one. It was on its hind legs but was hunched, lumbering straight toward us. "There's a bear," I whispered. "Be quiet."

I heard it getting closer.

I reached into my bag and felt the puck I had taken from the ice rink and threw it as hard as I could at the bear, but I couldn't see if I hit it.

"Ow," I heard someone say. "Um. What was that?"

Then I saw it wasn't a bear, it was Bearislav.

"Where's our mother?" I yelled. I had the feeling he might be there to hurt us. I was shaking very badly. I didn't want him to see me in my *I Love Lucy* nightgown.

"Um," he said. "She's inside. Did you just throw something at me?"

"Mom!" I yelled.

"Um. Can you not yell?" he said. "I brought you an extension cord for the television set."

"Yay!" Madding said.

"We need to speak to our mother," I said.

"Um."

A bear would have been smarter.

"I have a forty-foot extension cord but I might need more for it to work."

"You can lower the tailgate and put it on that," Madding said. "This is great!"

"Actually sleeping inside would be great." I didn't want to admit that having a TV out here would help.

He did what Madding said and set the TV in the corner. I found my flashlight and shined it in his face. The TV wasn't turning on. I scanned the grass with the flashlight, praying I wouldn't see a snake, and saw the puck lying there. I had carved *NP* + *SS* in a heart on it with a ballpoint pen. It took awhile and I had to press very hard with the pen and trace over it several times.

"Can you get that?" I said.

He lumbered over, picked it up, and handed it to me. "I'll get it to work tomorrow."

He left, and Madding and I just sat there with the bum TV.

"What's that?" Madding asked.

"It's a puck my boyfriend at camp gave me. He carved our initials in it."

"How did he carve that?"

"I don't know," I said. "Maybe with a pen."

"Why would you want a puck?"

"It's a token of his feelings for me," I said.

"It matches your nightgown." He pointed to the cartoon figures of Lucy and Ricky with their orange and jet-black hair against red hearts. "She doesn't like him," he said, pointing to Lucy, who was turning away from Ricky with her hands clenched under her chin.

"No, she does. She's just acting shy."

"They look like they're fighting. Do they get a divorce?"

"No," I said. "They have a baby named Little Ricky."

My brother had no trust in love anymore. Ricky looked menacing to him and Lucy looked like she was going to run away and meet some artist with a truck.

"Can I have this? Is the guy who gave it to you a famous hockey player?" Madding asked.

"No, he's just a kid. I have to keep it. But when I talk to him, I'll ask him to give you one."

We lay down and I thought about a time I was taking a taxi down Fifth Avenue at night and I looked up and saw a beautiful bed pushed right up against the window on the third floor of a fancy apartment building. I looked up at a lot of beds in a lot of apartments, actually. It was a big, fluffy bed with sheets printed with pink roses. It was perfectly made with a lot of pillows in ruffled shams. I always wondered who slept in that bed. Whoever slept in it was both safe and cozy and totally vulnerable and exposed to anyone like me passing by.

They were in the most beautiful bed in the most beautiful apartment in one of the best buildings in the world, but they weren't that different from a homeless bag lady right downstairs on the street.

I tried to convince myself that things weren't that bad and I shouldn't feel so sorry for myself. You are not homeless, I told myself. It's not so bad sleeping in this truck. Your brother is next to you and your mother is inside and your father is only a few hours away. We were a family, but we would never sleep in the same house again.

There was a constant low percussion sound that could have been from a rattlesnake.

You are in that bed on the third floor on Fifth Avenue, I told myself. If you listen very carefully you can hear the Delacorte clock.

Right before my parents got separated, my mother called me into the dining room. Our dining room was huge with an oval glass table in the center over the red Bukhara Persian carpet. There was one of those doors that swings back and forth like in a restaurant kitchen, with a round window that opened into our kitchen and an archway into the foyer. One wall was lined with black bookshelves with *The Joy of Sex* featured dead center, and one wall was all windows with a long, wooden, splintery desk and two leather desk chairs and two typewriters and some Murano paperweights. There was a giant dictionary on its own stand that was always opened to a page that had a picture of a blue butterfly. Palos Verdes.

The fourth wall was covered floor to ceiling with a painting the famous artist had made.

My father was sitting in his desk chair and my mother was in a black bentwood chair at the table and Madding was at the table drawing one of his sports pictures. He always drew football players who looked like robots with square helmets and bodies. Even the football was square.

"We need you to help us with a decision," my mother said.

"Pizza," Madding said.

"It's not about dinner," my father said. "We're in a predicament."

"I'm pregnant," my mother said.

I had recently gone through her pocketbook looking for money and had found a black, completely see-through shorty baby-doll nightgown. I'd wondered at the time if she had used that to have sex with my father.

"We're thinking of not having the baby," my father said.

"Give it to an orphanage?" Madding asked.

"No," I said, "that's not what they're talking about."

"I can have an abortion," my mother said.

"We love you and your brother very much but we're not sure we should have another baby. We wanted to see what you think." My father stood up and walked in front of a bookshelf with giant jade chess pieces behind him. It was like they had come to life and were in the room too. We were all human chess pieces.

"Can we still have pizza?" Madding asked.

This wasn't how a husband and wife announced they were going to have a baby, I thought. In a soap opera I had just watched when I had stayed home sick from school, the wife had come up behind the husband while he was pretending to read and she wrapped her arms around his neck, and he said, "What's for lunch?" and she smiled and said softly, "How about pickles and ice cream?" and he turned and looked at her with a complete expression of shock and wonder and pride, and he said, "You're . . . I'm . . . we're . . ." and she said, "Yes, darling," and then they immediately started making out. And in an afterschool TV special I'd seen, this woman wanted to tell her husband she was pregnant so she decorated their Christmas tree with tiny baby socks on tiny clothespins, and when he walked in and saw it, he touched the little socks and looked up at her, confused, and then they started making out. And Lucy told Ricky when he was performing at the Tropicana, and then he sang, "*We're having a baby, my baby and me,*" and they were both so happy. There was no coming into the dining room and talking to the kids and using the word *predicament*.

"So, Swanna, Papa, what do you think?" my mother asked. My mother had been trying to get us all to call my brother "Papa" because people called Ernest Hemingway "Papa," but no one did it but her. There was no way I was going to call my little brother the same thing I called my grandfather. It was a terrible name for a kid.

I looked at one of the empty chairs around the table and imagined a little girl sitting in it. That little girl would be my sister.

While my mother tried to explain to Madding what baby she was talking about, I saw my sister's perfectly achieved Farrah Fawcett hair, her report card strewn with A's in every subject, chatting away about how she had just been given the part of Clara in *The Nutcracker*. She would probably be a blonde like my mother.

"Do you want to have another baby?" I asked.

My father looked very grave. It was like the baby was already with us, wrapped in a tiny black shroud, in a bassinet tucked under my father's desk, or shoved in my mother's pocketbook with the black baby-doll nightgown.

"We certainly love having you and your brother," my father said. But he certainly didn't look like he loved it. He looked like he wanted to throw himself out of the dining room window the way I had just moments before disposed of my ripped-up Latin test.

"What if you have an abortion and then you just get pregnant again?" I asked.

"I would have my tubes tied," my mother said bitterly.

"Ba-by, ba-by, ba-by," my brother chanted. "Have it! Have it!"

"You would be the middle child," I warned him. "That's not good. That's like Jan and Peter on *The Brady Bunch*."

"I wouldn't mind," he said.

"I don't think you should have this baby," I said.

My parents looked shocked. "You don't?"

"You asked my opinion and I gave it," I said, suddenly feeling sick to my stomach. I felt like a boa constrictor was tightening inside of me, as if the umbilical cord had left my mother and entered me. The baby was attached to me by an invisible balloon string and I was responsible for it now. It would follow me like that creepy red balloon followed Pascal through the streets of Paris. Even to school.

Maybe it was even here in Vermont.

Lying there in the truck, I wondered if I was any different from an abortion. Was I even there? Did I even still exist? And did my parents have more love for that baby they aborted than they did for me? Somewhere along the way, they had aborted me too, they just took longer to do it.

10

Just when I was finally falling asleep, my mother suddenly appeared at the truck. She was wearing her nightgown with the long, skinny satin ribbons hanging from it. She looked like a maypole. Once I had to wrap a present for my art teacher. The present was a little mouse wearing a beret and holding a paint palette standing next to a miniature easel in a plastic display box. They had them for every hobby and profession. I hated mice and I almost always hated cutesy things like this, but I loved these mouse characters in all of their outfits. I had wanted the wrapping to be nice so I cut one of the ribbons off that nightgown and to this day she never noticed.

"What are you doing?" I said. She was struggling to climb into the truck.

"I'm bunking with you tonight."

"Bunking?" My mother had never said a word like *bunking* in her life.

"Borislav and I had a fight."

Now I was very interested. "Is it normal to have a fight with someone when you've only been dating for about five minutes?"

"I don't know," my mother sulked.

"What did you fight about?" I asked.

"I don't want to talk about it."

She started to wedge herself between me and Madding, but I told her to go on the other side so my brother was between us. She had not brought a pillow.

Madding woke up and looked confused. "I had a dream I grew up and I got a snake and then I got a wife," he said.

"I'd rather you just get a wife," I said.

"I meant I got a wife for the snake," he said, and then fell right back to sleep. He could sleep anywhere, anytime. He could sleep on two chairs put together in a restaurant.

"You woke up Madding," I said.

"This is cozy," my mother said. "I can't imagine why you would complain about this."

If we were in a concentration camp, my mother would say it was cozy and she didn't know why I was complaining.

"He was drunk," I said. I realized he had been drunk when he came out to try to plug in the TV. That's why he had seemed especially idiotic.

"No he wasn't."

"Yes he was," I said. "I saw him drinking and he was slurring his words."

"He wasn't drinking," she said.

"Yes he was!"

"You're not making this easier for me. It has not been easy for him to accept my children."

"I don't need to be accepted by him. Now that it's over, we should go home. Someone can take us to a bus tomorrow."

"*Ew*, buses," my mother said, like a little girl. She cried for about thirty seconds. "Anyway, I can't go home. I have to stay."

"Why?" I said.

"I'm his muse. He has a commission. If he doesn't work, he won't get the money. I have to be here for him."

"His muse?"

I assumed she was kidding, but apparently she was serious because she said, "That's right." She said it like it was an actual job description in the *Weekly Wag* "Help Wanted" section. She said it so seriously that you could tell she actually, without any irony whatsoever, really thought she was a muse. Like if I got her one of those mice it would be wearing a long white Grecian dress and be perched on a cloud or a clamshell or something. She had been painted by two famous artists. There was a painting in MoMA called *Val*. I always pointed it out when we went on a class trip. She had been hit on by her teacher when she was sixteen. I guess those were her qualifications.

I hated myself at that moment because I realized I wanted to be a muse too, and I would probably never be one. I was jealous of the girl on the Bob Dylan album cover, walking arm in arm with him on a cobblestone street. His hands are in his pockets and she's got both her arms looped around one of his, and he's leaning into her as if she's saying something very fascinating. I wanted to be that girl more than I wanted to be anyone. More than I wanted to be Andrea McArdle or Valerie Bertinelli or Gilda Radner, or Ally Sheedy who published a book when she was sixteen because her mother was a big-time literary agent, I wanted to be whoever that was on the Bob Dylan album. Maybe that's why I had sat in the freezing rink watching Nestor Perez all summer, because I was trying to be his hockey muse, but his coach had told me that I was a distraction and his friends called me Chestor. They always said, "Hey, Chestor, where's Nestor?"

I cringed thinking about it.

"Borislav," my mother said. "Borislav." She was just crying and saying his name over and over.

"Stop that," I said. "Just go back in the house."

"No. He doesn't take my feelings into consideration."

"But didn't you just say you're the muse?" I was starting to get exasperated. "He's not *supposed* to care about your feelings."

"What?" she said.

"Artists don't take the muse's feelings into consideration. Is the artist supposed to ask the muse how they're doing? If they need anything? If they're feeling all right? Does Cinderella ask her fairy godmother, 'Hey what are *you* doing tonight? Do *you* have any plans? What are *you* going to wear? What time do *you* have to be home?' Did Leonardo da Vinci ask Mona Lisa if she was bored sitting there and was that why she couldn't muster up a bigger smile?"

I wished I could think of some more famous muses.

"Did Shakespeare say to whoever his muse was, 'Hey, what are *thou* working on?'"

I was really starting to a-muse myself. I was my own muse. I actually often woke myself up laughing out loud because my dreams could have very funny dialogue in them.

"Enough about me, Muse, let's talk about you—what do you think about me? Did Alice say to Lewis Carroll, 'I'm bored. It's my turn to write a book about you,'" I continued. "I've never heard of a muse saying, 'Okay, I've inspired you enough, why don't you inspire *me* for a change.'"

"Shakespeare's muse was a man. He was a homosexual," my mother said. "I don't find this funny. Oh, Borislav."

"No one would date that guy," I said.

"Your guidance counselor would."

"I don't think so."

"Oh, she would. She knocked on our door. That's how the fight started. She wanted to join us."

"Join you where?" I said.

"In bed. She wanted to swing. A ménage à trois."

I was so shocked I couldn't say anything for a minute.

I heard a sound and sat up. A scary light was coming toward us.

"Who is that?" I said.

"Um, is your mom there?" Borislav called out.

"He's drunk," I whispered to my mom. "I can smell it from here. He stinks of booze."

"That's a very ugly word." I didn't know if she meant *stinks* or *booze*. "It's not booze. He was eating Muenster cheese."

"That's not Muenster cheese," I said. "That's booze. He's a bum."

"No, it's Muenster cheese," she said.

"Come back to bed now," he said.

"Borislav," my mother whimpered.

"She's not going back in there," I said.

"Borislav."

"Um, this is between your mother and I."

Your mother and *me*, I thought. "Obviously," I said.

Then, suddenly, Obvislav turned his back to the truck and pissed right there in front of us. He was holding his dick and a big arc of pee was coming out of him.

"Ew," I said. "Who does that?"

"Come to bed, Val. I'm sorry, baby."

Baby? She was about fifty years older than this man.

Then my mother, the Muse of Muenster Cheese, rose up and he lifted her out of the truck and put her on the ground right where he had pissed, and I thought I'd rather *have* a muse than be one.

11

In the morning I told Madding what had happened. "They had a fight but they made up."

"Who would make up with that guy?" he said.

"I thought you liked him," I said.

"You thought I liked Boring Slob? Let's go find Mom and tell her we want to go home."

I followed Madding inside the house and into the kitchen.

"We're not allowed to have food."

"We need protection," he said. He opened up a cabinet and pulled a pot out by its handle. "You need a helmet too." He handed me a metal colander that was hanging on a hook.

"This is for washing grapes," I said.

He put his pot on his head and I put the colander on my head. The pot covered his eyes. "Let's switch." He put the colander on his head. "This is good. I can see through the holes." I put the pot with the handle on my head. I felt ridiculous but I could tell Madding was really enjoying this. He handed me a lid for a shield and took one for himself. He put a bottle opener in the pocket of his shorts and gave us each a long wooden spoon. "Now we're going to save Mom," he said.

We walked upstairs to their room and stopped outside the door because we could hear they were arguing.

"You're not as beautiful as you think you are."

Madding stopped giggling.

"You're drunk," my mother said. It was only about eleven in the morning, so I guess she'd figured he hadn't hit the Muenster cheese yet.

Then Madding made some kind of crazy jungle noise and started banging his wooden spoon on the door.

"What the fuck is that?" Drunkislav said.

He opened the door and Madding ran into the room hitting the spoon on the pot lid and screaming, "Get away from our mom!"

My mother was lying on the bed completely naked. You could see her bumpy nipples and her triangle of pubic hair. Her ribs jutted out and she had very, very big breasts, which were like white mountains because the rest of her was tanned.

"Get the fuck out of here," he said.

"*You* get the fuck out!" Madding screamed. He charged with the spoon, but Muensterslav took the colander off his head and threw it across the room.

"Madding, stop," my mother said. She rose up out of bed.

"Put some clothes on," I said to my mother. I threw her kimono at her and she put it on. I grabbed my brother's hand.

"Keep your crazy fucking kids away from me." He stormed out of the room.

Madding struggled to get out of my grasp and went and got the colander and put it back on his head. He was crying and breathing hard. "I want to go home."

I hugged him.

"Borislav didn't mean what he said," my mother told him.

"Yes he did," I said.

"No. He really didn't. You shouldn't have attacked him like that. You scared him."

I noticed an easel knocked over on its side in the corner of the room and a canvas facedown on the floor. I picked up the canvas and was very surprised to see the beginnings of myself on it. There was an outline of my face, with eyes and eyebrows started. I felt a red heat rising in me, an anger I had never felt before in my life. It felt like an anger I would never recover from. It reminded me of a Roald Dahl story I had read once about a man who tries to shoot some ducks and gets so angry he turns into a duck himself. I looked up from myself on the canvas to my eyes in the mirror on the closet door. I was like one of those little children in Africa who was afraid of cameras because they thought it would steal their soul. Now it had happened to me.

"What is this?" I heard myself say.

"Isn't it wonderful?" my mother said. "Richard Henri wants to buy it when it's finished."

I couldn't speak. I turned and walked out of the room like the Roald Dahl duck man with Madding waddling right behind me.

My mother put on her pink flowy dress and came outside to the truck.

"If you don't take me home right now, I'm going to call the police," I said.

My mother laughed. "I'm going to call the police and tell them to arrest my thankless daughter. *How sharper than a serpent's tooth . . .*"

Thankless was my mother's favorite word. She was

constantly quoting *King Lear*. I practically knew all of *King Lear* by heart because she never stopped quoting it.

"This place is literally filled with serpents," I said. The dead snake was gone, which was almost creepier than having it lying there under the book.

"Tell it to the judge," she said sarcastically.

"Being thankless is not against the law, but child abuse is."

My mother laughed again. "I wouldn't call taking you bowling child abuse. In what way is this abuse?"

"If the bowling is in the state of Vermont, it is. Having to beg for food. Riding in the back of the truck. School is about to start. It's illegal to keep me out of school."

"The world doesn't revolve around you," my mother said.

"But it revolves around you?"

"Yes, it does. I'm in love. When you're in love, the world revolves around you. I had hoped you would be happy for me. After sixteen years of misery with that pervert, I am finally happy and you're not going to ruin that for me. I have met my Russian prince."

"He's just a drunk from New Jersey," I said.

My mother climbed up on the truck and sat on the mattress next to Madding. "Let's make up and snuggle," she said.

"We're not sleeping out here again," I said calmly. "There's snakes. This whole state is a snake pit. You'll have to pay for a hotel."

"It's child abusion," Madding said.

"Ms. Korn would call this neglect."

"I bought you everything you're wearing and sent you to a fancy theater camp. That's not neglect."

"You didn't buy me this barrette!" I screamed.

"Well, everything else."

"I can't stand it here another second!" I screamed, and stormed off.

I walked into the woods, picking up two big rocks along the way in case I saw another snake. I had eaten my meager toast so I couldn't leave bread crumbs. I inspected a log next to a stream and sat on it carefully.

I couldn't believe she had tried to take credit for my barrette, which I had gotten from the Japanese woman in our building who committed suicide. She lived in 16A and was always elegantly dressed with gigantic sunglasses. Once I saw her in the elevator and she said she would like to give me something and I should go to her apartment. She handed me a black lacquer box that was made up of three trays with a lid. In each of the trays there were beautiful barrettes and combs covered in pearls and crystals. She insisted I take it, and a purple kimono with big pink flowers all over it, and a delicious piece of cake. She asked me what made me happy and I thought about it and said I wasn't really a happy kind of person. I said having interesting and unusual experiences like being at her apartment made me happy, and getting presents and eating cake. I was always especially happy if there was a bake sale at school. Of course, I loved reading and TV and movies and Broadway shows and going to the zoo or Coney Island. And doing things for my brother. But I wasn't sure if those things made me happy exactly.

She said she had a sister in Tokyo. She was smiling a lot and trying very hard to come up with the English words for what she wanted to say. When I left she made me take the whole cake to share with my brother. It was in a bakery box with just the slice I had eaten missing from it. It was pink and had green grapes on it, which was a very strange thing to have on a cake but surprisingly delicious.

"Don't you want it?" I asked, and she smiled and said, "No, it doesn't make me happy," and I assumed she meant because of the grapes.

The next day, at seven a.m., she jumped out of her window. When I left for school there were police in front of our building. Roger the doorman told me she left a note that said, *I love everybody. Please do not worry about me.* He said she had no friends or family except her sister who had just died of cancer in Japan.

I asked how he knew that and he said she used to come down to the basement once a week and have coffee with him and this other guy, Tony, in the laundry room. She had given them stuff from her apartment too.

"I know something about the Asian people," Roger had said. "You know, because the mother of my children is from Thailand." I nodded even though I didn't know that. He was very nice but he was very unattractive and I felt sorry for the mother of his children.

"They are a very proud people," he said. "Respect is the most important thing to them, and like, you know, not to be too gross or nothing, but do you know why they are the biggest manufacturer of blow-up lady sex dolls in the world? Because the men ask out one woman on a date and if they get rejected or something like that, they never ask out anyone else again for their whole lives. Someone probably disrespected

Kimi and that's why she did it. But Kimi, she was very nice. She was all dressed up for work when she did it."

I wanted to stay in the lobby with Roger but I had to leave for school.

That was probably the thing that had surprised me the most. Seven a.m. seemed like a time you would be least likely to kill yourself. If you made it to seven you could just say, *Okay, it's morning, I made it through another night.* And it was especially surprising because my favorite thing in her apartment was a clock. It looked like a normal clock, but every hour on the hour, the face of it broke open like a lotus flower into four parts and four glittering children danced in a circle to music, and then after a minute, it closed up again. The tune had sounded familiar to me, but I only had one minute to figure out what it was. On my last visit there I had finally recognized it. It was *Hello Muddah, Hello Faddah, here I am at Camp Grenada,* which I thought was a very strange song for a beautiful Asian clock.

She had jumped at exactly seven, so the music would have been playing and the children would have been spinning.

I told my mother about Kimi and she said she was going to write a poem about her. My mother didn't even know her. That's how writers were. They were constantly using you. If something bad happened to you, they couldn't wait to write a poem about it. I told her not to tell Madding, but as soon as he walked in the room, she said, "The woman in 16A jumped out of her window." My mother loved to tell us gruesome things. Her favorite children's book to read us was *Struwwelpeter,* which was a German book of stories that warned you not to do things, like if you sucked your thumb, someone came with a big scissors and chopped it off; or if you daydreamed, you walked off a pier and drowned. She always read it in a scary voice even if we begged her not to. My mother didn't know anyone in our building except the people on our floor, a woman in 3B who had an affair with my father and a famous feminist named Adrienne Rich. How do you live in a building and not know anyone in it? I knew everyone in our building. Everyone, on every floor, on both sides of our building.

Thinking about my building was making me feel homesick. I should have been sitting on my bed instead of this log, and holding the receiver of my Trimline phone instead of a big red leaf. I heard a rustling sound and looked up to see a deer not far from where I was sitting, drinking from the stream. It looked right at me for a minute and then galloped off. I couldn't help but wonder if the deer was Kimi. I was an atheist but I still wondered things like that. I thought most atheists probably did.

I sat there for a while longer and then walked back to the house, went right into the kitchen, and picked up the phone receiver and dialed 911.

"What is the emergency?" a woman said.

"My mother and her boyfriend have, um, brought me to this place," I said quickly.

"What is your location?"

"I don't know," I said. My heart was racing. "I'm supposed to be in New York."

"Do not get off the line," the woman said. "Do you understand?"

"Yes," I said. "I just need someone to—"

"Do not hang up the phone. What is your name and age?"

"Swanna Elizabeth Swain. Fourteen. I'm with my brother, Madding Dylan Swain, he's eight."

I heard a beeping sound in the background.

"Are you hurt? Do not hang up the phone."

I didn't say anything. I suddenly didn't feel like dealing with any of this. I hung up.

I felt bad about Kimi. They had put up yellow police tape on her door, and I thought of all the beautiful treasures from Japan locked inside. Her apartment was like the lacquer box she had given me, filled with things she had carefully selected, except for what she had given away. Her apartment was like King Tut's tomb.

This life was the afterlife. The afterlife was this life. All we had were the things we collected along the way.

I heard a siren and went outside to see an ambulance speeding into the driveway.

Two men got out and walked quickly to the house. I ran to the front door and opened it. "I think there's been a mistake," I said.

Nadine and a couple of the artists rushed over.

"What's going on?" Nadine said.

"Someone called an ambulance," one of the guys said.

"I'm the director here," Nadine said.

"I called the police but I didn't call an ambulance," I said. Vermont could not get anything right.

"Is someone hurt?" the ambulance worker asked.

"No, I didn't request an ambulance," I said.

Madding came running over.

"Did you call 911?" the man said to me.

"Yes, I have to speak to the police."

"What's wrong?" Nadine said. She was glaring at me. "ArtCom is not responsible for this."

A green police car pulled up and two police officers got out. One was a woman. She had long brown hair tied in a ponytail and she looked unbelievably terrible in her police pants. They were hunter green with a beige stripe down the side, and the shirt was beige and brown with a yellow patch with a deer and a Christmas tree on it. It looked like it had been designed by a child. Both of the cops had guns.

"We got a call from a minor," the policeman said.

"I am she," I said, stepping forward.

"What's the problem, honey?" the policewoman asked.

"My brother and I were brought here against our will. Our father doesn't know where we are. We have to get back to New York."

"Is this your brother?" the policeman said. I thought it was pretty obvious that he was, because he was standing next to me holding my hand and he looked exactly like me, but I didn't make any sarcastic comments.

"Yes, officer," I said.

"Where in New York?"

"Manhattan," I said proudly.

He pulled a radio out of its holster and said some numbers into it. "Check missing children reports out of New York City," he said. "Manhattan. Swain, Swanna and Madding."

"Who brought you here?" he asked.

"Our mother," I said.

"Her mother is not a resident here," Nadine said.

He looked at the woman cop and then back at me. "All

right, everyone, let us talk to the kids alone. Thank you." He gestured for everyone to leave and they headed back to the house.

The director ran toward the studios, probably to get my mother. The ambulance drove away.

"Is Mom here on the premises?" he asked. I hated when people were talking to you and they referred to your mother as *Mom*.

"Yes, she's here with her alcoholic, druggy boyfriend. I just need for my father to be called so he can come and get us."

"Do you want us to call your father?" the cop said to Madding.

Madding shrugged. "I don't know. It's not so bad here."

I let go of his hand. "You hate it here!" I said. "We're not allowed in the house. We have to sleep in that truck. There's marijuana everywhere."

The cops looked over at the truck and the man wrote down the license plate number.

"How did you call 911?" the policewoman asked.

"On the phone in the kitchen."

"I thought you weren't allowed in the house?" the male cop said.

My mother was walking toward us.

"I'm allowed in to make a phone call," I said.

"Seems like a handful," the male cop said to the female.

"It's a very serious thing to call 911," the policewoman said.

"I know." I was getting angrier and angrier.

"What is it you want?"

"I want to call my father."

"Why don't you just call him from the phone you used to call us?"

"He's not answering his phone," I said. "He doesn't know where we are."

"What's going on?" my mother said.

The cops introduced themselves and asked to speak to her alone. We waited outside while they went into the house with her.

"Why'd you do that?" Madding said.

"Do what?" I said.

"Call the police! You could get Mom into trouble."

"She *should* get in trouble!" I said. "This isn't normal. It's not safe to drive in the back of a completely open truck. We could get killed. Didn't you hear all those cars honking at us? They were trying to get Mom's attention!"

"I thought it was fun. Remember when Mom killed the snake?" Madding looked like he was going to cry. He was acting like *I* was the one who was bad. Madding always forced me to yell when I didn't even want to. He turned me into a shrew.

"You're only eight. You shouldn't be in this environment. Leave me alone." My voice was shaking.

"I'm sorry," Madding said. He tried to hold my hand but I pulled my arm away.

I climbed up on the truck and started putting my things in my duffel bags because I was pretty sure I was finally going to get to go home.

The cops came out of the house with my mother and walked over to me. "We spoke to your mother and your father."

"He's not my father," I said, pointing at Smokislav, who was standing in front of the house looking at us and smoking a cigarette.

"We spoke to your father," the cop said.

"You called him?" I was trying not to look at my mother. She looked sad.

"Yes. He said your mother has every right to have you here."

"I didn't kidnap you, Swanna. You're my daughter."

"Then why are you always smoking pot in front of me and putting my life in danger with that alcoholic?"

"These are serious accusations," the cop said. "I think you should think about this before you go calling the police."

"I did think about it," I said. "Is my father coming?"

"No, we're going home next week," my mother said.

"Did you tell Dad I wanted to go home? I don't believe you talked to him!"

"Take care of your big sister, okay, buddy?" the cop said, and patted Madding on the head extremely condescendingly. I would actually kill someone if they patted me on the head.

"I will, Officer," Madding said. He looked at me but I looked away.

"Your mother is allowed to have friends," the male cop said. "You have to cut her some slack. She's an attractive lady." I realized I had handled this very badly. I should have had evidence. Maybe taken some photos with my Vivitar camera or interviewed some witnesses. I had interviewed Curtis Sliwa from the Guardian Angels for a school project. He was very nice.

"Don't you think you should put her in juvenile detention?" my mother said, in her scary voice.

"I'd rather be in juvenile attention than here. At least I'd have a bed and some food." There wasn't even any such thing as juvenile detention. This wasn't the fifties.

The cop laughed. "Juvenile attention. That's funny."

"What?"

"You said juvenile attention."

I stormed into the house, picked up the phone, and dialed my father's number. It rang and rang.

"I really have to ask you to leave the kitchen," Nadine said.

"I'm just calling my father," I said. "It's a collect call."

"You're making a lot of noise and causing distraction for residents. This is a place to create. A sanctuary."

"Hello?" my father said.

"Collect call from Swanna," the operator said. "Do you accept the charges?"

"Yes," my father said.

"Dad?" I said.

Nadine grabbed the phone receiver from my hand and hung up.

"Why'd you do that!" I screamed. I stormed back out of the house, grabbed my jean jacket and army-navy bag from the truck, and started walking. The cops were gone and my mother didn't try to stop me.

12

Of course, hitchhiking could be safer than walking alone on a completely deserted road where a person or a bear could pull you into the woods. In New York, if you found yourself alone on the street—like if you were coming home by yourself after ballet or a debate tournament and you thought someone was following you—you could walk right in the middle of the street where there were always taxis, or go into a restaurant.

The road was very hilly, black tar with a yellow dotted line down the middle of it, a few houses by its side with land between them. Nothing too impressive.

I walked in a straight line, not turning on any of the side roads called things like Upper Samsonville or Lower Bone Hollow, because I knew I would end up just going back to ArtCom and I didn't want to get lost. There was nothing to look at except stupid nature. Trees which were nothing but furniture for birds. I wasn't really going to leave my brother there. If there had been a car, I didn't really know what I would do anyway, actually put out my thumb? In old movies the woman would lift up her skirt one inch above her knee and the car would come screeching to a halt, but I was wearing jeans and sneakers.

I watched two chickens literally cross the road.

Then a car drove by while I was standing looking at the chickens. I froze. I wasn't really going to do it. I had my small army-navy shoulder bag I had gotten at Canal Jeans with five dollars and some change in it, and my contact lenses, saline solution, and sanitizing machine, just in case I got up the guts to do it, but I wasn't going to do it.

I turned around to walk back toward the artist colony and saw a car coming toward me. I kept walking but the car stopped a little ahead of me and the driver said something out his window. He was on the other side of the road and I couldn't hear him, so I kept walking.

"Everything okay?" he asked as I was passing his car.

"Everything's fine," I said. I knew in the country you had to smile and wave and talk to everyone and say "Howdydoo" or whatever people said out here. You couldn't just walk by.

"Hey, Elton John, it's me. We met at the bowling place."

"Oh, hi," I said. It was the nice dad. "Bruce Springsteen."

"Right!"

"Where are you going?" I asked.

"Why, do you need a ride?"

"No, not really. I'm just taking a walk," I said. "I just wondered where you're driving."

"Cumby. Have to pick up some things."

"Like what?"

"Cottage cheese for my wife. You need anything from there?"

"Yeah," I said. "Can you take me?"

He leaned over and opened the door for me and I got in. "I don't usually pick up hitchhikers," he said.

"I'm not a hitchhiker. Although I do have to get back to New York, so maybe I should be."

"New York!" he said, smiling at me. He was pretty good-looking with his feathered hair. I had to remember what he looked like so I could tell Jacquie Beller. I would say he had light-brown hair, but she would call it dirty-blond. It was dark gold. "That's four hours from here. By car," he said. "Manhattan?"

"Yup."

"What neighborhood? Let me guess. Upper East Side?"

"Upper West."

"Columbia?"

"Yes." I was smiling and I knew the gap in my top front teeth was showing. I usually tried to smile with my mouth closed. He looked at his digital watch and I saw the gold wedding band on his finger.

"Ah, so you don't drive because you're from New York. That makes sense. All right," he said, "I'll go to New York."

"Really? We're going to New York?"

"There's a painting at the Met that reminds me of you. *Salome*. I'd like to show it to you."

"So we're going?"

"No," he said sheepishly. "I guess not. You got me there. I like the idea of it though. But my wife really needs that cottage cheese."

I felt a little mad at myself for falling for his joke. But I was also relieved. I didn't want to go without Madding. When we got to the store, I could call my father and he could come and get us.

"But seriously. You shouldn't hitchhike. It's dangerous."

"Why?" I said. "I got in your car and you're not dangerous. Are you?" This came out very teasingly. I was very good at making my voice sound sexy because my favorite thing to do, besides answering the ads in the back of the *Wag*, was call into the Dr. Ruth Westheimer radio show every Wednesday night and ask ridiculous made-up sex questions. I had to keep changing my voice because the producers would make you ask your question first before they let you on the air. I always had two questions prepared—the one I would tell the producers and then the ridiculous one I would ask Dr. Ruth. I wasn't sure, but I thought he was getting a hard-on because he had to shift all around.

"No! I'm the opposite of dangerous."

"Right," I said. "You're a doctor."

"So New York City, huh?" he said. "Something big waiting for you there? A boyfriend?"

"Maybe." I said. "I'm just trying to get home. Do you know where I could get a bus schedule? I'll probably take the bus back with my brother."

He laughed. "You sound like a runaway."

"I'm not a runaway. I'm the opposite of a runaway. I'm running *to* home, not away from it. I've been kidnapped by artists, if you want to know the truth. Hey, do you ever need a babysitter?"

He pulled into the parking area of the Cumberland Farms.

"I'm not sure how my wife would feel if I brought you home to babysit," he said.

I didn't know what he meant by that but I didn't appreciate being called a runaway by a married dad with an erection. "Well, that's too bad because I'm very good at it." If I could have babysat, I could probably make enough in one night to get two bus or train tickets home. "Thank you for the ride," I said, opening the door. "Give my best to your wife. I'm going to use the phone."

"I'm going to get some gas before I run in there," he said.

I really didn't care what he did. I was an extremely experienced and fun babysitter. I was annoyed by the runaway comment. I headed to the phone booth, put in a dime, and pressed 0 and my father's number. "Collect from Swanna," I told the operator.

The phone rang about ten times. The operator came back on but I hung up before she could tell me that he wasn't there. I went into the store to get change for a dollar and to buy M&M's for Madding. I was going to try to call Port Authority and see if I could find out how to take a bus and how much it would cost.

"Do you know where there might be a bus stop near here?"

The man behind the counter had no idea.

"Any luck with your phone call?" the married dad asked me.

"No," I said. "Do you think you could drive me back to where you picked me up?"

We got back into his car. "I'm very sorry I can't take you to New York." He was smiling shyly at me. "I'm sorry I called you a runaway. I thought about it and that wasn't nice. Not cool. I hope that didn't upset you."

"Not at all," I said. "Why would it upset me? If you think I'm a dangerous runaway and your wife wouldn't want me to babysit, I understand."

"I did upset you," he said. "I knew it." He looked very upset himself. "What I meant is, you're a knockout. My wife would not like that I'm talking to a beautiful woman."

I smiled a little because I hadn't thought of that.

"My wife's very beautiful too. Don't get me wrong. I'm a very lucky man."

He didn't look too lucky. He looked very upset.

"I really would like to help you get back to New York. I mean, if my grammar's been okay. I haven't used any double negatives, have I?"

"Not yet," I said.

"Maybe I could make it up to you. I could figure out the bus schedule. Drive you and your brother to the bus stop. Can I call you?" He reached behind him and emptied the contents of the Cumberland Farms bag—a box of garbage bags and the cottage cheese—and handed me the brown paper bag and a pen.

I wrote my name on the bag and then I realized I didn't have a number to give him.

"It's a house with a lot of people in it. There is a number but I'm not sure what it is. You'd have to ask for me and they might not know who I am."

"Swanna," he said, looking down at my name. "That's pretty. You're pretty. I'm Dennis." He tore off a piece of the bag, wrote down his number on it, and handed it to me. "This is my office phone. Please call me."

I took his number and put it in my jeans pocket. I thought about the Mistress Amber column Jacquie and I had read where PhD asks for her phone number and she says, "Do you want to kiss me?" and he does.

Now I *knew* he had an erection. I leaned toward him and I knew he could see down my shirt a little. He put the torn bag on his lap.

"This is crazy," he said. "I don't know what it is about you."

"Do you want to kiss me?" I asked, in my sexy Dr. Ruth Westheimer voice.

"Yeah I do, but I can't. It's not a good idea," he said.

"*I* think it's a good idea," I said. I had to remember every minute of this to tell Jacquie. That was the thing about life. If I hadn't gotten stuck in Vermont, something like this would never have happened to me. I would never have known what this was like. "I can't kiss you. I'm married. I really don't do things like this."

"But what if I want you to?"

"Jesus." He looked in the rearview mirror. "I can't."

"Yes you can."

Then he leaned over and kissed me. It was very slow and I closed my eyes.

"Oh my God," he said. "I want to see you again and I don't even have your number. Can I take you to dinner tonight?"

"Tonight?"

"Do you have plans?"

I shook my head. I wondered what excuse I could give to leave, and what the dinner was going to be.

"I could pick you up at seven. Then we can talk more. Talk about getting you home to New York."

"Okay," I said.

He dropped me off at the art colony and I saw that the truck was gone and Madding was watching the TV where the truck had been. He was just sitting on the grass all alone watching the little olive-green TV with its cord snaking all the way into the house through a window.

"Where were you?" Madding said.

"I went to try to call Dad," I said. "I got you these, but I was still right to call the police." I gave him the M&M's.

"Thank you!" he said. I smiled because I always got a kick out of it when he said please and thank you. He was really a very polite little kid. But it also made me a little sad at the same time. "Those cops were cool," he said.

I went into the house to pee. When I got out of the bathroom, I saw the truck had pulled up and Bozoslav was walking toward the house carrying a bag of groceries in his arms, probably purchased with my mother's money. I was relieved it wasn't a Cumberland Farms bag. This was very awkward considering I had just called the cops on him.

I was going to have to face him sooner or later, so I just stood there.

"Um, you're back," he said.

I looked at him and then looked away quickly. He wasn't like any man I had seen before. I had known several drunks and potheads, but none like this. Only his eyes seemed drunk. His eyes looked hurt. His cheeks were wide and flat like they'd been under a rolling pin.

"I'm sorry I called the police," I said. "But I really don't appreciate being painted against my will. If you ever paint me or my brother again, you'll be very sorry. It's illegal. My grandfather's an attorney." I was so angry I was shaking.

"Ooooh, heavy threat," he said.

"How old are you?" I asked him. I wasn't good at guessing people's ages. He acted like he was about five.

"Um. You probably think I'm too young for your mother, but I don't think age has anything to do with love."

"I don't think love has anything to do with love," I said nonsensically. I had never regretted asking anything so much in my whole life. Now he was saying they were in love. My parents weren't even divorced yet. They were separated. "I was just asking how old you are. It's a normal question."

He lifted two six-packs of beer out of the bag, wrote a *B* on each can with the marker hanging on a string on the wall, and put them in the fridge. Writing your initial on a beer was probably the most pathetic thing a person could do.

"Um." He sort of gulped like a cartoon frog. His voice reminded me of a song called "Tubby the Tuba" on a Danny Kaye record I used to listen to. "I don't really like to give out personal information about myself."

"You won't tell me how old you are?"

"When you're a Russian living in the US, it's not the wisest thing to do."

I doubted he would ever know the wisest thing to do. "I thought you were born in New Jersey."

"My mother's Russian," he said.

"What's your father?"

"German."

"So you're American of Russian and German descent," I said. "Same as me. Same as everyone."

He looked at me with his stoned eyes. "Um," he frogged.

"I wasn't exactly going to call the Kremlin and tell Brezhnev your age." I was, however, going to make a point of stealing his wallet the first chance I got and looking at his driver's license. Dennis had told me his age without having a paranoid fit. When we were in the bowling alley he had said he was thirty-seven.

"I'm not worried about Brezhnev. Jimmy Carter was the problem," Traitorslav said.

"Yeah, right, Jimmy Carter's the problem," I said back. "Our family is all Democrats, by the way. My father campaigned for McGovern. I really don't think Jimmy Carter cares about any personal information about you."

"What are you two talking about?" my mother said, coming through the swinging kitchen door. We had a door like that between the kitchen and the dining room in our apartment, and my brother and I were always getting slammed in the face by it because we weren't tall enough to see through the round glass window.

"He refused to tell me his age."

"Why would he tell you anything when you tried to have us arrested?" My mother glared at me with a look I was very familiar with. It meant the last thing she wanted me to do was to bring up the fact that she was obviously about a million years older than this jerk. If I ever revealed my mother's age to anyone for any reason, she screamed at me. Even though she looked very good for forty-three. She said a woman never revealed her age. I wasn't even sure she knew her age anymore. She was the opposite of a feminist. It was amazing she was actually good friends with Erica Jong. "Don't ask rude questions," she said.

"I met someone I know from camp at the bowling alley," I said. "Her family is taking me to dinner tonight. And I might sleep over. But Madding can't sleep alone in the truck."

"He'll be fine with the TV," my mother said.

"You have to let him sleep here. He can't sleep in the truck by himself. And he has a very loose tooth. You have to put money under his pillow if it falls out."

"Madding knows the tooth fairy isn't real, and he is much braver than you think. I think you're the one who's afraid," my mother said.

13

Dennis came to pick me up right at seven. He pulled the car up and I got in. I had been standing at the entrance to the driveway. He was wearing the same jeans with a different button-down shirt and he smelled very good.

I loved sitting next to him in the car. It was big like my grandfather's.

"There's a place I like. Very casual. Is that okay?" he asked when we'd been driving for a while.

"Okay," I said.

"To be brutally honest with you, I almost didn't show up."

"Why?" I asked.

"This isn't New York. It's a small town."

"You consider this a town?" I said.

"Very funny. My point is, I know everyone here. I don't want my wife to find out I'm taking you to dinner."

"Then drive me back," I said. I wanted to eat in a restaurant, but it wasn't going to be worth it if he was going to be paranoid about his wife the whole time.

"Driving you back would be something I would regret for the rest of my life."

The radio was playing softly. "Book of Love" was ending and "Sloop John B" started. "*This is the worst trip I've ever been on . . .*"

"Well, that's quite apropos," I said.

He grinned. "'Runaway' ended right when I pulled into the driveway," he said.

He drove us to a diner with big booths and giant plastic menus. There was a jukebox on every table.

"This is great," I said.

"Really? My wife hates this place."

"How could you hate this place?" It was called the Galaxy Diner and there was a mural with planets and stars on the wall. The planets were not in the correct order but I didn't say anything. I was trying to be less judgmental.

"She says she can make everything they have on the menu at home. When she goes out to eat, she likes something fancier."

"That's logical," I said, even though it was the stupidest and most boring thing I'd ever heard. Why wouldn't you just eat what you felt like eating? When I was an adult, I was going to eat everything I wanted to every second of every day.

"After that night at the bowling alley, I thought about you," he said. "I'll admit I drove past that artist place a few times. Even wondered if I should go to New York, hang around Columbia looking for you."

"You wouldn't find me," I said.

"But I *did* find you. That's the amazing thing."

"It is pretty amazing," I said.

"I want to hold your hand really bad," Dennis whispered. "You've cast a spell over me."

I felt myself blushing. "You can," I said. I had been playing with the wrapper of my straw and I stopped and laid my hands palm down on the table. They suddenly felt like the most valuable things in the world. Like two *Mona Lisas* in the Louvre. He put his hands palms down on his side of the table. Our hands were like planets floating in the black speckled galaxy that was the diner table.

"I can't," he whispered.

I could feel electric currents connecting our hands, but they didn't move.

We ordered grilled cheese and tomato sandwiches and welldone fries and Diet Pepsis.

"Do you mind if we change seats?" Dennis asked.

"Okay," I said. "Why?"

"I'd just feel better if I could see the door."

"I thought your wife hated this place."

He stood up. "I'm just nervous and—"

"Dr. Whitson!" a woman said, coming up behind him.

"Shit," Dennis said, plastering a big fake smile on his face. A man and two little boys had followed her over to our table.

"How are you?" the woman said. "How are Kathy and the kids?"

Dennis smiled. "All fine, thanks! How are you guys? You're getting so big," he said to the kids. Kathy, I thought. Kathy and Dennis.

"Dr. Whitson delivered both our boys," the woman told me. She was smiling so hard with this big, gaping gummy smile that she might as well have gotten down on the floor right there in the restaurant and spread her legs wide apart to reenact the happy memory.

"Best-looking babies I ever saw," Dennis said.

"Sorry to interrupt you," the woman said. "Or were you leaving?"

"I didn't see your vehicle out front," the man said. "You still driving a Lincoln?"

The waitress came with our sandwiches and fries and put one plate down in front of me and one down on the other side of the table.

"Thank you, looks good!" Dennis said, like he had never eaten in a diner before. He could be very fake. He sat down, smashing into the corner of the table.

"We're the Kroegers," the woman said to me. She started telling me everyone's name.

"I'm Swanna," I said. "I'm going to be babysitting for the Whitsons."

It was fun calling families by one name like that, the Kroegers and the Whitsons. We didn't do that in New York. In New York, mothers usually had their own last names. I looked up at the dad, who was staring at my chest.

"We'd love to hire you too," the mom said.

I gave an *I told you so* look to Dennis.

"Great to see you all," Dennis said.

"Nice to meet you," I said, looking at the husband and smiling the way I knew my dimple would show. Then I noticed Dennis give the dad a weird look, and the dad looked away quickly. They started to go but I suddenly remembered I had two blue-and-purple lanyard bracelets in the snap pocket of my denim jacket that I had made at camp—a box stitch and a zipper stitch. "Oh, wait!" I said.

"What are you doing?" Dennis whispered. He was sweating even though we were sitting under a ceiling fan. They turned back around.

"Would you like these?" I asked, handing a lanyard to

each of the boys. I could give them away because I had another one in my bag for Madding. "I have to tie it around your wrist," I said.

"That's so nice!" the mom said. "What do you say?"

"This is cool. Thank you," the older kid said, when I'd finished knotting his.

"This means we're friends. I can show you how to do them when I come babysit."

The dad shuffled his family away like a sad sheepdog. "I told you I'm a great babysitter," I said.

"That wasn't fun," Dennis said. "I'm sorry."

"You looked like you thought I was going to blow your cover or something."

"That guy Kroeger was looking at you," Dennis said.

"No he wasn't," I said.

"Yeah he was. I almost punched him in the face. He's lucky he's still alive."

"Didn't you take the Hippocratic oath? Wouldn't you have to save him?"

"I'm not going to sit here and let some jerk look at your tits like that!" Dennis said. "I can knock him out and *then* I can save him."

I liked seeing Dennis jealous like that. Men looked at me all the time, but I'd never had someone get upset about it and want to punch anyone. It felt very romantic. He was really great-looking, I thought. When I really liked someone, it took me awhile to fully see them sometimes. It was almost like I was seeing them in slow motion, like a flip-book, and then they suddenly came together, like when they showed a flower blooming on a science show with time-lapse photography.

"I'm taking an oath right now to protect you," he said.

I laughed, but I was smiling and I felt happy, especially when he told me to eat my sandwich, which I was having trouble doing in front of him. I was hungry and it was delicious and I was glad he went to the men's room so I could finish it. I doubted his wife could make a grilled cheese and tomato sandwich taste as good as that. I wiped my mouth and put on my Lip Smacker root beer–flavored lip gloss. I wanted to touch him. I was glad we had eaten but I wanted to sit in his car and kiss him again.

Nobody had ever said they wanted to protect me before.

We left the restaurant and got into his car. "I should take you back," he said.

"I don't want to go back."

He held my hand. "This is going to end in tears."

"Yours or mine?" I said.

"You're a tough cookie," he said.

Weirdly, that was what my father called me. It was pretty much the only thing he called me that I didn't mind.

"I don't usually like a lot of people," he said. "But I liked you the minute I met you. I really like you."

"I can tell that," I said.

"Oh yeah? How can you tell?"

"Because you're married but you're here with me."

"That's true. You produce funny feelings in me."

"What kind of feelings?"

"I don't know, joy, exhilaration, mad jealousy. Like I'm on an alpine slide whooshing down a mountain."

"Jealousy?" I said.

"Yes, jealousy."

"Who are you jealous of?"

"Everybody. That jerk Kroeger. I'm jealous of New York. I don't want you to go."

I nodded solemnly because I understood being jealous of New York.

"What are you thinking about?" he said. "You've gone quiet on me."

"I'm having fun," I said.

"Me too," he said.

But he didn't look like he was having fun. "You don't know anything about me," I said.

He laughed even though I wasn't kidding. "I suppose that's true. I know you go to Columbia and you're writing a novel."

"I don't go to Columbia," I said. I wasn't writing a novel yet either, but I planned to.

He looked confused. "Where do you go?"

"High school. Bronx High School of Science."

"Wait. How old are you?"

"It's okay," I said. I was starting to get annoyed by how shocked he looked. "You just made a whole alpine-slide speech about whooshing down a mountain and now you're having a heart attack just because I said I'm in high school."

"I'm old enough to have a heart attack," he said. "I should take you back."

"I don't want to go back. Let's hang out in your car. Let's go to a motel."

"Swanna, I shouldn't. You're in high school. I'm married."

"Can you just get me a motel room for the night? I don't feel like going back there."

We drove in silence and I didn't know if he was just going to take me back to ArtCom or take me to a motel.

"I never told you I went to Columbia," I said after a while.

"You asked me if I live near Columbia and I said yes. I don't live that near, actually. Thirty blocks or so."

I saw a sign for the Black Swan Motel.

"That motel had my name on it," I said, but he kept driving. Then he pulled over on the side of the road.

He just sat there saying nothing for a few minutes. "Bronx High School of Science. Is that how you know about the Hippocratic oath?"

I shook my head no. "*M*A*S*H*," I said.

"How old are you?"

"Almost eighteen," I said. "Haven't you ever seen the movie *Manhattan*?"

"What year were you born?"

"1965."

"Jesus. Why don't I take you back to the art place now and then we can go out again tomorrow and talk about things."

"If you don't like me enough to take me to a motel, then forget it." I knew I sounded like a kid. "I don't want to have to talk you into it. Maybe you should take me back."

"Don't be mad," he said. "I'm just trying to figure out the right thing to do."

"I'm not mad."

He didn't say anything. Then he made a U-turn and drove into the parking lot of the Black Swan Motel.

"You're pretty good-looking for a high school kid, you know that?"

I smiled. He leaned in to me and I leaned in to him and we kissed. I closed my eyes and felt his tongue on mine. His stubble was rough on my cheeks. I had never felt anything like that before.

"So, do you want to go inside?" I was smiling and teasing him. I looked at the bulge in his pants. I pretended to start to take my shirt off, and his eyes got wide and he grabbed my hands.

"Stop. Man, you're a barn burner. Fine, let's go inside," he said. "I'm going to check in. Wait here."

He got out of the car and I watched him go into a door that said *Office* at the end of the row of doors. He got back into the car and started driving and I thought we were leaving, but he was just parking in front of what was going to be our room. I had never been to a motel although I had seen them in movies. He got out of the car and walked around to open my door and I got out. He opened the motel room door and I walked in first.

The room had a lot of brown wood in it, a desk and a TV, a big bed with a brown stiff cover on it, and a brown couch.

I sat down on the edge of the bed and kicked off my high heels. He sat down next to me and kissed me. I touched his hard-on through his pants and he took my shirt off and then my bra. He was breathing hard and squirming around a lot, and I just kept looking him right in the eyes and smiling. I was feeling extremely confident, considering. I took off my jeans and lay down on the bed and he took off his clothes and lay down on top of me. He was heavy and I could feel his hard penis pressing into my panties. His chest hovered over my face.

"I've never done this before," I said quietly. "I'm a virgin."

"We don't have to," he said.

"I want to," I said.

He smiled at me and kissed me. "I've never wanted anyone more in my entire life." He touched me through my panties and then put his finger in me. "You're unbelievably wet," he said.

I wasn't sure if that was a good thing. I was also moaning even though I was trying not to.

"I want to go down on you," he said.

I shook my head no. "Just put it in me," I said.

"You're only seventeen," he said. "We should wait."

"Till I'm eighteen?" I teased.

"Maybe. Or until you're ready."

"We don't have condoms," I said.

"Actually, we do." He sounded embarrassed. "They had them in the office." He got up and picked up his jeans from the chair and took a little packet out of the front pocket. "You sure you're seventeen?" He stood in the middle of the brown carpet with his hard-on and a helpless expression on his face.

It was pretty amusing. "Why? Do you think I'm older or younger?" I wondered if he could tell from making out with me that I was fourteen.

"What grade are you in?"

"Eleventh," I said.

"Wait," he said.

"I mean I finished eleventh. I'm starting twelfth."

"What are you taking in math?"

"Precalc," I said. "Why? Are you going to give me a quiz?"

"What's a polynomial function?"

"You really want me to talk to you about positive powers of x?" I said. "Or do you want me to do *this*?"

He was standing by the bed now, so I sat up and kissed the tip of his dick. He moaned. "I've never cheated on my wife before. I don't want you to think I'm a terrible person. I honestly don't know what's happening to me. I've just been so unhappy for so long. And when I met you, I felt something I haven't felt in a long time."

"I don't think you're a terrible person," I said. "Just maybe not the best conversationalist right now."

"We should put a towel down," he said. "If it's your first time."

I nodded and he went to get a towel from the bathroom. He was saying there was going to be blood. I knew that although I hadn't really thought about it. But he was an obstetrician. He could handle this. I was in good hands. I had made a good choice.

In *Forever* by Judy Blume, she finally loses her virginity on page 115 after an agonizingly long time on a multi-colored rug at his friend's house, but there was no way I was going to do it on the brown shag carpet of the motel. That page had been playing in a loop in my mind since the first time I'd read it. Her first time was occurring simultaneously with mine, like we were losing our virginity together in different rooms of the same house. I had to worry about both of us.

I loved that book, but if I were her I would have lost my virginity by about page sixty.

He put the towel down, brown of course, and started

pressing against me. "I've never been this turned on," he said. "But we should wait."

I took off my panties and shook my head. "I want to do it with you."

"It might hurt," he said.

"I know," I said. "I know everything about it."

"Oh you do, do you?"

He rolled on the condom and I closed my eyes. He did it to me. It felt like being shot. My eyes filled with tears and I gasped. Don't cry, don't cry, I told myself. You wanted this. You're not a stupid virgin anymore.

"Does it hurt?" he asked.

I shook my head no. "It feels so good." I watched him shaking over me like Poseidon moving the sea. I had never felt so powerful. I had done this to him. I was in complete control of him. I was more powerful than Poseidon. I was more powerful than anyone.

He put his face in my hair and kissed my neck. "It's going to get better," he said. "Next time will be easier."

I couldn't speak. Do not cry, I commanded myself. I imagined myself turned to stone.

"I'll do anything for you," he said, lying next to me and touching my lips with his finger. "I'll drive you to New York if you want. I'll keep you here. I can give you money if you need it."

I shook my head and kept my lips pressed together so I wouldn't cry.

"No matter what, I want you to know that I know you're amazing."

"You don't even know me," I said.

"I know I've never met anyone like you before."

I nodded that that was true.

"Tell me something about you. Why are you named Swanna?"

"My mother's a writer," I said. "She was reading *Swann in Love* by Proust when she was pregnant with me."

"What's your brother's name? Marcel?"

"Madding."

"Was she reading *Far from the Madding Crowd* by Thomas Hardy?"

I nodded again. I was impressed he knew about Thomas Hardy.

"What's your last name?"

"Swain. But my mother doesn't like it. When she met my father, she tried to get him to change his last name to Twain, but he refused."

"That's kind of crazy," Dennis said. "My last name is Whitson. I guess if we got married she'd want me to change it to Whitman."

"Definitely."

"Swanna." He kissed me. "Swanna in love."

"I don't know about that," I said.

"I do," he said. "What we have here is undeniable. My feelings for you are far from just sexual."

I went into the bathroom and had a stinging pee. There was blood on the toilet paper. I looked in the mirror for a few minutes. I was a woman. I wasn't a kid anymore. I'd had sex with a man. A married man. A doctor. More than twice my age. I smiled at myself because I loved myself at that moment.

"Come here, darling," he said when I finally came out of the bathroom. "I can figure out a way to spend the night here with you." He stretched his arms out to me.

"I think you should take me back to ArtCom," I said.

"What? No. I thought you didn't want to go back there."

"I'm worried about my brother." I suddenly just wanted to be next to him in the truck.

"Okay," he said. "But promise you'll let me see you tomorrow."

"Aren't you worried about your wife seeing your car in a motel parking lot?" I asked when we left the room.

"She wouldn't be at this motel," he said, smiling.

"What if she drives by and sees it? Or one of your friends does?"

I was actually very good at lying because I had the ability to think things through from other people's points of view, which is something my parents were both terrible at. My brother couldn't lie because he blushed and pursed his lips into an involuntary *O* every time he tried it. It was hilarious. I blushed too sometimes if I wasn't concentrating. Blushing was one of the worst things that could happen to a person.

I knew it was probably a bad idea to be asking these kinds of questions about his wife finding out, but I was very curious. I was sure she was a terrible wife. From what I could tell, a lot of wives were. And he wouldn't want to do this with me if she was giving him a lot of sex. But I felt very competitive with her and with all of his past girlfriends, who I could practically see in front of me—studying with him in his dorm and the library. I had read *Love Story* by Erich Segal and *One L* by Scott Turow, so I knew everything about what college and law school were like— studying and falling in love and looking up from your torts to gaze at each other—and I was sure medical school was the same.

I wanted to ask him where he went to college but I was afraid he might start quizzing me again.

"You act like you're an old pro at this infidelity stuff," he said.

"Oh I am," I said.

"Well, I'm not, I've never done anything like this before. But if you want to know the truth, this isn't my car. I traded cars with a friend of mine at the hospital. For exactly the reasons you outlined. You didn't notice you were in a different vehicle?"

I looked around me and I realized the leather seats were tan and not black. As a New Yorker, I had zero awareness of cars.

The only car I knew was the Datsun 280ZX. I memorized that one in case anyone ever asked me what my favorite car was.

"You knew we were going to a motel?" I asked.

"No! I was worried enough about the restaurant. I like that you don't care about cars. You're not materialistic," he said. "My wife only cares about who has an in-ground pool and whose house is bigger than whose."

"Do you have an in-ground pool?"

"Yes," he laughed. "I wish we could swim in it together."

"Do you have a Jacuzzi?"

He nodded. I was still thinking about what he'd said about my not being materialistic, and I was pretty sure that wasn't true. My number one goal in life was to be famous.

That wasn't so much a goal as a feeling. Whenever I had any money, I spent it on books at Eeyore's or B. Dalton, or I bought earrings at the Postermat on 8th Street or P.S. I Love You on Broadway. I stole a lot of my clothes from Reminiscence, Unique, Canal Jeans, and Antique Boutique. Sometimes my dad gave me money if I told him it was for a bat mitzvah present for someone. My father hadn't noticed that I'd been to about thirty-five bat mitzvahs this year, and several of them were my friend Liza Jacobs's.

"I would love to put you in my Jacuzzi," he said.

"Maybe you can one day," I said.

"I don't want to take you back yet."

"So don't."

He pulled over to the side of the road next to a closed ice cream stand. I wished it was open. I was feeling much better than I had felt in the motel. I wished I had just kept my mouth shut and stayed in the room with him. Sometimes I got in such a sad mood, and I'd leave a sleepover or a party and then I'd regret it. If I could remember to just relax and be quiet, it would probably pass. There was still a very bad burning pain deep in-side of me. Of my vagina. I had wadded up some toilet paper in my panties because of the blood. I was very sore.

I thought about him breathing hard over me, and my stomach turned over and I closed my eyes involuntarily and took a deep breath. He was looking at me. His breathing had changed too. "I don't want to say goodbye. This night was too incredible. You're too delicious."

He pushed his seat back and I climbed on top of him, facing him. I put my arms around his neck and kissed him.

"Oh my God," he said.

"I have to tell you something."

"Lay it on me."

I really wanted to tell him the truth. I didn't want our relationship to be based on a lie. "I'm not seventeen," I whispered.

He groaned. "No precalc?"

I shook my head. "Nope. Geometry."

"You're sixteen?"

I shook my head no. I wanted him to know I was fourteen. "I'm fifteen," I said.

"That's too young," he said.

"I don't feel too young."

He buried his face in my neck and my whole body prickled.

"We have to slow down," he said.

I was grinding into him, and I felt the wedge of toilet paper and my jeans rubbing against me and I felt him through his jeans.

"I've never been hornier in my entire life," he said.

I paused for a moment because I normally hated that word more than anything and was embarrassed by it, but hearing it now had the exact opposite effect on me. I was going to come on his lap. I pressed into him harder.

"Can you come for me?" he whispered. He was breathing really hard.

I couldn't open my eyes. I was clutching his neck and he was holding my butt through my jeans. I was going to come.

"Are you coming?" he whispered.

I nodded, my eyes closed tight.

We both moaned at the same time. I opened my eyes. Nothing had ever felt that good. We sat like that for a while and then I climbed off of him.

The stinging started again but I didn't care. I was pulsating. My thighs were shaking which surprised me because I had very strong legs from ballet. I'd been *en pointe* since I was eleven.

"Do you still want to go home?"

I nodded, trying to forget the bitter irony that home was now a mint-green pickup truck in the middle of nowhere.

"You have to call me tomorrow, because I can't call you," he said.

"I will," I said.

"You spoiled me tonight."

I laughed because it was funny to think of a kid spoiling a grown-up.

"And now I have to figure out how to deal with the come in my boxer shorts."

"You're a doctor. You can figure it out."

"I don't remember studying that."

He pulled up in front of the sign that said *ArtCom* and I got out of the car and closed the door as quietly as I could, now noticing that the outside of the car looked completely different from Dennis's car. For someone who wanted to be an actress, I was the least observant person on the face of the earth. I climbed into the back of the truck but Madding wasn't there. They must have let him into the house. If I had known that, I would definitely have stayed with Dennis at the motel.

I walked up to the house but the door was locked, so I went to sleep in the truck alone.

14

When I woke up, Madding and my mother were standing there.

I'm not a virgin, I thought.

"What happened to your sleepover?" Madding asked.

"I mixed it up. They wanted me to come over to their house last night but not sleep over. They invited me to sleep over tonight," I said.

"Hurry up and get ready," my mother said. "I signed us up for the yoga class. I made a new friend and she teaches it."

"Do you even know what that is?" I asked her.

"It's a new kind of exercise from India. It's like that Jane Fonda workout."

I was extremely dubious. "I can't," I lied, "I have my period."

"What is your period?" Madding asked.

"It's when you're a woman and you bleed every single month for the rest of your life. It's normal. If you ever see a girl in your class who has it when you're older, you should never make fun of her."

"Where does the blood come out of?"

"Your vagina," I said.

"I'd like to make a movie of that," Madding said. "What do you mean, if I see a girl who has it?"

"If you ever see a girl when you're in sixth grade and she's wearing a white skirt or pants and there's a red stain, you should just pretend you didn't see it and give her your sweatshirt to wear around her waist."

"Okay, I will," Madding said.

"Meet me at the barn in an hour," my mother said.

"Is there any breakfast?" If I had stayed with Dennis, there would have been breakfast. Maybe we could have gone back to the Galaxy.

Thinking of him made me catch my breath and close my eyes for a second. I thought of him pushing into me. I felt the ache between my legs. I could still be there with him if I hadn't stupidly decided to leave.

I wondered if he was thinking about me right now. All I wanted was for everyone to stop talking so I could close my eyes and think about him. I wanted to remember all the things he had said to me.

He said he loved my lower lip. He had reached out and touched it with his finger.

"I lost my tooth but the tooth fairy didn't come," Madding said. "Maybe she left something in New York."

"Are you sure?" I glared at my mother. "Your pillow's here." I pointed to it next to me on the mattress.

"I used a rolled-up T-shirt for a pillow last night," Madding said. "In Mom's room."

"Well, the tooth fairy isn't going to know that a rolled-up T-shirt is a pillow, is she?" I was getting a headache. "Look under your pillow here."

He climbed up onto the truck bed and lifted his pillow. "There's a dollar!" he said, his eyes very big and wide.

I smiled. He never would have found it if I hadn't come back. It was lucky I hadn't trusted my mother, and put the dollar there myself before I'd left.

"If I don't have breakfast I'm going to die," I snapped at my mother. "This is ridiculous that there's no way for me to eat."

"Don't speak to me that way," my mother said.

"I need food!" I yelled.

"We've been waiting for you to wake up so Borislav can take the truck and go get us some breakfast. We weren't sure if we should wake you."

"I told them to wake you up first!" Madding said.

"You mean he was just going to drive the truck with me sleeping in the back?" I yelled.

"Yup," Madding said.

"But I'm wearing my nightgown. I would have been at the store in my nightgown."

"You would have had the surprise of your life," Madding said.

"I'm not sleeping here again," I said. "I'm sleeping over at my friend's tonight and then I'm driving back to the city with them in the morning. I'm not spending another night here."

"You're hurting my feelings," my mother said.

"I'll stay with you, Mom," Madding said, putting his hand into hers.

Elvislav came out of the house with his huge, gross, pillowy lips and dumb flat face like he was a street urchin in the olden days pressing his face up against glass, looking in. If I had to see him or hear his stupid voice one more time, I was going to go crazy. For a Russian from New Jersey, he sounded suspiciously like a valley girl from California. *Um, grody, gag me with a, um, spoon.*

"Um, what can I get everyone?" he asked.

"A bacon, egg, and cheese," I said.

"Um, I was just going to get sandwiches," he said.

"That *is* a sandwich," I said in total disbelief. I turned to my mother, hoping she could deal with her moronic boyfriend. "How about turkey or a nice chicken salad?" she said. "You don't need to be eating bacon."

"And you don't need to be smoking pot." I grabbed my toiletry kit, my smiley face towel, and some clothes, and climbed down out of the truck. "Bacon, egg, and cheese on a roll, and a Diet Coke if they don't have Tab," I said, and stormed toward the house. Luckily the door was open and the bathroom was empty. I brushed my teeth, pulled my *I Love Lucy* nightgown off over my head, and looked at my body in the full-length mirror. There was blood between my thighs. I looked pretty good. I had lost a couple of pounds since leaving camp, I thought. No ice cream sandwiches and slushies every night.

My plan had been to take a shower in the motel, but I hadn't done it and I really didn't want to take one here, although I didn't have much choice.

"You're so seductive it's incredible," Dennis had said to me. "You're a damn genius."

I washed my hair and shaved my legs with Wella Balsam shampoo and someone else's razor, and put on someone's Tickle deodorant.

"You're wicked. Ingenious. Has anyone ever called you a genius before?"

I had nodded.

"I bet they have," he'd said, laughing.

I didn't know what he was laughing at. I'd been called a genius a bunch of times.

The shower felt good. I wrapped myself in my towel and used someone else's to dry my hair. I got dressed and remembered a dream I'd had the night before. I was playing catch with Madding with a heavy softball. But we were on two separate roofs on top of two separate skyscrapers, throwing the ball to each other across a busy avenue.

I left the house and went to the truck to spray Love's Baby Soft on my wrists and then walked over to the barn where the yoga was. I saw my mother standing by a big stack of rolled-up yoga mats, staring down at them.

"What do we do?" she asked a woman who was spreading hers out like a beach blanket on the floor. My mother always had to ask for assistance, no matter the situation. She could never just figure out something on her own.

Whenever we went to a store, she always had to ask the salesgirl's opinion about everything and tell her whole life story. Instead of just looking at the shoes in the shoe store herself, she'd say to the salesgirl, "John Ashbery and David Kermani and the publisher Christopher MacLehose are coming to dinner," and it would begin, the whole story about what shoes she wanted, and where she was going to wear the shoes, and the history of every pair of shoes she'd ever owned, including plenty of information about her feet and anything she'd ever had published.

"Spread out your mat like this," the woman said.

I walked to the other side of the gigantic room and unrolled my mat and lay flat on my back on top of it, looking up at the enormously high barn ceiling. I imagined Dennis lying on top of me. It was very mysterious how you could go from not even knowing someone to thinking about them night and day like that. I felt like my head was a museum and Dennis stood on a pedestal cast in marble in the center of it, a permanent exhibit that had always been there and always would be.

"Let's make up," I heard my mother say. I opened my eyes to see she had brought her mat over to where I was.

She was wearing a black scoop-necked leotard and pink Capezio tights and a batik wraparound skirt which she took off and laid out on top of the mat for no reason, then she lay on top of the skirt and started to point and flex her feet a lot. She was wearing her ballet shoes. She only took ballet because I took ballet.

Right before the summer, my mother had decided to take adult ballet on Saturdays and afterward always told me how she had no idea how I could remember all those combinations because she would just stand there confused. Adult ballet was the most pathetic thing on this earth. I always looked in on them on my way to Advanced Intermediate and swore I would never be one of them. They all stood trying to suck in their stomachs and do a plié in fifth. They didn't even bother to put their hair in buns half the time and their elastics were all sewed in wrong in their ballet shoes. I didn't know which was worse, the moms who took Adult Beginner or the ones sitting in the hall, digging around in their purses for grapes in plastic baggies or quarters for the juice machine.

"Now what is this called? Kuu-muu-muu yoga?"

"Kundalini," I said. The name was written on a sign—

Kundalini Yoga with Shura. If my mother didn't know a word, she just made up any word to put in its place. A few other people were setting up near us and I had just decided to leave when a woman who was clearly Shura, wearing white baggy pants and a white tunic and a lot of white material wrapped in a turban around her head, stood at the front of the room right in front of me and my mother. For some reason I had assumed this was the back of the room, which was why I had chosen it.

I looked down at my left arm. There was a small patch of skin on the upper part of my arm that was exactly like my father's skin. It was freckled and fairer than the rest of my body. Every single time I looked down at my left arm, I thought of him because I was reminded he was a part of me.

"Just lie on your back in Savasana with your eyes closed and breathe," the woman said. "Corpse pose."

"So morbid," my mother whispered.

I lay on my back and closed my eyes and took a deep breath. It was hard to breathe deeply when the person next to you reaked of pot and was dressed like Gelsey Kirkland. It was so embarrassing.

"We will begin with a five-minute meditation. Please sit up straight." The woman hit two tiny cymbals together that were attached by a leather string.

"I hope there's some exercise involved in this," my mother whispered to me loudly.

The teacher chimed the cymbals an annoying amount of times and then just smiled at us as people stirred and shifted behind me.

"This is my daughter," my mother announced. My whole body tensed in horror.

"Oh, this must be Swanna. I've heard all about you. I was raised that way, doing yoga with my mother in the commune. It was just natural. I've been doing this for so long it's now a part of me. Just looking at you all, I know everything about your bodies. For instance, I can tell, just by looking at you, how each and every one of you likes to make love."

I felt myself blush, and in my discomfort I accidentally turned my head and made eye contact with my mother, who had never looked so pleased. I thought of Dennis shaking on top of me. I thought of him holding my knees in his hands.

"We're all unique . . ." the teacher began. "But you, mother and daughter, are built just the same. You make love the same way."

Everyone in the class—the six or seven other women— was staring at me.

Everything that happened at this place was horrible. I could not believe this.

The creepy teacher kept smiling at me. I wondered if she could tell that I had done it. I knew that was impossible. Even a doctor probably couldn't tell, or the next boy I had sex with. So far, the way I liked to "make love" was through my jeans, straddling a guy in a fancy car. I doubted that was how my mother liked to do it. I shuddered thinking of her disgusting boyfriend and his gross truck.

I started to get a little turned on thinking about Dennis. I had to get out of this class and call him.

"Okay, to open our hips for lovemaking, and in honor of Swanna, let's start with Swan pose," the teacher said.

"I have to go," I said.

"I hope I didn't embarrass you," the teacher said, but I was already out of there and everyone was flapping around on the ground getting their hips open.

When I walked through the barn door, I saw that the truck was back. Boris-slave was walking toward me with a small brown paper bag.

"Thanks," I said, grabbing it from him. I tore open the bag like an animal and sank my teeth into the sandwich. It tasted a bit countrified but still delicious. The bacon was crispy and they had buttered the roll. I had secretly hoped they would butter it, but I didn't have the guts to mention butter in front of my mother. "It's good," I said with my mouth full. I had actually never tasted anything so good. I wondered if it was more scrumptious because I'd had sex. The colors around me seemed sharper, which was strange since I had slept in my contact lenses and I'd never smelled anything better than that bacon. I wished I had asked for two. I was going to have to try to get half of my brother's.

"Um, you know your mother and I are in love," Dracuslav said.

I took another bite and glared at him the way I glared at the construction workers on Broadway who made disgusting comments at me. It was a specific expression I'd perfected that really looked like I was going to throw up at the sight of him.

"My mother's in love with a famous artist," I said. "He just got another woman pregnant, which is the only reason she's here. He's going to marry the other woman because my mother had her tubes tied and his existing kids aren't enough for him apparently."

"Um," Umislav said, taking a moment to think this over, even though he would need at least a year to think anything over. Second graders seriously made better conversation than this guy.

"My mother's trying to get over him, but she won't. She never does. She'll probably be back with him before the baby even gets born."

"I don't want to have more children," he said, completely missing the point.

"What do you mean *more*?" I asked. "You don't have any."

"I have a son."

"Where is he?"

"He lives with his mother in New Jersey. He doesn't talk to me. Your mother and father are divorced and she wants to be with me now. I'm sorry if that upsets you, but we're all adults here."

"First of all, I'm not an adult. I'm a kid. Secondly, they're not divorced. They're separated. My father hasn't even moved his things out yet." I thought of his clothes in his closet, his black socks in the top drawer of his dresser all rolled into balls. And his Phillips Academy graudation ring and his gold wedding band. I had actually taken those and put them in a drawer in my room. He came to take me to dinner every Wednesday and he did a load of laundry in the basement and we went to the Cuban Chinese restaurant while his clothes were in the dryer. His temporary apartment didn't have a laundry room.

This conversation was actually managing to ruin my sandwich. I held the last bite between my thumb and forefinger, a tiny piece of roll with a microscopic speck of bacon inside.

15

Nadine was gone for the day so I walked around the studios. Why would anyone want to come here and paint or write in a tiny wooden box with nothing but a small lunch in a paper bag for sustenance? How bad would your life have to be to want to leave wherever you lived and come here? My mother had told me you had to *apply*. Apply for what? I thought.

"Swanna," I heard a woman say, "I'm sorry if I put you on the spot in there."

I turned around to see Shura, the yoga teacher. "You didn't put me on the spot," I said. "I just forgot I had to make a phone call."

"I read your mother's chart. Not a typical mama. Passionate but not necessarily well-suited."

I stood there completely confused. Was this something Ms. Korn had written up about her on a chart? Had she somehow seen my permanent record?

"I'm an astrologer," Shura said. "I'm here writing a book about it. Do you know what astrology is?"

I nodded. "My father's an astronomer."

"They're very connected," she said.

"He wouldn't agree with that. I do tarot cards and he thinks that's moronic."

"He's wrong," she said. "The three wise men in the Bible— Gaspar, Melchior, and Balthasar—were astrologers. Tell him *that*."

My father thought the Bible was made-up fiction, so that wouldn't make a difference.

"Do you want me to do your chart?"

"Why did my mother want her astrology done?" I asked.

"Because she's in love."

I could not imagine my mother sitting with this woman looking at a chart. If she was so in love, then why wouldn't she be with him instead of with this woman? Unless he was busy pooping in the woods, and she had some time to kill.

"How do you make a person's chart?"

"I use an ephemeris, which is a list of where the planets are located at midnight in Greenwich, England, and a table of houses to calculate the ascending, midheaven, and house cusps. I use interpolation and a calculator. It's simple math based on latitude and longitude in an atlas, and the corresponding time zone. Hours plus or minus from Greenwich mean time."

I looked at her as if all this made perfect sense.

"Come to my studio later," she said, "and I'll give you a reading. Your mother already gave me the day and time of your birth."

"Thanks," I said, "but I'll probably be on my way to New York by then."

I wanted to talk to Dennis. I went into the house but a woman I hadn't seen before was on the pay phone.

I couldn't believe there was only one phone. I lived in a family of four, well now three, and I had my own phone line in my room, although that had only been since my dad left. I had convinced my father to get me a phone so he could reach me anytime. I had been pretty manipulative about it.

The new woman's bags were by the door—a suitcase and a jumbo shiny black LeSportsac weekender and a big tote bag with those B. Kliban cartoon cats wearing sneakers on it. I actually had a calendar of those cats in my room. "It's good to get out of New York," the woman said into the phone. "I'm not going to settle for half. Yesterday my aerobics instructor said half of my body is strong. My agent said my novel is only half-finished even though it took me half a decade to write. Tomorrow I'll have been alive half a century. I'm living a half-life."

She went on and on giving more examples of halves, and I noticed a newspaper sticking halfway out of her tote bag. I brushed by it and toppled it onto the floor. It was the *Weekly Wag*—but only half of it.

I took off my denim vest and dropped it over the paper, and then scooped them both up and headed back out to the truck. I shoved it into my duffel along with the clean clothes I had left, four pairs of panties that said *Bloomie's* on them, two white V-neck T-shirts from my father's new Hanes three-pack, my Hawaiian skirt, my T-shirt from the King Tut exhibit at the Met, and my socks that had the tops of sneakers printed on them so when you wore them you looked like you were wearing sneakers but you were just wearing socks. I was dying to see the Mistress Amber column, but that would have to wait.

I went back into the house to find the half-wit woman thankfully gone. I picked up the receiver of the phone and put in a dime. I dialed the number from the scrap of paper bag that was in the front pocket of my jeans. A woman answered.

"Dr. Whitson's office," she said.

"May I speak to him, please?"

"This is the answering service. Is this an emergency?"

"Yes," I said.

"Do you need an ambulance?"

"No. I just need to speak to the doctor," I said. I hoped they wouldn't send another ambulance.

"Phone number?"

I gave her the number on the phone. I was relieved to see it written in pencil in a little slot above the rotary dial.

"Name?"

"Swanna Swain. It's very urgent."

"Symptoms?"

I hesitated. "It's a viral infection," I said. My friend David's mother was a nurse and he had a stack of signed doctor notes he'd stolen and always used *viral infection* as an excuse, which was how I'd thought of it.

"The doctor will call you right back," she said.

I thanked her and hung up. I stood by the phone guarding it. The walls were covered with pink-flowered and -striped wallpaper, and on top of that were dozens of framed book covers. One of them was by Richard Henri, I noticed. It was called *Openmouthed Bison*. There was a Bic pen, which was of course tied onto a string that was taped to the wall. What kind of place felt the need to tie up all its pens? I wondered. Not a good place. I ripped the pen off the wall and used it to scratch the word *IDIOT* into the wallpaper with an arrow pointing to Richard Henri's book, as I had done with the hockey puck. Then I dropped the pen with the string still attached into a vase of pussy willows.

My dream was to write my initials in wet cement on a New York City sidewalk, but that was very hard to achieve.

The phone rang.

"Dennis?" I said.

"I'm at the hospital," he said. "Are you okay?"

"Can you pick me up?"

He didn't say anything for a second. "Now?"

"Yes," I said.

"I can't now. I'm delivering babies."

I tried to think. It hadn't occurred to me that he would say no. He sounded like my father.

"I was hoping we could go to the motel," I said.

"I would love that. How about in the morning?"

"I was hoping to spend the night there with you."

"Let me see what I can do," he said. "I'll call you back in an hour."

I went into the screened-in sunporch which was off the kitchen and lay down on the rattan daybed and waited. Ring, I thought. Ring, ring.

I fell asleep and had a terrible dream, which is why I despised naps. In my dream I was in charge of barbecuing for a lot of people. I put a live baby pig and a live puppy on the grill. They didn't want to lie down on the hot flaming coals but I coaxed them down with my poker. At first I was gentle and said, "It's okay, it's okay, just lie down and go to sleep," but they kept getting up and I got frustrated and poked them and yelled at them harshly until they finally lay down for good.

The phone rang, waking me, and I sat up, startled. I'd imagined it ringing so much, I couldn't tell if it was real or just ringing in my head. I was relieved the terrible dream was over. I stumbled into the kitchen.

"Hello?" I said.

"It's me." Hearing his voice felt like oxygen. "I can meet you at four this afternoon for an hour or two."

My body was tingling with relief. He wanted me. And I was getting out of here.

"I actually saw you early this morning on the way to the hospital."

"You did?"

"From a distance. I stood in the driveway. You were sleeping in the truck. It was three in the morning."

"What do you mean?"

"I wanted to wake you up so badly and carry you into my car."

"So why didn't you?" I challenged.

"It would have scared your brother!" he said. "I didn't want to get arrested or shot for trespassing. I have a surprise for you."

"What is it?"

"You have to find it."

"How?"

"Go to the *ArtCom* sign and think, *Cinderella*."

"Cinderella," I said, smiling. "And are you supposed to be Prince Charming?"

"Don't be such a wiseguy," he said, and I could hear he was smiling too. "Be a good girl and do as you're told."

"Or what?" I asked.

"Or I'll give you a spanking."

The half-dead woman came in. "I have to use the phone," she said.

"Just a half second," I said.

"Use tradecraft."

"What's tradecraft?" I had to remember not to ask him the definitions of vocabulary words because it made me sound like a child.

"It's what spies use. Like the CIA. To be secretive."

"Okay, I'll use tradecraft."

"For instance, you shouldn't say *tradecraft* out loud if someone is listening."

"She's only half listening," I said.

"I've really got to use the phone," the woman said, looking at me strangely. I had used tradecraft quite well already to steal her *Weekly Wag*.

"I'll see you at four," Dennis said.

My heart pounding, I walked out the door and over to the *ArtCom* sign at the beginning of the driveway. There was a bug on it that literally looked like a cartoon caricature of a bug with huge round eyes and stripes.

Cinderella, I thought. Then I saw a cinder block with a tiny pumpkin sitting on top of it next to a rusted chair. I hoped the pumpkin wasn't my present.

I lifted the cinder block and behind it there was a gold box. I picked it up quickly and looked over my shoulder. No one had seen me.

I walked pretty far into the woods. A tree had fallen and I kicked it a few times to make sure there were no snakes or bears hibernating in it or anything, and then I sat down and looked at the box. It was gold with gold lettering that said, *Godiva Belgium 1926*. Also in gold was a drawing of a naked woman with long hair riding a horse. The box was tied with a stretchy gold cord with a red silk rose attached to it.

I opened the box—it was chocolates. I had never seen chocolates that beautiful before. Some were square, some round, some had golden G's on them, or the shape of a nut tucked under a blanket of caramel, or a dusting of a leaf, or a cherry stem sticking out. They sat on a waxy board and under that was a whole second layer. I popped one called a *champagne truffle* according to the little booklet into my mouth and it tasted expensive.

I leaned back and ate seven more and thought about sex. I wished I could call Jacquie Beller and tell her about Dennis. She had said that when you have sex with a man it feels like they're fucking your brain and that was where the expression "fucking your brains out" had come from. I had said that was ridiculous, fucking had nothing to do with your brain. But when I'd had sex with Dennis, I realized it really did feel like that. When he entered me and was pushing all the way inside, I couldn't think. I felt like my brain was literally going to explode. Maybe it even had. He had penetrated my brain from inside of me. He was permanently a part of it now. I wished I could call Jacquie and tell her she was right. She was 100 percent right about everything.

I went to find Shura to have my astrological chart read, because I was definitely in love.

16

"I can tell you hate math, but you're good at it. You're good at systems, patterns, logic. You would make a good astrologer," Shura said.

I laughed out loud, thinking my father would rather I turn out to be a Times Square hooker than an astrologer. I had a tarot card deck and I liked to give readings and he always looked completely disgusted if he came into my room and I had the cards spread out on my bed. I was not good at math, but when you were forced to sit between Nathanial Steinberg, literal US chess champion of the world, and Thor Yaloff, who had walked over to the new computer the first day it was brought into the classroom and showed everyone how to use it, it was hard not to feel retarded.

"Do you want to hear the good, the bad, and the ugly?" she asked. "I always like to say that. The good, the bad, and the ugly."

I got a nervous feeling but I said I definitely wanted to hear whatever she had to say.

"Jupiter is transiting your seventh house, bringing in someone who is going to be very much in love with you. But

Venus in Capricorn, twelfth house, means you are a girl who feels unlovable. You're terrified that it's not going to happen. It's like being born with a hole in your heart, similar to the black hole in the Milky Way. You're going to meet someone older. An older man. Mars opposes Pluto at the moment of your birth. You are deep, penetrating, soulful. You live with one foot in the underworld. You are attracted to the strange characters of the world. You are born to be unique, original, peculiar. Your life won't be staying home and cooking." She let out a huge laugh, as if me staying home and cooking was the most ridiculous thing she ever heard. She was really cracking herself up with that. "You have a soul hunger for the deep and dark. You go underneath the rock, exploring deep, dark places. You're like a house with rooms no one knows are there. This man who is coming in, he is not going to be able to resist you."

My mother, I was sure, had eaten all of this up. For a minute, I actually forgot about Dennis, and I wondered if the older man was Nestor Perez. He was two years older.

"I hate dark places," I said. "I love views. That's why I have no desire to have a town house. I would rather have a penthouse with wraparound windows." I pointed at the pie chart on the table with its symbols and stars and lines, like string art. "Does it say I hate all bugs and snakes? I would never look under a rock."

"I'm talking about the older man you will meet. How can I say this? You are a person who will always live for desire. For you, desire is not meant to be fulfilled. It's meant to be stoked like a fire. It's almost like you will desire desire itself. To be in a state of desire. You will learn to live with that. Desire will be an exquisite pain. You will always see the beauty in desire. Mars-Pluto people are hungry. You will always be hungry. You will overeat, be prone to stomachaches, nausea, vomiting. You'll have to guard against getting fat."

I was sure my mother had told her to say that. "That doesn't sound good," I said. I actually did get a lot of stomachaches.

"You already know this. Do you have stomachaches?" I nodded.

"This is interesting. You were born on the world axis. You will be famous."

I nodded again because I knew that was true, and it made the stomachaches and always being hungry better, and being in love with Hades or whatever she had said. She talked very fast. She made me sound like a crazed Persephone, being too hungry to resist the pomegranate seeds and throwing up on the way down.

"You will have children, but childbirth will be difficult. Intervention will be needed. Moon in Uranus. You'll need to be cut by a surgeon. Uranus women want to be cut."

I wanted to ask if I would be tall, but I suddenly didn't want to hear the answer. I'd heard enough of the good, the bad, and the ugly.

"You're about to embark on a time of discovery and adventure. And when it's over, you're going to say to yourself, *I can't believe I just did that.*"

When it was almost four, I went into the house to tell my mother I was leaving. I heard her talking to Stupislav in the kitchen. "She's sexual," I heard him say.

"Don't be ridiculous," my mother said.

I wondered who they were talking about. If they were talking about Ms. Korn I was going to throw up.

"I see her Marilyn Monroeing at me," he said.

"I think it's very strange and suspect that you would talk about my daughter like that," my mother said in her angriest voice.

"*Ooooh oooooh*," he said in a baby voice, presumably imitating me or Marilyn Monroe. I didn't sound anything like that.

"Stop that," my mother said.

"She's fourteen," he said. "She's a sex bomb."

I turned and ran out as fast as I could.

17

"I'm sorry I'm late. I had to stop home first," Dennis said. "What did you say to your wife?" I had told myself I wouldn't ask about her, but I was too curious.

"I told her I was going to the dump." He grinned at me and gestured behind him. "I have two big bags of garbage in my trunk. The funny thing is, I was so excited to see you, I started to drive away and then I realized I had forgotten the garbage. Thank God I remembered it."

He looked like a little kid at that moment. I imagined his wife seeing the garbage left behind and yelling at him, or maybe she was a great sport and would just laugh about it. When I got married, I would always be a great sport, I decided right then. I imagined she was probably pretty beautiful because he was very good-looking himself, probably dirty-blond because he was dirty-blond. I had never been to a dump before. I pictured it like the dunes in Wellfleet, but made out of garbage instead of sand.

We were in his original car. There was a leather doctor bag in the backseat.

"Do you want to go get something to eat?" he asked.

That sounded great to me. I was starving. I had only had the bacon, egg, and cheese for breakfast and a mini box of

SWANNA IN LOVE

Frosted Flakes and skim milk for lunch. And all the chocolate. I wanted to go to the Galaxy Diner again. I was wearing
my Hawaiian skirt and the second white V-neck T-shirt from
the three-pack and my blue high heels. The T-shirt looked
great with my tan and the black bra I had shoplifted from
Bloomingdale's with matching panties. I had shaved my legs
which were covered with mosquito bites, but I had used my
mother's Clinique undereye concealer to cover them.

"Whatever you want to do is fine with me," I said.

"Well, I don't have much time," he said sheepishly.

I knew he didn't want to get something to eat. "So
whatever you want," I said. I kind of wanted to see the dump.

"Really? Whatever I want?"

"Well, I guess that depends what you want," I said.

"I want to kiss you again. That's all I've been able to think
about."

He took his eyes off the road and looked right at me
when he said that, and I knew it was true. I pictured him in
bed with his wife thinking about kissing me and of course
jerking off in the shower.

My stomach did this involuntary flipping-over thing it
did, which people in books always described as butterflies
but felt more like an astronaut turning over in a spaceship.

"Then I guess it depends on where you want to take me,"
I said.

He pulled up to the Black Swan Motel. "Is this okay
again? We don't have to go here. I'm being very forward."

"I see that," I said.

He leaned over and kissed me and I kissed him back as
sexily as I could. Kissing him was different from kissing

Nestor Perez. Nestor Perez had been sort of aloof, I guess the word was. He was quite cocky. I guess he felt that if a girl watched him push a puck around on the ice for two hours, making out after would be pretty inevitable. He had come and seen me in the play I was in too, though, and every girl in my bunk had been amazed. It was the first time a boy from the hockey camp had come over to the theater side. And he had given me his huge jersey that said *Perez* on the back to wear in the rink when I got too cold. I never knew if Nestor Perez would want to make out after his practice or not—we never had a plan—but we always did. We never didn't.

When Dennis kissed me I could hear his heart pounding in his button-down shirt. I could see his hard-on in his jeans. He looked at me like I was the greatest thing that had ever happened to him.

"You stay here. I'll be right back." He got out of the car and went into the motel office. I opened the glove compartment, which was jammed with maps. There was also a lipstick. It was a very light pink color called Copa Cabana. His wife was definitely blond.

The night Nestor had come to see my play was also the night my father had driven up. I could see the stage lights reflect off my father's glasses in the audience and I was nervous. I had wanted to introduce him to Nestor after the show but Nestor had waved from a distance and gone back to his cabin, and my father took me to the Red Lion Inn in Stockbridge, Mass., for dinner.

It had been one of the best nights of my entire life. In the morning my father had come back to camp and taken me out on the lake in a kayak. Then he had driven all the way back. Now he didn't even know how to find me if he wanted to, which he clearly didn't.

Dennis got back in the car and handed me a key. "You go in first, if that's okay. I'll follow in a few minutes. Room nine." I took the key and went to room nine and let myself in. It was the same as the other room we had been in, but everything was reversed like a mirror image. *Through the Looking-Glass*, I thought. I had stepped through to the other side.

There was a soft knock on the door and I opened it and Dennis came in quickly, holding his doctor bag.

"Why do you have that?" I asked.

"If anyone sees me, I thought maybe I could say I'm seeing a patient."

"Now I'm your patient? You make motel calls?"

"Look, I'm sorry. I wish things were different."

He put the bag down on the dresser. When he turned around, I pulled my shirt off over my head and stood in front of him.

"Oh my God," he said. "You're incredible."

I looked down because I suddenly felt overcome with happiness and luck. I was glad we hadn't gone to the diner or the dump. I was glad he had brought me here to the room on the other side of the mirror.

He sat on the couch and I climbed onto his lap, facing him, and we kissed like that.

"What's that?" I said. There was something vibrating underneath me.

"I'm sorry, that's my pager." He lifted me off him and pulled a black box out of his pocket. "I'm sorry, baby, just a minute." He picked up the phone on the desk. "Can I get an outside line?" he said into the phone. Then he dialed a number that he read off a little screen on the black box.

"Dr. Whitson," he said into the phone. "Acute? Temperature? I'm not on call, is there . . . Okay, I'll get there as soon as I can." He got off the phone and frowned. "I think I have to go." He pushed me down on the bed, climbed on top of me, and kissed me. He kissed my neck.

"I thought you had to go," I said.

"I do. I don't know how long I'll be there. I should take you back."

"What about the dump?" I said.

"Oh yeah, that's what I'm actually most disappointed about."

"You're not disappointed about missing *this*?" I kissed him and he groaned.

"Don't make this harder for me. What if I told you I got you something?"

"What is it?"

"A present." He got up and took a little box out of the bag. "I ducked into a jewelry store during lunch. I used tradecraft."

My whole brain flushed with pleasure. It was like jumping on a wave in the ocean. He had thought about me. I opened the box. It was a necklace. A gold star on a delicate gold chain with a ruby in the center of the star.

"It's eighteen-karat gold and that's a ruby," he said. "It's handmade. I know the jeweler. I took a risk . . ."

Before he could ruin the moment, I stood up on the bed and kissed him. Standing on the bed, with him standing on the floor, I was taller than him. "Thank you," I said. "I obviously love it. Can't someone cover for you?"

"I'm working on a plan."

"Maybe I should stay here alone."

"I'm going to be at the hospital all night. But tomorrow night I can come for you and we can be together."

He checked out and we got back in the car. "Oh, I have this for you," he said, grabbing something from the backseat. It was the *Weekly Wag*.

"Where did you get that?" I asked.

"One of my patients had it. She's a New Yorker on vacation here and she started to have fetal trauma."

I took the newspaper from him and looked at the date— *August 18*. I was happy to see it wasn't the same issue as the one I'd stolen from the kitchen.

I didn't know what caused fetal trauma, but anyone who would "vacation" in Vermont was an idiot. The fetus was probably traumatized by how boring it was here and worrying about the family vacations to come. I felt sorry for this woman, leaving New York and coming to this awful place, clutching her *Weekly Wag* like a child's security blanket, her only reminder of normal society, while her fetus begged for death.

"Don't worry," he said, "I saved her." He beamed at me.

I smiled back because his doctor arrogance was quite adorable. I was proud of Dennis for saving that woman and proud that he had come to be with me right after. "I'm impressed," I said.

He nuzzled his face in my neck.

"There is nothing more impressive than your tits. And your ass. Which belong to *me*."

"I have to read this," I said, and found the Mistress Amber column. There was the drawing of the whip and the bustier in the circle next to her name.

Of course you dominate his heart, but do you dominate his apartment? Today I helped my favorite PhD move out of the home he has shared with his wife for fifteen years and into a little love nest downtown. I will admit his former abode was impressive—a Steinway in the living room, a massive dining room with a telescope taller than I am even in stilettos, wondrous views, and more books than you could read in a lifetime. With all that reading, it's no wonder he's getting a divorce. "Leave these here," I instructed. "You won't have time to read them."

The boy's room had a basketball hoop and the girl's room a ballet barre at perfect handcuff height, but we were in a rush to get out of there. This is the kind of apartment you only see in Woody Allen movies. After a quickie on his rock-hard marital bed, under the Warhol painting—a quadruple portrait of his wife—we were off to start his new life downtown.

I put the paper down. I felt sick to my stomach.

"Are you okay?" Dennis asked.

I was in a state of shock. This couldn't be true.

We had a piano and a Warhol of my mom in four colors. But the Warhol was in the living room, not in her bedroom. My ballet barre wasn't in my room, it was in the foyer. We had a telescope and my father believed in firm mattresses. And we had everything else she had described. It was him. She was writing about *us*. My father had moved out. He had taken a real apartment. In New York, signing a lease was the most serious thing a person could do.

Jacquie had told me that he would be completely moved out when I got home, and I hadn't believed her. "That's what summer camp is mostly for," she had told me. "That's why they pay the big bucks. You'll see. There won't be a scrap of him left in your house and they'll have given your room an upgrade. I assume you got your own phone when they separated?" I had nodded. "Good. Well, now you'll have your own TV or the new beanbag chair you've always wanted. I got an amazing canopy bed and new carpet and my sister got one of those beds that you can make go up and down by pressing a button. That's what she wanted. She's so weird."

My father had been living in an apartment he had borrowed from a colleague. He said it was temporary, to give my mother and him a chance to figure things out. He hadn't figured *anything* out! My friend Jacquie had figured it out. I couldn't believe she was right.

"Don't expect your new room in your dad's new place to be that great," she said. "Real estate prices are very high right now. It could very well suck. I've heard of parents having to sleep in the living room."

It's a third-floor walk-up, so I made him take off his shirt. If I have to walk up three flights of stairs, I at least expect to be entertained. Let's just say that the only thing I let him unpack were the condoms.

Wait, so it wasn't my father! It couldn't be him, I thought. Because my mother had made him have a vasectomy.

I breathed a literal sigh of relief. He hadn't moved out. He hadn't gotten a real apartment. He was still in his colleague's place while the guy was on sabbatical and his stuff was still at home. My father would never have moved without telling us.

"What's wrong?" Dennis asked.

"I follow this column in the *Wag*," I said.

He looked over at it. "Mistress Amber. A dominatrix?"

"It's a funny dating column. For a minute, I actually thought she was writing about my father."

"Wow, your childhood sure was different than mine."

Different *from*, I thought. Dennis looked sad and I got angry the way I had when he called me a runaway. I hated when people criticized my childhood. That was only for me to do. Not for anybody else.

18

Because Dennis had to be at the hospital, that night I told everyone my sleepover was canceled and I went into town with my mother, Madding, and Fraudislav.

"What are you wearing?" my mother said, looking at me. She could see very well what I was wearing, very nice pink satin shorts with black stripes on the side and my very nice black T-shirt that said *Treasures of Tutankhamun New York '78-'79* on it with a cool gold picture of King Tut looking a little like a lion. I was also wearing Corkys and I looked good. The T-shirt was from the King Tut exhibit at the Met a few years ago so it was very tight now.

"I'm wearing perfectly normal clothing," I said.

"I mean your necklace. Where did you get that?"

I touched the gold and ruby star that Dennis had given me. "Dad gave me this," I said, using tradecraft.

My mother took Madding into an art supply store but I convinced her to give me ten dollars and I went into a café and sat in the window so I could people-watch. It felt normal there. I ordered pink lemonade and a sandwich that had turkey with cranberry sauce on some kind of peasant bread. It came with homemade potato chips which were thankfully a lot better-tasting than they sounded. There were people walking around who didn't look like they were from the Wild West. I had overheard someone say that everyone in Vermont had a gun, but I didn't see any holsters. The girls were pretty. I don't know if it was the light, but every single girl who walked by looked like a Hollywood movie star for some reason, even if she was wearing a flannel shirt. It made me feel beautiful too.

I finished my sandwich, which was absolutely delicious. I wanted to write in my diary about Dennis but I knew my mother would read it, so I didn't.

My brother saw me in the window and came in to tell me about a very cool store he wanted to show me. I paid my check and followed him into a candle store called Wax & Wayne. It was filled with things that didn't look like candles but had wicks sticking out of them—turtles and skulls and planets. Madding got a big kick out of one in the shape of a penis. I wanted one in the shape of a wizard with a staff and a long beard. It was $4.50.

"I can buy it for you," Madding whispered. He was so funny. Whenever he had any money, he was always trying to spend it on me.

"You have to spend your money on yourself," I told him.

"We should get Dad this one." It was a candle that looked like the moon.

I wished I could just be alone in the store and not have to talk about every single candle and who would like it. "Why don't you ask Mom to get you ice cream," I said. "I'll catch up with you."

"Don't you want ice cream?"

"Not right now." I didn't want to tell him I had eaten a huge amount of chocolates.

He left and wind chimes sounded as he walked out the

door. One of the best things about leaving Vermont would be no more wind chimes.

Then the wind chimes clanged again and a couple walked in. "It will take two minutes," the woman said crossly. I turned around and found myself face-to-face with Dennis and his wife. We both froze.

I didn't say anything, but I must have looked very shocked because she glanced at me and then at Dennis with a weird teachery smile on her face.

"Do you know each other?" she said.

"Yes, hi, Dr. Whitson," I said. I slipped my star necklace under my T-shirt.

"Hello," he said. He sounded different, like a husband, but he smiled at me. "This is my wife Kathy. Kathy, this is . . ."

"Swanna," I said. I didn't know if he had forgotten my name or was just pretending he had. "Nice to meet you."

"Isn't this such a neat store?" she said.

I had always hated people who said the word *neat*. *Neat* and *cute*. I was right about her being blond. She was pretty but she had frown lines raked on her forehead even when she was smiling, like lines that suddenly appear in the sand at the beach out of nowhere. She was wearing a preppy pink button-down shirt that matched her lipstick from the car.

"It *is* a neat store," I said. Your husband's dick is neat, I thought, looking at Dennis. It's neat the way I can make him come in his off-white boxer shorts just by sitting on his lap.

"How do you two know each other?" she asked.

"Bowling alley," Dennis said. "The kids hit it off with her little brother." He picked up the same wizard I had liked.

"Fun!" Kathy said.

167

"I like your lipstick," I said. "Is that color called Copa—"

Dennis gave me a look like I should take it easy, and I suddenly felt really angry. He was sweating again. Luckily, she had become engrossed in the candles and had forgotten all about us.

"Okay, I like this one, should we get this one?" he said to Kathy. "Gift for someone," he said to me, nodding at the wizard.

"No, definitely not that one," his wife said, shaking her head. She had a very loud, cackling voice. "What is that, a troll? All these super-cute candles, and he picks the worst one. Maybe we should ask Wanda. It's for my niece, who's probably around your age. We're going to visit her in London tomorrow. Which one would you like if your aunt and uncle were buying you a gift?"

"It's okay, Kathy, just pick the one—"

"No. Let Wanda choose."

Was it possible I'd just heard that he was going to London? They stood frozen in front of me like the wax Prince Charles and Princess Diana at Madame Tussauds with wicks sticking out of the tops of their heads. His wife was a nightmare. I was glad he was going.

"London, England?" I said.

"Yes," she said. "And we're not even packed. We should hurry home, Den."

I looked at him and he shook his head, almost imperceptibly. "Maybe this one," I said, pointing to a candle in the shape of a sundae. It was supposed to look like a tall glass with three scoops of wax ice cream, wavy fudge, and the wick like a stem sticking out of the cherry on top. As if I had turned into the wizard, I could see Kathy's niece's room in front of me, with its pink walls and floral curtains and this candle on the shelf over her desk. "I have to go. Really neat to meet you." I gave Dennis my construction-worker look and brushed past them and out into the wind chime world. From unfeeling wax to heart pounding in flesh. I let out a moan. My heart was in pain like it had just lost its virginity too. Like it had its brains fucked out.

I hated him. My cheeks were hot. I thought of his pager going off in the motel. Maybe it had been a lie. Maybe there hadn't been an acute patient who needed him. Maybe his moronic wife Candle Kathy had just wanted more cottage cheese. Now he would never see me again. I walked down the main street in the direction of the lot where the stupid embarrassing truck was parked.

Sitting in the back of the truck next to Madding, I could barely speak.

"Will you read to me tonight?" he asked.

I closed my eyes and ignored him.

Ever since I was a kid, I would do this thing to sort of calm myself down. I would recite the children's book *Eloise* in my head—but all of a sudden I couldn't remember the words. *I am Eloise. I am six.* I couldn't come up with anything else. I thought of Eloise losing her virginity and I felt sick like I was going to throw up.

Then, just before we pulled into the driveway, I saw a car parked on the side of the road. It looked like it could be Dennis's car, but we drove by too fast for me to see it well enough.

"You had ice cream, so you have to go in and brush your teeth," I told Madding. "Then I'll read to you."

He went into the house with my mother and Bozo-the Intruder and I grabbed the flashlight and went to the driveway.

It's not Dennis, I told myself. He was home packing.

I rounded the bend cautiously.

"Swanna," he said. He was standing next to his car. "You ran away before I could catch up to you. You must have walked fast."

"I'm a New Yorker," I said. *I am a city child. I live at the Plaza.* "And I have a feeling you didn't exactly *run* after me."

"I wanted to. But what could I do? Leave my wife standing there while I run after the foxiest lady in Vermont? I felt so paralyzed, I fucking hated it. It was horrifying, painful. You must think I'm a total wimp. You must think I have no balls."

"No, I don't," I said, even though I did. "Did you buy the sundae candle?"

"No. Her niece has anorexia nervosa. Do you know what that is?"

"So which one did you get?" I wanted to tell him I had liked the wizard.

"I don't know, Swanna! I don't give a shit! The penis. Who the fuck cares? Who the fuck wants a candle? I see you dressed like this and you think I care about candles?"

I shrugged. "You shouldn't have come here. It's dangerous."

"You have no fucking idea how dangerous this is," he said.

"It's not just dangerous, it's disastrous. It's madness. It's insane."

"So why *did* you? You should stop seeing me," I said, starting to turn to walk back to the truck.

He grabbed my arm. "I couldn't stop if I wanted to. You make me feel like the heavyweight champion of the world. Everyone deserves to feel like this at least once in their lives."

"Well, you're going to London. And I'm going home to New York."

"I'm not going to London," he said. "I'm going to tell her the doctor covering me had an emergency. He's going to call the house at four thirty a.m. I'm going to drive her and the kids to the airport and send them to London without me. There's no way I'm going to fucking London when I could have you here in my bed. I have to go now, but I'm going to come get you tomorrow and bring you to my house and make love to you in my fucking bed."

"I'll have to think about that," I said.

"From the way you're looking at me right now, it looks like you already are. Thinking about it," he said. "Now I have to go home and pretend to pack."

"I don't think you should pick me up here. You shouldn't come here again." I thought about what Pervislav had said about me. I couldn't risk anything going wrong. "Is there someplace close to here where we could meet?"

"Nothing close," he said. "If you take a right out of the driveway, and you walk straight for about two miles that way, there's an old closed-down tire store called Tetta's. It has a bench out front, I think. Do you want me to pick you up there? Five tomorrow?"

"Yes," I said. "I'll be there. I just walk straight that way?"

"Yes."

"I have to read to my brother now." I turned and walked back toward the truck.

SWANNA IN LOVE

That night we lay on the mattress in the truck and I read *On the Banks of Plum Creek* from the *Little House on the Prairie* series out loud to Madding. Every time I read the name *Nellie Oleson*, he shouted, "That *bitch*!" at the top of his lungs. I never laughed so hard in my life.

19

"**M**adding," I said, "my friend Debbie is going back to New York. I'm going to sleep at her house and then go back to the city with her family. Are you okay here? If you're not okay, I'll stay."

"I'm okay," he said.

"Make sure you ride with them in the front of the truck," I said.

He nodded obediently. "Ray is going to pitch a tent and we're going to camp."

"Who's Ray?"

"My favorite grown-up friend. He got four splinters out of my hand."

"Okay," I said. "Make sure they give you lunch."

"It's okay, I'm not hungry."

"I mean every day. Even if you're not that hungry. You have to eat breakfast, lunch, and dinner." My mother would rather sit in the corner of Bumislav's art studio, watching him sculpt his gaseous tar into roads than get anyone a PB&J or bother to cut up a cucumber. "I'm going to pack some of my things."

I dumped the smaller of my two duffels out in the back of the truck and packed just the nicer, cleaner things and all my toiletries and contact lens stuff. I packed my glasses, but I wouldn't wear them in front of Dennis. I'd sleep in my contacts even though I wasn't supposed to. My father had died of shock at the price of the contacts, so he wouldn't also get me new glasses at E.B. Meyrowitz. My eye doctor said it was very dangerous to sleep in my lenses, but I had done it a thousand times. I hated when he warned me like that because it made me think of Chekhov's gun.

"What do you miss most about New York?" Madding asked.

"Chinese food," I said.

"Do you miss Roger?"

"The doorman? Yes, I do. Do you?"

"No. Do you miss Scarlett?"

"Who's Scarlett?"

"Your doll."

"Madding, I'm fourteen. I haven't thought of that doll in years." She was actually still in my room, though, in her box in a drawer. She was supposed to be Scarlett O'Hara and she had a blue silk ball gown with a matching hooded cape. She was from Harrods. That summed up my parents perfectly. They would buy me a million-dollar doll I didn't even want that much, but they wouldn't buy me new glasses.

"When I get home we can look at her," I said.

"Nah," he said, "I miss Big Bird."

Right before my dad had moved out, my mom inexplicably bought a nine-foot plant. A neighbor was moving out and had put up a sign about it on the bulletin board in the mailroom. Except for small marijuana plants, and the lima bean plant I had grown at school, we'd never had a plant in our house before. "What have I done?" my mother had sobbed. It was coming in the morning and she and my father had a huge fight about it. She said she couldn't handle taking care of another living thing, and my father said she had never taken care of a living thing in her life. She was up all night with a tension headache and couldn't stop throwing up and had to take a Compazine suppository. When the neighbor delivered the plant, my mother was too sick to come out of the bedroom and Madding and I had to tell him to put it between the windows in the living room. Madding asked the man if it had a name and the man said he called it Big Bird. "I didn't water it so it would be lighter to carry. Tell your mom to water it today." Madding and I had looked at each other because it was impossible to imagine our mother watering Big Bird.

When she finally came out of her room she wouldn't look at it, and when Madding told her its name was Big Bird, she started crying and moaning again and went back to her room. My father left to stay at a friend's house that day and never came back. After that, every time I looked at the plant I remembered we were divorced now and I would start to cry too. We had lost a father but gained a plant, a plant that was about three feet taller than my father was. That plant must have thought we were crazy. I almost cried now even thinking about it.

I finished packing and put on my cowboy boots because my father had always told me to travel in my heaviest things. I was wearing what I had worn to town because Dennis had seemed to really like it, with a bathing suit underneath because he said he had a pool. I left all the rest of my stuff in a heap.

"Okay, I have to go, Debbie's father is coming. Tell Mom I'm going back to New York. Have fun camping." I hugged my brother until he squirmed away. We used to play this game where I would hug him as tightly as I could and say, "I love you, Madding, but I can't just hug you all day. You have to go out into the world and be a man," and he would pull and struggle to try to get away and scream, "I'm trying to leave!" but I wouldn't let him go and I'd say, "I mean you can't just stay here with your sister all day long, you have to stop hugging me," and finally he'd manage to get away.

20

A mile was twenty city blocks, so two miles was forty blocks. I sometimes walked from my apartment on 93rd Street to my ballet class on 61st. That was thirty-two blocks. I could easily walk eight additional blocks. Although I always stopped for pizza and ice cream or a hot chocolate when I walked that far and I had sometimes gotten on the 104 bus if it wasn't the one driver who checked for bus passes. I had lost my bus pass in October. I loved walking down Broadway past Woolworths and the 84th Street Quad and Morris Bros. and Liberty House and the Ansonia and the McDonald's on 72nd Street, and Lincoln Center and O'Neals' Baloon Saloon.

It took a long time to walk that far. I should leave at five o'clock, I thought. My dad hadn't let me bring my new Swatch to camp because he said it would get stolen. I was the only kid all summer who had no idea what time it was, and camp was the opposite of anyplace where anything would get stolen. In fact, the girls in my bunk actually gave me things because my parents didn't send me anything all summer, and Janie Rand showed me how to use conditioner, which I hadn't even known about until then. She gave me a whole bottle of Fabergé because she said I had very thick hair and should use half a bottle each time. I went to the truck and grabbed my bag, walked up the driveway, and turned right.

I didn't know how long I had been walking when I saw the sign for Tetta's Service Station and Tires. I was sweating and incredibly thirsty. I should have stolen a Coke from the refrigerator. The road had been very winding in places and cars drove by me fast. I had walked in a cloud of gnats like Pig-Pen. I tried to pretend I was in New York seeing all the things I would see on Broadway. I also sang a lot of Bob Dylan songs very loudly. "It's All Over Now, Baby Blue" and "Stuck Inside of Mobile with the Memphis Blues Again." I felt exactly like Bob Dylan felt in that song, except I was about to be free. I saw the bench Dennis had told me about and sat on it. Then I opened the *Weekly Wag* I had stolen from the kitchen.

I turned every page until I found it. "Men and Mores," the headline said, "by Mistress Amber."

I looked at the words in disbelief.

The dreaded Labor Day is almost here and I almost feel as if I am in labor. PhD's chicks are coming home to our downy nest and the pressure is on. It seems I am required to meet them. I have never wanted children of my own, but the thought of rearing another woman's offspring fills me with dread. My therapist says some of the healthiest relationships she knows are stepchild and stepparent, but I am skeptical. I'm more the wicked type and I'm not afraid to admit it. I have memorized their ages— eight and fourteen—and their names and interests. For journalistic purposes we will call the girl Cygnet and the boy Gosling. Cyggie is a brainiac nerd and Gos likes basketball and cars. If my loving PhD thinks I am going to take them under my wing, he's sadly mistaken. I want no part of his gaggle. The best thing his wife ever did was force him to get a vasectomy.

Suddenly there was a loud scream behind me. Behind Tetta's, there was a small lake and three swans were floating on the water. They looked like trumpeters. Two males were competing for a female. The two males started screaming again, then flapped their wings and rose up out of the water and brutally smashed into each other. The female turned her back on them. The fight continued until one of the swans seemed severely injured. He stopped screaming and sat very still on the lake while the other two swam off together. I wished so badly I hadn't seen it.

21

Dennis pulled up in his car and helped me with my duffel. "That bag is bigger than you are," he said.

"I know. I have an even bigger one in the truck. You either bring huge bags like these or a trunk." My dad had bought it for me at the last minute at Morris Bros. on Broadway. It was the last one they had. I had to sew on all my name tags myself the night before camp because my mother had a tension headache. I had also done all of Madding's.

"Bring where?"

"Oh, I was at camp."

"Bennie and the Jets" came on the radio, which I liked, followed by "Please Please Me," "You Can Do Magic," and then my favorite song of all time, "Vienna" by Billy Joel, and Dennis started to change the station. "Stop! That's my favorite song," I said.

"What?"

"That's my favorite fucking song," I said.

"Oh is it, now." He let out a big exaggerated laugh but he let me listen to it. "Here we are," he said a few minutes later.

His house was at the end of a very long driveway. I followed him in through the garage, kitchen, and a big dining room and living room. He put *The Stranger* on the stereo. He pulled the record out of the sleeve like he was operating on a patient. He held it carefully, the correct way, so he wouldn't scratch it, like he was holding a baby's head and watching out for the soft spot. Men were always weird around records. I picked up the empty album cover and pretended to look at Billy Joel wearing a suit, scrunched up on a bed, looking down at a Japanese Noh mask on a pillow. I knew the cover by heart but it was comforting to look at something I had at home.

Even though I knew Dennis was married, and I had met his wife, I hadn't realized how married he was until I was in his house. His wife was everywhere. Her pocketbook was slung over a chair in the kitchen. Straw hats hung from pegs by the front door. Ladies' magazines were fanned out on the gigantic coffee table, flowery wallpaper and ceramic tiles with pears painted on them in the kitchen and an actual apron, hand towels with scalloped edges and matching scallop shell soaps in the bathroom and a big box of Tampax. My mother didn't have any of these things except the Tampax.

My mother had books and art and a desk with a typewriter and reams of white paper. Her beautiful coat and boots and black braided leather pocketbook from Bergdorf's were in the closet. Aside from three half-naked photos of herself with a very, very bad haircut taken by a famous photographer named Jill Krementz, who took the pictures in a book called *A Very Young Dancer*, you wouldn't have known a woman even lived in our apartment. We got the *New Yorker* and the *New York Times*, not *House Beautiful* and *Victoria Gardens* or whatever the hell those magazines were. Same with all my friends' houses. I couldn't even imagine Dennis lived here. Except for all the stuff in the garage—fishing rods and tackle boxes, skis and surfboards, tents and coolers and weights and tools. Maybe he lived in the garage. Or maybe he had switched houses with a friend the way he had switched cars when he first took me to the motel. Except I knew it was his house because there were family photos everywhere and he was most definitely in them. I kind of wished we were back in the motel, but he seemed excited to have me here.

He gave me a glass of Tab with cylindrical ice cubes in it. "Make yourself at home," he said. "Is it weird being here?"

"I love your place," I said.

"Do you?" He smiled at me. "Scenes from an Italian Restaurant" had ended and "Vienna" was starting.

"Thank you for having me."

"I'm going to have you, all right."

There was nothing I could think to say to that because it was pretty much true. "You sure you wouldn't rather be in merry old England?" I said.

"I think I'm going to have a bloody marvelous time right here," he said in a Cockney accent.

He leaned over and kissed me and I immediately relaxed. He liked me and that's why I was here. He had made the plan. I had nothing to feel insecure about.

"I thought we were going swimming in your in-ground pool," I said.

"Let's do it."

The living room had big French doors that led to the pool and patio. There were a lot of kids' toys lying around and a big basket of rolled-up striped towels.

"This is beautiful," I said, the way my mother always did when she went to someone's house. "I love this wavy-shaped pool."

"It's called kidney-shaped," he said.

I took off my King Tut shirt and my cowboy boots and shorts to reveal my white bathing suit. It was scooped way down low in the back with a big white bow right above my butt. I had my back to him and I knew he was looking at that bow. I hadn't even wanted to try on this suit in the store because my mother said white wasn't slimming and the bow seemed ridiculous, but the annoying French saleswoman had talked me into it and I had never looked better in anything in my entire life. I usually liked bathing suits with pictures of boats or polka dots on them, but this one was very sophisticated and the saleswoman had said it was "superb."

I started to walk toward the pool steps without looking back at Dennis, but before I could put my toe in the water he was behind me, kissing my neck with his hands all over me. He tugged the top of my bathing suit down and turned me around to face him. He sat down on a chaise and pulled me down onto his lap. I had never felt so grown up as I did right then with my arms around his neck. No one had ever looked at me like that before.

"I promised myself I would wait until after dinner to attack you," he said.

"Mmmmm, there's dinner?" I said.

"I'm grilling for you. Do you want steak or swordfish?"

"Hot dogs," I said. When a man looks at you like that, you might as well ask for what you want.

"Okay, hot dogs it is," he said. "But I get to pick the music."

We kissed for a little while but he didn't take off his clothes. He played with the bow and then he reached his fingers inside the suit and touched me until I came.

"That was so incredibly sweet. Your face. Do you want a glass of wine?" he asked.

I'd never had wine but I knew it always gave my mother a headache. "I'll stick with this," I said. My suit was wetter than if I'd already been in the pool.

"Why don't you take a swim and I'll get the hot dogs on deck," he said. "We don't have to rush anything. We have all the time in the world. And this is already the best vacation of my life. I can't believe that tomorrow I'm going to wake up and see you next to me."

Dennis went into the kitchen and I eased into the Jacuzzi, watching my limbs go as white as my suit. Under the swirling water, my legs looked like the chicken bone Hansel stuck out of the cage to fool the witch. My back had been killing me from sleeping on the soft mattress in the truck. My father and I liked extra-firm mattresses for our backs. Tonight I would sleep in a real bed with a gorgeous guy and nice covers and no risk of anyone peeing. This was much better than the motel. Dennis was happy. He didn't seem to care that his wife's stuff was all around.

Why had he chosen her? I wondered. What made someone pick one person over everyone else in the world? It seemed like an impossible choice to make. I always wondered that whenever I took the subway. I'd look at a woman across from me, fat and tired-looking with an ugly mole or weird twisted-up toes or fleshy upper arms, and I'd stare at her wedding ring and think, Someone proposed to this woman. Someone has sex with her and sleeps in bed with her every night. That's what I thought about in school for I'd say thirty-nine out of the forty-five minutes of every period, if the teacher was married. Did their husband or wife now feel it had been a terrible mistake? I couldn't stand looking at a teacher for forty-five minutes five times a week, let alone for a lifetime.

I closed my eyes, and when I opened them I was ecstatic to see Dennis coming out of the house with a big platter of not just hot dogs, but hamburger patties too.

There was corn on the cob and something wrapped in tinfoil and buns. My mother was completely against buns. She was against everything but the corn.

I got out and wrapped myself in one of the big towels from the basket and asked if there was anything I could do to help. I prayed he would say no because I had never barbecued anything in my entire life. I knew how to use a can opener and a toaster oven and I could make whipped cream. Once, the playwright Edward Albee was at our house for a dinner party and I was making whipped cream and Edward said I should add more vanilla and I said, "Edward, I don't tell you how to write plays, so you shouldn't tell me how to make whipped cream."

"I think I can handle this," Dennis said. "Do you want to get dressed? I put your bag in the bedroom upstairs."

I took my empty glass and went into the house. My hair was dripping water on everything. I walked to the kitchen to get myself some more Tab and opened what was the biggest refrigerator I had ever seen. I had never seen so much food in my life. There were some things I'd seen on TV, but we would never have like I Can't Believe It's Not Butter and frozen Lender's bagels and frozen pizza and chicken pot pies and Cool Whip. There was a whole drawer full of the rounded ice cubes—and the pièce de résistance, a whole drawer of dozens of cans of diet sodas. It was a drawer designed for cans! I wondered if Jacquie Beller knew about this and if my father might get a fridge like this now that we were divorced. He really should.

I closed the giant door and looked at the magnets and more photos and a list of *Kid-friendly Places to Eat in London.* She was wasting her time with that because London had terrible food. That's why she probably didn't bother to bring the list. The one good place, Pizza Express, wasn't even on the list. You could order the Fiorentina, which had an egg on it.

When I turned to leave, I saw something that stopped me dead in my tracks. On the shelf over the kitchen sink was the sundae candle from the shop in town. There were three of them—the sundae candle, the banana-split candle, and a slice-of-cake candle. Besides the candle she got for her niece, she had spent twenty-seven dollars on candles for herself. Who would do that? And what would it be like to be married to Dennis and live in this huge house and buy three of anything you wanted? I suddenly felt sick from all the food and photos and knickknacks and lists. I wanted to go home.

Dennis came into the kitchen and put his arms around me, squeezing me in my towel. It felt warm and good. I loved his chest.

"What's wrong?" he said.

"Nothing."

"Come on, tell me what's wrong. You seem upset." He looked very lovingly at me and he kissed me.

I shook my head in his chest and unbuttoned two of his shirt buttons. If I started to cry, I would never forgive myself.

"If something's bothering you, I want you to tell me," he said.

It's a cliché to say I was fighting back tears, but I was fighting them harder than Muhammad Ali. There was no reason for me to be upset about candles. There was no reason for me to be jealous.

"Come on," he said. He took my hand and led me up a flight of stairs to his bedroom. My bag was on the bed. It was a huge room and seemed more like him, with two big club chairs and a big green comforter on the bed. There was a TV and bedside tables and lamps and closet doors I was dying to open. I was starting to feel like myself again.

"Are you okay?" he asked.

"I'm excited for dinner."

He laughed and I had no idea what he was laughing at, because I really was. "I can't believe I'm saying this, but you should get dressed and come downstairs."

I put on the maroon flowery dress my Aunt Judith had bought me at the Galleria in Houston. It was low-cut with shoulder pads and I felt pretty grown up in it.

"Whoa," Dennis said when I came downstairs. "I dig that dress."

I was dying to know what was in the tinfoil packets on the grill. We were eating outside.

Dennis started chopping wood. "I can make a fire later," he said. "The nights are getting cooler."

I sat with my legs stretched out in front of me on the chaise. It was made of white plastic cords that had given the backs of my thighs red stripes when I was just wearing a bathing suit. I watched him pick up an axe, put a log between two stones, and split it in two. He had taken off his shirt.

"Is that hard?"

"What?"

"Chopping wood."

"It can be a little tricky, I guess," he said.

"Is that axe hard to handle?"

"What this?" he said, holding it up. He was trying to look serious and not smile. "This is just a little hatchet."

"It looks like a big axe to me."

"I bet it does," he said. "I bet it does."

He finished chopping and brought the wood into the house. Then he cooked on the grill for a while.

He put a hamburger and a hot dog on my plate, both with buns.

Suddenly I heard a man's voice from behind the fence— "Hey, dipshit, you home?"

"What the hell?" Dennis said.

"Who's that?" I said.

"Dennis, man, you there?"

"Oh Jesus," Dennis said.

The gate opened and three guys walked into the backyard.

Dennis looked terrified. He put his barbecue tongs down and they slid off the side of the grill and made a clattering sound on the bricks. He was trying to put his shirt on.

"The doctor is in," one of the men said. "Did you forget about us?"

"Hold on, hold on," Dennis said. "I didn't tell you I was in London?"

"You're in London?" the second guy said.

"We should go," the third guy said. "He's in London."

"Hey, I brought beer," the guy who'd opened the gate said.

He was very good-looking even though he had a beard. He was wearing a baseball cap that said *Brattlebrew* on it and carrying a big cardboard box. I couldn't stop looking at his black beard, and his eyes were so blue, they looked artificial like the freeze pops at camp. I'd almost never been around anyone with a beard before, let alone three beards in one place. There was a blond one, a salt-and-pepper one, and a black one. It was like *Charlie's Angels* but with beards.

In New York, absolutely no one had a beard.

"My friends call me Pop Can," the guy with the box said. He had the Jaclyn Smith of beards, definitely the best-looking one.

"Pop Can? What, are we in an S.E. Hinton novel?" I asked. Nobody knew what I was talking about. "Why do they call you Pop Can?"

Pop Can looked at Dennis. "An outtastata?" he said.

Whatever that was, it sounded like a bad thing. Dennis looked very uncomfortable.

"What's an outtastata?" I asked.

Pop Can looked back at me with his Disney eyes. "Someone not from these parts. If you want to know, they call me Pop Can because of the size of—"

"That's a story for another time. This is Swanna. That's Pop Can, Guts, and Bobby."

"Hi," I said. "I'm sorry I don't have a beard."

No one laughed. The one called Guts walked over and picked up the tongs and put them back on the side of the grill. Pop Can had gone into the house with the cardboard box and now he came back without it. "Let's go. He's got Barry White on in there, for Christ sake."

"I know you guys are going to try to make a big deal . . ." Dennis started.

"None of our business," Bobby, the blond Farrah Fawcett–beard guy, said. "See you, Denny." They started to leave.

"Thanks, Bobby. I know you wanted to lose some money tonight. I'll make it up to you."

"Lose some money?" I said.

"Poker," Bobby said.

"Texas Hold'em?" I said.

"Does she play?" Guts asked.

"Yes, I do play," I said. If we played, I could make enough for a bus ticket.

"Oh shit," Pop Can said, "she plays. We're staying. You two go ahead and eat, I'll put some more burgers on the grill. I've got a two-four of tall boys in the truck. What's your name? Swanna? We'll just play a few hands and get out of your feathers right quick."

"I hope your poker skills are better than your repartee," I said.

"*Repartee*," Pop Can said. "Where'd you find this one?"

"I'm a first-year resident at the hospital," I said confidently. "I had a bad day. Was feeling very homesick for New York, and Dr. Whitson said I could come by for a home-cooked meal."

The three men stared at me. I'd been working on it in my mind for a few minutes and I thought it came out pretty good.

"Where'd you go to medical school?" Guts asked.

I was deciding between Harvard and Columbia and was about to say Harvard when Dennis said, "Guts is a Harvard Med man like me."

"Columbia," I said, praying it had a medical school.

"You must know Harry Lowe," Guts said.

"I'm going to take a dip if nobody minds," Pop Can said.

"I mind," Dennis said. He looked upset.

Guts walked back over to the grill and started turning over the tinfoil packets. His beard was equally black and gray, with two stripes on either side of his mouth that came down from his mustache to his beard. It almost looked designed like the lanyards I made at camp.

Pop Can threw his baseball cap on the ground near the pool, pulled off his shirt, and stripped down to his underwear.

"Dude!" Dennis said.

I knew my cheeks were red. I looked away as he took off his underwear and dove into the pool.

"Jesus, nobody needs to see that," Bobby said.

"Swanna," Dennis said, indicating for me to follow him into the house. "I'm sorry about my friends," he said once we were inside.

"At least I covered for us pretty well."

"You mean when you told Dr. Gutowski, the head of the hospital, that you work there?"

My heart started pounding. "He doesn't know everyone who works there."

"Yes, he does."

"Then I'll leave," I said. "I don't really care."

"You don't care?" He let out a strange laugh. "I'm risking everything I have."

"Well, if you're embarrassed about me, I'll go. Can you call me a taxi?"

"You know I don't want that," he said. "It's difficult to explain. I'm married."

"Is that why you don't have a beard? Your wife is against beards?"

"Maybe."

"So are you embarrassed that I'm here or proud that I'm here?" I pressed. I didn't care what he answered. I thought he was very immature to care what his stupid friends thought.

"Both, I guess. I mean, you're young."

"They don't know that."

"That's true. I didn't know it when I met you."

"Does your wife call him Pop Can?"

"She calls him The Sociopath."

I remembered an article I had read in *Seventeen* magazine that said giving your boyfriend a nickname is a key to seduction. Why should Pop Can be the only one with a cool nickname?

"I thought of a nickname for you," I said. "But I don't want to tell you in case you don't like it."

"What is it?" he said.

"You have to promise to tell me if you don't like it."

"I promise."

"I was thinking I might call you Axe," I said.

"I like that." But he didn't just like it. I could tell he *loved* it. I had never given anyone a nickname before. "Hey, Axe."

"Yes?"

"Just trying it. I don't have to call you that if you don't want me to."

"No, I want you to."

"Should I call you Dennis or Axe in front of your friends?" I said teasingly.

"Let's stick with Dennis. And if he asks about Harry Lowe again, say of course you know her."

"Her?"

"Harriet. You can't go to Columbia and not know her."

"Hey, where's Guts?" Dennis said when we got back outside.

"He left," Pop Can said. He had gotten out of the pool and was wrapped in a towel.

Dennis looked upset. "How come?"

"He mumbled something about being a family man and not wanting to stand by. Can't stand seeing anyone happy."

Dennis didn't look happy. "What does that mean?"

"Don't worry about that uptight prick," Pop Can said.

I put mustard on my hot dog and ate it. Dennis opened a beer. Someone had opened a big bag of Wise potato chips. I hoped they would drink something a lot stronger than beer, because my plan was to try to win.

They talked about the Bosox, which I figured out was the Boston Red Sox, and someone named Dale Earnhardt who seemed to be like some kind of Evel Kneivel type. I was being quiet because I was still a little mad at Dennis and I was trying to remember all the rules of poker.

"Where are the cards?" I asked.

"Inside. We eat first and then go downstairs."

Good, I thought. They would be drunk before we even started.

22

"**A**re you sure you don't mind this? I can throw them out. Or we can just leave if you want. Go to the motel," Dennis said when I carried my plate into the kitchen. "I'm having fun," I said. "They're nice."

"What if you like them better than me?"

"You're the best looking," I said.

The Cutter mosquito repellent mixed with my Love's Baby Soft reminded me of camp. I missed having red bug juice from a giant drink dispenser with dinner. I had noticed a tub of Kool-Aid in the kitchen and I'd gone in when the conversation turned to politics and quickly made myself a glass, but I'd used two big scoopers full and it was thick and gloppy.

"But you can't leave tomorrow. You have to stay as long as possible."

"I will," I said.

"I want to fuck you," Dennis whispered.

"I know," I said.

The guys all came lumbering in with their plates. Pop Can had put on his pants. They went downstairs and Dennis leaned in and kissed me, putting his tongue in my mouth.

"Did you just have Kool-Aid?" I nodded. "I keep forgetting you're a kid," he said, kissing me again.

I ran upstairs and got my four dollars and then went down-stairs to the basement, which was carpeted, with a big sectional sofa, TV, pool table, and a bar. There was a giant buffalo head on the wall. They were all sitting at an octagonal poker table. Dennis was drinking a beer but the others were drinking amber-colored liquor. I was nervous.

"How do I buy chips?" I asked. I put my four dollars on the table.

"I can buy in for you," Dennis said.

I thought for a second. "Maybe if I run out of money."

"Oh, you're going to run out," Pop Can said. "How are you with losing money?"

"I wouldn't know," I said. I might not triple my money, but I wasn't leaving here without my four bucks.

I had never played at a table like this. It was covered in soft green felt and had a cut-out circle where your drink could go. I had learned poker at the Playboy Club in New Jersey. My grandfather was a member because they had golf there. I would lounge by the pool all day. My grandfather always tipped a hundred. A few times when it was cold out, one of the bunnies said I could hang out with her in the dressing room, and that's where I learned how to play. She was prac-ticing to be a dealer in Las Vegas. I won a lot of money in that dressing room, and everyone said I was a natural.

I stacked my red, white, and blue chips in my own personal built-in tray and Dennis shuffled and dealt me in. My plan was to fold right away a few times, unless I got a monster hand. Then I started playing for real, and quickly lost my four dollars and most of the twenty Dennis gave me. I was making mistakes. Worse than anything, it was starting to dawn on me that Brenda, the *Playboy* bunny, had lied to me. She had told me I was good to butter me up so my grandfather would keep giving her hundreds. She had just treated me like a stupid kid.

We were taking turns being the dealer, which was nerve-racking. I had almost put down the flop too soon and everyone yelled. Now it was Dennis's turn to deal again. I picked up my cards. A pair of aces—the best hand on this earth. Pop Can put in a red chip, which was fifty cents. Bobby called. Dennis folded. I raised two blue chips, which were a dollar each. Pop Can called and Bobby folded. I felt Dennis tense up a little next to me. He thought I was playing badly.

Dennis dealt the flop. Another ace, a king of spades, and a two of diamonds. I had three aces now. Everybody checked, including me, even though it hurt me to do it. Pop Can and Bobby were talking about the Bosox again but I wasn't listening to them. Dennis turned over a queen of hearts. Pop Can bet a red chip. I just called, slow-playing my set of aces.

Dennis dealt the river, a queen of spades. I had a full house and the only thing that could beat me was four queens.

"Who shuffled these things?" Bobby said.

Pop Can smiled slightly, which made me think he now had three queens. He put down two blues. I went all in with my last four blues and two reds.

"Easy does it," Dennis said to me.

My father was always saying things like *Easy does it*. Like if I was playing baseball and I was up at bat, he'd say, "Easy does it," as if that would at all help me to make contact with the ball. Pop Can called, which was the right thing to do if you had three queens and were playing against someone you didn't know to be any good.

I turned over my cards.

Pop Can threw his cards down without turning them over. I gathered all my chips from the center of the table and stacked them quietly while Pop Can picked up the deck to shuffle and deal. Pop Can not showing his cards made me think he didn't have three queens. I was pretty sure he'd had nothing and couldn't bring himself to fold. If that was the case, he would be easy to beat, but the others really knew what they were doing and I should probably stop while I was ahead.

"Sorry I'm late," a voice said at the top of the stairs.

"Santiago," Bobby said, "make yourself a drink. We just watched Pop Can get kicked in the back of the pants by this young lady."

I had also kicked *him* in the back of the pants, but I didn't think I should point that out.

"Hello," the new guy said with his mouth full. He was holding a cheeseburger in each hand. "The front door was locked so I came in the back. I'm John," he said to me.

"Hi, I'm Swanna."

He was wearing a black sleeveless T-shirt and had a lot of tattoos. One was of a snake, which I thought was a swan for a minute. He had a little patch of beard.

"She's a friend of Dennis's," Pop Can said, smiling.

They all stared at him smiling, except Dennis who got himself another beer from a small fridge.

I hoped no one would bring up that I was a doctor. I regretted saying that more than anything. I had thought about it more, and it made me way too old.

Before Guts left, he and Dennis had discussed someone's blighted ovum requiring a scraping, whatever the hell that was. I had almost asked what a blighted ovum was, but of course I would already know.

"I thought you were in New York," Dennis said to Santiago.

"He got done with that," Bobby said.

"I've got someone collecting my unemployment. I'll go back in a few days and move my stuff out here."

"Are you going back to New York?" I asked him. I could feel Dennis looking at me.

Santiago looked at Dennis and then at me. "Yeah, next week sometime, why? You want to go with me?" He smiled.

"Maybe," I said.

Santiago finished his burgers and poured himself a big drink, and the others drank more too. I folded the next four rounds even though my hands were decent. As I predicted, Pop Can lost all four hands. Dennis and Bobby were both up. I liked Santiago. He had a New York accent and attitude.

"What job did you have?" I asked him.

"Mailroom at Goldman Sachs. My old lady's pissed as shit. How can you lose a job in the mailroom?"

"Your mom is mad at you?" I said.

Everyone laughed. "Not my mom. My wife. Girlfriend. Whatever the hell."

I got an ace and a king. I raised a blue but I knew I shouldn't bet if I was talking because that meant I wasn't concentrating hard enough.

"The fucked-up thing was, I never dealt with no mail. All these douchebag traders would order takeout dinners and I had to bring it up to them on a fucking cart. There were like two or three hundred food deliveries a night."

I called. I had a straight but Dennis had a flush. I always forgot about flushes. That was my weak point. Sometimes I even had a flush and didn't realize it because I forgot all about them. "They make so much money. Rich kids. Nervous, can't look you in the eye." Santiago started twitching and screaming in a nerdy whiny voice, *"Where's my fucking Caesar salad? Where is it? If my spaghetti and meatballs don't get here by the count of three. . ."* It was pretty funny, but no one was paying attention to him. "You make a million dollars but you're crying over a salad. Then they'd get upset because the delivery guy would eat half the food. There'd be a dirty spoon and a few bites taken out of the container, and the shithead would be coming to me saying, *Hey, how come there's no turkey in my turkey club?* Hey, delivery boys get hungry too. It's good these guys weren't police detectives, 'cause not a lot of crimes woulda got solved."

I was interested in this story because we ordered in a lot of Chinese food and the containers always came filled to the top.

"What's your name, Juana? You Spanish?"

I shook my heard. "Swanna. Swanna Swain. I'm also from New York."

"Oh yeah? Swanna Swain from New York," he said, smiling. "Where in New York?"

"I really should take Swanna back to her place," Dennis said suddenly. "Didn't you say you have six a.m. rounds? You guys can keep playing. But don't stay too long. I have an early morning too."

"I have to cash in my chips," I said. I had no idea why he was making me leave.

Bobby counted my chips and gave me my winnings. Ten dollars. Probably not enough to get home.

23

"Where'd you learn how to play Texas Hold'em?" Dennis asked when we got in the car.

"My grandfather's a member of the Playboy Club in New Jersey," I said.

"You go to the Playboy Club?" Dennis said, as if that was the craziest thing he'd ever heard.

"Yes. Basically, you just lounge by this huge pool and have bottomless virgin piña coladas . . ."

"I had a bottomless virgin the other night," he said.

"Do you want to hear about it or not?"

"Yes, but I also want to think about the other night. While I'm hearing about it."

"Suit yourself. All these *Playboy* bunnies wait on you hand and foot . . ."

"Jesus Christ."

"And after you're done at the pool, you have dinner at a buffet called a smorgasbord and then you can watch men playing poker."

"So you're lying by the pool and *Playboy* bunnies are bringing you drinks?"

"Yes, and it's like ninety degrees and they have to wear pantyhose and high heels and tight costumes with ears and a bunny tail. Their ears are the same color as their leotard. Everyone wears a different color but they don't get to pick, it's assigned to them on their first day of work. You have to be a certain height and weight to work there. It's very sexist but a lot of them are very smart, like they're going for their PhDs."

Dennis laughed really hard. "Going for their PhDs," he said.

"What? You don't believe me?"

"No," he said.

"Well, you can come with me. When you're in New York. My grandfather will let me bring you."

"I don't think your grandfather is going to want to take me to the Playboy Club, Swanna. When I come to New York, we're going to have to be secretive. Do things just the two of us."

I nodded but I wasn't convinced. We could say Dennis was my camp counselor or something. Papa wouldn't mind.

"You would like my grandfather. He's a gambler. His law partner is Elizabeth Holtzman's father."

"The woman who ran against D'Amato?"

I nodded. "My grandmother married him because he carried a big wad of hundred-dollar bills in a silver money clip on their first date. They're divorced now." I put my feet up on the dashboard. It was nice to relax and be alone with Dennis without all those other guys. I hadn't realized how nervous I had been. I had a lot of tension and I got hives and eczema and headaches quite easily.

"My childhood was very different," he said.

"Why, what was yours like?" I asked. He had gotten a little judgmental like this before, so I made myself ready.

"Fishing trips, boarding school."

"Like Holden Caulfield?"

He smiled. "No, nothing like Holden Caulfield. Good student, played a lot of sports."

"Ice hockey?"

"No, football."

"They don't have that in New York," I said.

He laughed as if I was kidding, but we really didn't have it. "I wasn't too lucky with women. Lost my virginity when I was eighteen. Worked too hard in college and medical school to really be with anyone."

"How long have you been married?" I asked.

"Six years."

"Wow. You have a six-year-old." This was making my Playboy Club story seem boring. "Did you love your wife when you got married?" I stared out the car window, keeping a lookout for any bears or foxes.

"No," he said.

"Why'd you marry her?"

"She got pregnant," he said. "She's seven years older than I am. We had already been dating for three years. It was her last chance to have a baby."

"So why don't you get a divorce?"

"I'm a father now," he said. "I don't want my children to grow up with the worst parents."

"I don't think you would be the worst parents," I said.

"I didn't say the worst parents. I said *divorced* parents. I don't want them to grow up with divorced parents."

He didn't realize it was an insensitive thing to say to someone who was about to grow up with divorced parents herself. I turned my head away from him and saw the ghosts lining the road.

"Do you still like me?" he asked.

"Yeah," I said.

He took my hand, putting his fingers through mine. I caught a glimpse of myself in the side mirror and I was surprised for a minute. I looked a lot younger than I felt. I wasn't wearing any lip gloss and my face looked a little fat.

"Santiago liked you," he said. I didn't say anything to that. I had actually thought Pop Can liked me the most until I beat him. "He kept saying you have nice hair."

"I didn't notice that," I said.

"Yes you did."

"No, I really didn't." I got that compliment several times a day. If Dennis did come to the Playboy Club with me, he would hear about fifteen bunnies tell me how jealous they were of my hair. "Who cares if Santiago likes my hair?" I said.

"I might."

"I'm pretty sure he also likes other things about me," I said.

"Stop."

"When you said you wanted to take me home, I thought you were angry at me. I thought you were going to take me back to the . . ." I hesitated because I didn't even know what to call what he would be taking me back to. I couldn't imagine going back to the truck now.

"I could never be angry at you," he said. "This is ridiculous. Let's go back. You can wait out by the pool while I get rid of them."

We returned to his house and I went around the back to

the pool, and Dennis went in the front door. I was supposed to stay put in case the guys were still there. I sat in a chair and looked up at the stars. I thought about Pop Can swimming naked in the pool and I wanted to do it. I wanted Dennis to come out and find me like that. I took off my clothes and slipped into the pool and did some ballet and jumps and kicks to try to burn some calories. I had eaten another hot dog when I was clearing plates in the kitchen.

I heard the men saying goodbye and leaving. They must have been outside, in front of the house.

Then Dennis came out of the kitchen and over to the pool, but it wasn't Dennis. It was Santiago. He picked up his pack of cigarettes from the table and lit one. It was dark and he didn't notice me. I tried to swim as quietly as possible to the side so I could hang on, but I was a little out of breath and he heard me.

"Hi there," he said. "I left my cigarettes."

I didn't think he could see me too well but I wished more than anything that I was wearing a bathing suit. Dennis was going to be angry if he came out here and saw us, even though he had just said he would never be angry at me.

"I thought you were going home."

"I forgot my key, so—" I began, but he interrupted me.

"Don't worry. Your secret's safe with me. It's none of my business what two consenting adults get up to. How old are you anyway?"

"Twenty-one," I said. "Why, how old are you?"

"Come on, you ain't no twenty-one. You legal? I don't even think you're sixteen."

"I think I know how old I am."

"You may know how old you are, but I wonder if our man Dennis the Menace knows. In New York fifteen will get you twenty, maybe out here with the cows and the chickens things are different."

"Where's Santiago?" I heard Dennis say.

"I don't know what you're talking about." I knew it was a weak comeback, like something my mother would say.

"Where do you hang out? In New York, I mean," Santiago said.

"Around Columbia mostly, or in the Village. Bars, dancing. Why do you ask?"

"What bars?"

"Puffy's. I like their sake."

"What the hell is sake? Listen, if you want a ride to NYC, call me at the Maple Inn. My old lady owns it. I have a sister who's sixteen and I wouldn't want her floating around in this pool."

"I'm not sixteen," I said.

He took a towel from the back of the chaise, folded it, and put it on the side of the pool next to the ladder. "Maple Inn. I got stuff to do in the city anyway." Then he walked out the back gate and I heard a motorcycle rumble off.

24

I opened my eyes to see Dennis standing by the side of the bed looking down at me.

"Good morning," he said. He was very blurry because I had taken out my contact lenses. He had actually forced me to, saying he was a doctor and he wasn't going to let me ruin my eyes. He had distilled water in his garage so I was able to clean them in the machine I had brought.

He put a mug down on his wife's bedside table.

"What time is it?" I asked.

"It's ten. I've been up for hours."

He opened the curtains and sun came pouring in. I hadn't slept that late in so long, with beautiful pillows and sheets and covers. I stretched sexily like Scarlett O'Hara in *Gone with the Wind* after she's had sex with Rhett. I was naked because my *I Love Lucy* nightgown smelled like the truck and I hadn't wanted to put it on.

I got up and went into the bathroom to pee. I wished I had put my bag in the bathroom so I could brush my hair, but I brushed my teeth and put in my contacts. The phone rang and I heard Dennis answer.

"Hi, honey . . . Yes . . . Big Ben, that's funny . . . Right. Right . . ."

I left the bathroom quietly and looked at Dennis. He put his finger to his lips. I felt like I was in a Woody Allen movie.

"I was there all night. I'm going to sleep now."

I wasn't sure what to do. There was a coffee-table book about Marilyn Monroe by Norman Mailer that I flipped through. We had that book at home.

I picked up a clay pumpkin from the dresser. It was made by a child, lopsided with carefully carved grooves and a fat, squat stem. It was glazed a rich orangey brown. It was the size of the pumpkin Dennis had hidden the box of chocolates under.

"I miss you so much. And now it looks like I might have to go to New York for a few days. Leon wants me to consult on a patient . . . No, please don't get me that . . . Because I don't own a French-cuff shirt, for one thing. I'm not going to wear them. Just buy yourself something."

He wasn't wearing any shirt now. He was lying on the bed in gym shorts, with the phone cord stretched across his chest. Besides being completely quiet, I didn't really know what to do. I could pretend to read but that felt stupid. When he got off the phone, I wanted to call my dad, but then I wondered if his girlfriend would be there.

"Yes, I love you. Tell them I love them. We should get off the phone because this is going to cost about a hundred pounds . . ." I put the pumpkin back on the dresser, thinking how annoyed I'd be if my father's girlfriend was touching any of my stuff. But then I thought that my father probably didn't have any of my stuff at his new apartment. There was a clear plastic cube on his desk and every side of it had a picture of me or my brother on it, and I wondered if he had brought that with him. I had actually made quite a few things out of clay, and now that I thought of it, I didn't know where they were.

Once, a teacher had told my father that I was a perfectionist and needed to relax, so my father bought me a pottery wheel.

I had to kick it to make it spin and it was the most stressful thing imaginable, but I made a few things. One vase I had given to Adeline, my old babysitter, but where had the other things gone?

I was starting to get really annoyed standing there looking at his kid's pumpkin while he talked on the phone to his wife long distance.

"Which one of your kids made this?" I asked, when he finally got off the phone.

"I made it, actually," Dennis said. "My mother just sent me a box of things from my childhood. She has early signs of dementia. She's doing a lot of sorting. I guess my wife put it there."

Suddenly, when he said that, my heart softened in my chest like wet clay in a bucket. I thought of Dennis as a little kid, Madding's age, forming the clay in his little hands, concentrating on the stripes, using a tool to angle the tip of the stem and make it flat. I thought of him bringing it home to his mother, who kept it like a treasure. It was very stupid of me, but I hadn't thought of him as being a kid once. I realized I had been a little suspicious of Dennis. I had been a bit of a wisenheimer around him. But he was still the little boy who had made this pumpkin. I climbed onto the bed next to him and touched his soft hair and the stubble on his face very gently and kissed his forehead.

He closed his eyes and smiled.

"I'm really having fun," I said. "Thank you."

"I'm sorry about that call."

"You don't have to be sorry about anything. What did your wife want to get you?"

"Cuff links. I guess one said *Fish* and the other said *Chips*. Absurd." He looked so miserable and helpless even saying the words.

"What are we doing today?" I asked.

"What can we do that would be fun for you? We could go tubing or horseback riding. There's a lake."

I thought of the terrible swans. I looked at the coffee mug on the bedside table. I didn't drink coffee but I was curious to at least try it.

"I've never had coffee before," I admitted, picking up the mug. But it wasn't coffee. It was delicious hot chocolate. The most delicious hot chocolate I had ever tasted.

"I know you don't drink coffee," he said.

"When did I tell you that?"

"At the diner, our first night. I was secretly fantasizing about bringing you coffee in bed when the waitress asked if we wanted coffee and dessert, and you said you didn't drink coffee."

He leaned over and took the empty mug from me and put it down. Then he climbed on top of me.

"I want to know everything you like and don't like," he said.

"For one thing, I don't like tubing, horseback riding, or lakes."

He looked a little hurt and I thought of the pumpkin.

"But I'd like to try," I said.

I waited for him to get in the shower and I called my dad. I didn't call collect.

"Hi, Dad, it's Swanna."

"Oh. Hi," he said. "How're you?"

"Fine," I said. "I'm at a friend's house."

"Oh that's lovely. Is Madding with you? Mother?"

"No."

"Oh?"

"He's not really a friend. He's a counselor, actually. He's driving back to New York so I thought I'd catch a ride. I don't know when Mom is going back. He offered to drive me."

"How lovely. You must thank him," he said, as if I hadn't thanked him. I thanked him with my virginity, I thought. I thanked him with a really spectacular blow job.

"Of course I thanked him," I said.

"Is it the young man I met, the Braverman fellow?"

"No," I said, trying not to laugh out loud. David Braverman was the camp tennis teacher. He had told my father I was good at tennis, which wasn't true. It was a theater camp and I was practically the only one who had played tennis all summer. I'd tried it a few times but it was at the same time as stage makeup, which I thought was much more important. To take stage makeup, your parents had to pay an extra forty dollars and you got to go home with a full Arthur Gold stage makeup kit, which I had left in the truck. On the last week of camp, famous stage makeup artist Arthur Gold himself came and demonstrated how to use everything. Of course my father was more interested in if I was good at tennis than in my performance as the drunken actress Gay Wellington in *You Can't Take It with You.*

"Did you get a new apartment?" I asked.

"Yes. How did you know that? I was going to surprise you."

"I was just wondering. Is it nice? Where is it?"

"It's in the Village. On Sullivan Street."

"Is it near Mister Cacciatore's down on Sullivan Street, across from the medical center?"

"What? I don't think so."

I rolled my eyes. He had probably never even heard of Billy Joel, so it wasn't worth trying to explain it. My father hated all popular music. When he first heard the Beatles, he predicted they would never make it.

"Does it have a big fridge?" I asked.

"What? It's close to the D train."

I started to get a bad feeling about the new apartment. In New York, when the only thing someone could tell you about their apartment was what train it was near, you could bet it wasn't going to be too impressive.

"Mom met someone," I said. "I think he might move in with us."

"Well, I wish him luck." I could hear the kissing sound of an unimpressive refrigerator door being opened and closed.

"Have you started dating anyone?" I didn't know why I had asked that when I already knew and didn't want to hear the answer.

"I'm seeing someone," he said.

"What's her name?" I gulped out. This was the worst part. This was worse than when he'd made the speech that he was moving out and it had nothing to do with me. Tears were flying out of my eyes like bats. This was hard. Even if you already knew about it and didn't care, it was hard. For a second I was worried he would actually say her name was Amber.

"Her name's Amanda. She wants to meet you."

"She knows I exist?" I said. It came out very harshly.

"Yes."

I felt like we were having a fight. I could see the drunk birdlike movements of his head. Like the bird head on a beaker toy I had that tipped over and drank from a glass of water.

"Am and I are heading to the Cape for a few days. We're renting the house in North Truro for the week. When are you coming home? Maybe you could come for a day or two, even if you have to miss school. Maybe two or three days on the Cape with Am and me."

Not the whole week, I clarified for myself. It sounded like Dr. Seuss. *Green Eggs and Am. I and Am. Am I am. A day or two or two or three. A day with you and Am and me.*

"I can't miss school," I said. "When are you leaving?"

"We're leaving today."

"What day does school start?"

"I don't know, I'll have to look. I got a letter out of the blue from the Smalls saying the house was available, so I took it."

"The house? *Our* house? You're going to our house?" The Smalls owned the house we had rented for the whole summer every summer since I was born, except the year we lived in London. We hadn't rented it this year because of the divorce. I couldn't believe he was taking Mistress Amber there. "I should get off the phone," I said. "This is long distance."

"Oh my. Yes."

"Bye," I said, and hung up.

I went into the bathroom and cried for a long time. I looked at all the medicine in the medicine chest. I recognized the Valium. My mother had that. I had no idea why I was crying because I didn't feel sad at all and I couldn't care less if my dad was going to the house. I was usually bored out of my mind there. When I was a kid, I used to sit in the car on the broken shell–covered driveway and pretend I was driving home to New York. It was a nice house though. It was on a hill and from the deck you could see the shape of the whole Cape in the Atlantic. With my dad's telescope we could watch whales spouting and we could also see other planets. I was surprised Mistress Amber would want to go where my family went, but then I realized that was a bit hypocritical because I was here in Dennis's family's house snooping through his medicine chest, looking at his wife's prescription for Monistat cream which was for a yeast infection. If you're in love with someone, you want to see where they live and know everything about them. I wanted to go back to New York but I also wanted to stay with Dennis as long as possible, especially if my dad wasn't even going to be home.

I put on my Gloria Vanderbilt jeans and tried on one of Dennis's button-down shirts and rolled up the sleeves, but it was way too big.

"I like it," he said, coming into the bedroom. "Here, try this." He opened a drawer and found a shirt and handed it to me. "It's too small for me."

It said *Bread and Puppet Theater* on it and had a picture of wheat stalks. I put it on and tucked it into my jeans halfway. "I love it," I said.

He untucked it and took it off me again, making me put my arms up over my head like I was a little girl. He unhooked my bra and took it off. He looked at me.

The doorbell rang.

"Who's that?" Dennis said. "I cancelled the housekeeper."

The doorbell rang again. "Wait here." He did the annoying finger-to-his-lips thing again and went downstairs still holding the shirt.

I walked quietly to the top of the stairs so I could hear who it was.

"Hiya," I heard a woman say.

"Hi, Sandy," Dennis said. From where I was, I couldn't see who he was talking to.

"I hope I didn't wake you. I called but the phone was busy, so I figured you were up."

"That's weird, we have call waiting. Should work because I spend three dollars a month for it. Haven't been to sleep yet. Just got home a little while ago." I realized he was pretty good at lying.

"You poor thing! I know Kathy's away so I brought you something."

"That's incredible, wow." Dennis sounded annoyed. "This really wasn't necessary. What is this?"

"A lasagna. Want me to heat that up for you? I wrote down the instructions."

"I think I can do it," he said. "Thank you, Sandy, really."

"It's nothing. I made it and Ellie announced she's suddenly a vegetarian. You'll see when you have a teenager.

She'd probably be happy if I came here and ate it with you tonight and let her have the house to herself."

"Unfortunately, I'll be at the hospital. But thank you so much."

I was dying to know what Sandy looked like. It was literally killing me.

"It's been stressful with the news about Dan. I was going to ask you if you could prescribe something for me so I can get some sleep."

"I can do that," he said. "I'm actually on the phone with a patient. Let me finish the call and I'll put a prescription in your mailbox."

"I can wait. I was hoping we could catch up. How's your game these days?"

"Let's get together when Kathy's back," he said.

"Okay," she said. "Enjoy the lasagna."

I heard the door close. I didn't move. I just stood frozen at the top of the stairs, topless.

"*How's your game?*" I mimicked when he came upstairs.

"Jesus, that was harrowing. That was no joke. Were you standing here the whole time?"

I followed him into the bedroom and he pulled the velvet curtains closed.

"So we're just going to sit here, huddled in the dark," I said.

"That's probably the best idea."

"Who's Dan and what's the news about him?"

"Dan is her ex-husband and I have no idea what the news is. I was trying to get rid of her. I had to hide my erection with her lasagna."

"Well, where is it now?" I asked, pressing my hand on the front of his jeans.

"I have to get over how horrifying that was. I was scared shitless."

"But nothing bad happened," I said. I hadn't thought about if I sneezed or coughed or she had just come upstairs and seen me standing there.

"I don't think you realize how serious that was."

"It wasn't," I said. "Are you going to tell your wife that woman wanted to have dinner with you?"

"No, I'm not going to tell my wife."

Dennis looked miserable. This wasn't romantic at all. I thought of a math problem I hadn't done yet that was in my summer math packet. You had to pick three friends and give them different head starts and figure out who would finish the race of a certain distance in a certain amount of time. I suddenly felt like Dennis and his wife and this idiotic neighbor had a big head start. I was wasting my time.

"I think I should go." I put my bra on and grabbed my King Tut shirt from the chair.

"What?!"

I put on the shirt.

"Because of *her*?"

I went into the bathroom and grabbed my stuff and threw it in my bag. I felt this low-down feeling of anger and sadness, below the pit of my stomach, almost like it was between my legs. It was a familiar feeling but it didn't have a name.

"Swanna, I'm sorry, that just really freaked me out."

"I don't want to be the cause of you being freaked out," I said. "I have to go."

"Now I'm freaked out that you're going. Please."

My bathing suit was out by the pool. I had to get it. I loved that bathing suit. I had a crazy idea that I could go to the lasagna lady's house and make up a story that I had to get to the bus station and she could call me a taxi, or probably she would actually drive me there. If I got home tonight, I could find my father's apartment and go to Cape Cod with him or stay in his apartment alone while he was gone. Or I could go home to my mother's apartment.

"Swanna, please, please don't go. I'm sorry." He blocked my path by getting down on his knees in front of me. He bore the top of his head into my stomach like a golden retriever. Our neighbor had a golden retriever and Madding always said *golden intruder* instead of *golden retriever*. "I'll take you wherever it is you want to go, but please, please, please stay with me."

"I don't think you can handle my being here," I said.

"I can. I'm gonna show you I can."

"What if that lady climbs through the window?"

"I'll very calmly ask her to leave," he said.

"What if she pulls out a gun and tells you she'll shoot if you don't heat up her lasagna and have sex with her?"

"I'll get out my own gun and tell her to leave me and my girlfriend alone."

"You have a gun?"

"Of course I have guns." He lifted up my shirt and kissed my stomach. He unbuttoned my Gloria Vanderbilt jeans and traced the gold-stitched swan on the side pocket with his fingers.

"You have a girlfriend?" I said.

"I have an incredible girlfriend," he said.

He pulled down my jeans and I stepped out of them using the top of his head to keep my balance. He moved forward on his knees, nudging me, making me walk backward over to the bed. We got undressed and we had sex. It felt different. I was more used to his size and there was this feeling like we both knew we had come close to losing everything.

"You have to come this time," he said. "I'm not going to stop until you come."

I wasn't even thinking about coming because I didn't think I could do that and have sex at the same time.

"I don't care if the whole neighborhood stops by and all the wives at the club and the volunteer fire brigade show up, I'm not stopping until you come."

"Maybe I'll fake it," I said.

"I'll know. I'm a doctor."

He gently pushed in and out of me until I couldn't stop myself and I came quietly under him.

"I know where I want to take you," he said.

Please don't say hiking, I thought.

"Rudyard Kipling's house," he said.

"Is that a friend of yours? I thought you didn't want me to meet your friends."

He laughed even though I wasn't kidding.

"I think you'll like it. He wrote *The Jungle Book* and *Gunga Din*."

"I know who Rudyard Kipling is," I said, even though I had no idea. "I want to go there. But first I want to see your guns."

25

"Why do you have guns?" I asked.

"Grew up with them. Hunting, self-protection," he said.

"Where are they?"

"Hall closet. I keep them locked up so my kids don't get into them."

"Can I see them?"

"Why are you so interested? Do you want to go hunting?"

"No," I said. "I would never shoot anything."

"What about an intruder?"

I thought about that for a minute. "I'd rather just die myself than kill anyone," I said.

"Hmmm. That will change when you have children."

I had no idea why Dennis seemed to think everyone on earth was a different person after they had kids. My parents were the same as before they had us, although my father was very depressed and now he drank a lot, but he had probably been that way before. And my friends' parents seemed like the same boring people they had always been. I didn't know them before but I studied their wedding pictures and they seemed just as boring.

"So if a robber broke in, you would shoot him?"

"Yes, I would," he said.

"Have you ever thought about killing yourself?"

"Actually, I have," he said. "But I think everyone thinks about that sometimes."

"That's what they say."

"Being in a bad marriage makes you feel incredibly lonely. Much worse than being alone."

I thought about Kimi in my building again, jumping from 16A.

I was pretty sure my mother would kill herself over the famous artist she was in love with. I certainly hoped she knew better than to kill herself over the Slavmeister.

I followed Dennis into the hall outside the bedroom and watched him open the closet and pull down two leather cases. "Do you want to see a rifle or a handgun?" He opened the cases and laid everything out on the bed. "These are handguns. This is a Glock 19."

"Can I hold one?" They looked just like my brother's toy gun. My mother didn't believe in guns, but Madding had traded something and gotten one from a friend. Ironically, he traded this male doll he had named Peter. He had a toy stroller for Peter and instead of lovingly feeding and changing him, he would use the stroller as a catapult to see how far he could throw him. My brother was always getting things taken away from him at Dalton by the teachers. They wouldn't give them back for the whole year. Then when he went back to school in the fall, there was a plastic box waiting for him in his cubby filled with all the things that had been confiscated the year before. He was so proud bringing it home. He laid everything out to show me on the oval braided rug in his room—a

Weeble pirate, a little velveteen dog someone gave him in a liquor store once, a pink Barbie purse, a fake emerald ring, a brass Viking helmet key chain, a miniature bat he had gotten at Yankee Stadium on bat day, and the gun.

I was suddenly overwhelmed with missing Madding. I wished I could just enjoy myself without worrying about him all the time.

"Should we go outside and shoot them?" I asked.

"Well, it would make a lot of noise. I'm supposed to be at the hospital."

I rolled my eyes. "This again?"

"What?"

"You didn't worry about noise when you had me screaming and moaning in there a few minutes ago."

"This is madness," he said. "We can go shooting later. Tomorrow."

"I should go home tomorrow."

"We'll shoot clay pigeons before you go home. Or there's a felled branch out back we can shoot."

Felled, I thought. I had never heard that word before. "Does Santiago have a gun?"

Dennis looked annoyed. "Yes, he does. Why do you ask?"

"Does Sandy have a gun?" I said the name Sandy very sarcastically.

"Yes, she does."

"How do you know?"

"I helped her buy it."

"Does Pop Can—"

"Everyone in the great state of Vermont has a gun," he said. "Didn't they have riflery at your camp?"

I looked at him as if he was crazy. "It's a theater camp. The circus department has a gun. When you shoot it, a flag comes out that says *Bang*."

He laughed.

"Shhhh," I said, "someone might hear you."

"I can really see you with that clown gun."

"I can see myself with this." I picked up the Glock 19. "Chekhov said if a gun is introduced in act one, it has to go off in act three. But I don't believe in any rules like that," I quickly added.

26

We got in the car and pulled out of his driveway. Dennis put on his sunglasses with one hand while holding the wheel with the other, and tossed the case back on the dashboard. I wished we were in LA or somewhere more exciting than Vermont, but other than that, this was fun. It was now September, I had to remember that. I didn't know when school was starting although it was harder and harder to imagine choosing my first-day-of-school outfit and taking the subway and walking into that building. I had to buy a binder and I liked to start the year with a new LeSportsac, but that didn't seem possible now. It would be hard enough to get to New York before school started, let alone Bloomingdale's. Jacquie Beller said they had come out with shiny purple.

"What are you thinking about?" Dennis asked.

"Nothing. I'm just enjoying the drive."

"It's nice you can be quiet."

"What do you mean?"

"My wife never stops talking. It's nice to just drive with you and not have to talk and respond all the time."

"So get a divorce," I said.

"I can't. I couldn't do that to my kids. But I wish things were different."

"Do you know who Dorothy Parker is?"

He laughed. "Yes. First Chekhov and now Dorothy Parker?"

I had been thinking about Dorothy Parker because she had a famous poem about suicide, which was pretty much the only poem I liked. "She said never grow a wishbone where a spine should be, or something like that."

"Very clever. Are you saying I don't have a spine?"

"I'm just saying what Dorothy Parker said."

"Maybe you're saying I'm a turkey?"

"I don't think you're a turkey." I regretted bringing any of this up. I didn't mean to say that I wanted him to get a divorce. I was just wondering why he didn't if he liked me so much more than his wife. "I wasn't thinking about it so literally."

"Remember when you said that you felt bad for your brother because he's seven years younger than you are so he's having seven years less of your parents being married?"

I nodded, desperately wishing to change the subject. Madding was *six* years younger.

"I couldn't stand not to live with my children."

You could stand not to go to London with them, I thought. I really didn't want to talk about this anymore. All I ever thought about was divorce. Dennis was definitely going to get a divorce eventually, but I didn't have to be the one to let him know that. He could find that out for himself soon enough.

"You're a great dad," I said, even though it wasn't true.

The day my father told us, I had come home from school on the 96th Street crosstown bus. My father said, "Can you come in here, Swanna?"

He was in Madding's room. Madding was sitting at his white round kids' table in a kid's white chair.

"We're having a family meeting," Madding said.

We had never had a family meeting before, except for once when my father announced that we weren't getting enough exercise and we were going to be doing calisthenics every morning before school. That had only lasted about one day but it was horrible.

"Where's Mom?" I had asked.

"She's not here," my father said.

"I thought it was a family meeting," I said.

"It's not easy for me to say this. I'd rather say it without your mother here because we have very different views on how to pay attention to children. Swanna, sit down, will ya?"

I sat in the other white chair. My father sat on a red stool next to Madding's easel.

We used to share that room but then our nanny Adeline got married and moved to Brooklyn, so I moved into her room, which was the maid's room. Madding needed the bigger room because he had a basketball hoop and the easel and a pull-up bar and a pogo stick and a punching bag, and I only needed books and a bed.

"Sometimes grown-ups stop feeling connected to each other," my father said.

My brother started to cry.

"First of all, I want to stress this isn't your fault. It's very important you understand that. Your mother and I are happy with you but we're not happy with each other."

Madding was crying hysterically.

"Madding, come here," my father said.

My brother rushed into his arms. That was the worst thing about being a kid, being forced to be comforted by the person who was hurting you in the first place. I wanted to protect him from that but I was frozen stiff.

Dennis had been talking and I hadn't even realized it.

"One day I'll take you to the Algonquin Hotel in New York and buy you your first martini," Dennis said.

"How do you know I've never had a martini?"

"What restaurant do you want to go to? I want to take you to dinner and a Broadway show."

"I've heard Café des Artistes is very good," I said.

"I can't wait to do these things with you."

"Can you stop the car? Please! There's a yard sale!"

On someone's lawn there were tables set up with tchotchkes on them and a small cluster of lamps and a rocking chair. I had finally found something good about Vermont.

He pulled over to the side of the road. "Are you serious? Can I stay in the car?" He handed me a five-dollar bill and I rushed out of the car. I was very competitive and didn't want someone else grabbing the good stuff. There weren't any other cars or people, but that didn't stop me from feeling competitive.

I picked up the first thing I saw, which was a white plastic night-light shaped like Jesus. There were old-lady flowery bathing suits on a rack with big, stiff, pointy bosoms. There was a fake deer with bullet holes in it.

"How much is this?" I asked.

A fat man in a plaid shirt got up out of a plaid chair, actually groaning as if that was the hardest thing he'd ever had to do, and walked over to me.

We both looked down at what I was pointing to, a giant two-story toy garage with a ramp and an elevator to take the cars up and down.

"Elevatah works," the man said.

"How much is it?" I asked.

"Four dollars. You from outtastate?" He tried to look at Dennis's car but it was blocked by a tree.

"No, I live over by the Maple Inn," I said.

He nodded. "Then I'll take a one-dollah bell."

"I want this too," I said, holding up the Jesus night-light. "Both for one money," he said. I had no idea what he was saying, but when I gave him the five-dollar bill, he gave me four singles back.

Dennis opened the trunk. "What'd you get?" he said.

"A garage for Madding and a Jesus night-light for me."

"Now I'm definitely driving you back to New York," he said. "You can't take that thing on a bus."

"I have to get it home." Madding was going to love it.

"We need gas," Dennis said.

We drove to the Cumberland Farms and I sat in the car and watched Dennis pump gas through the sideview mirror. His hair looked blond in the sun. Seeing him through the mirror, I could really study him. He looked very manly handling the gas thing and I felt lucky all of a sudden. If I had taken the camp bus back to New York, I never would have met him. He went into the store and came back with a Tab for me and an iced coffee for him. He looked at me and smiled. He didn't have chips or Oreos or anything, but that was probably for the best.

He got in the car and a Black couple pulled up on bicycles. The man was staring at a map he had taken from his backpack. The woman was very voluptuous and was smiling and talking even though the man was concentrating on the map. She looked really happy. Then, right before my eyes, she reached over and grabbed him through the front of his jeans. The man gave her an annoyed but sexy look and the woman threw her head back and laughed.

What I had just seen was the height of sophistication. It was adult. I felt like I had gone through a portal. I had joined a grown-up club. I had witnessed the secret handshake. I had seen people happy and in love. It seemed like the most human and normal thing in the world because, I realized, I was happy and in love too.

I suddenly felt really bad for Madding being alone in the land of crazy with my mother when I was out in the normal world. I shouldn't have left him.

"I feel bad that I left my brother," I said.

"You're a really good person," he said.

I wasn't sure if that was true. "I was in the middle of reading him *On the Banks of Plumb Creek*. We were almost at the end. It's one of the *Little House on the Prairie* books." I had just been feeling adult and now I was talking about a kids' book.

"You like that kind of stuff? Is that why you wanted to see my guns? The father probably had a lot of guns. What was his name?"

"Pa," I said.

"Right, Pa. And what was her boyfriend's name? Something silly."

"Almanzo," I said. "I think you look like him."

"He probably had a beard down to his knees."

"No, he did not," I said. "I love him."

"You love him? Then I have something to show you."

He drove for a while and pulled up at a little school.

"This is an old one-room schoolhouse," he said.

I read the sign, *Established 1857.* "Can we go in?"

"I think so," he said. "If it's open. It's a museum but it might be closed in August."

We got out of the car and I walked toward the school very reverently, the way Laura Ingalls Wilder would have. The doors were locked.

"We can look in the window," Dennis said. He walked up to one of the windows along the side of the little building, and stood in a clump of long grass, not caring about ticks.

I went and stood there too. Inside were rows of desks with inkwells and slates like Laura used and Mary, before she went blind. We weren't up to Mary going blind yet. That was going to kill Madding and I was not looking forward to that.

Slowly my eyes adjusted to the dim room. I looked at each little desk and imagined an old-fashioned kid sitting at each one, older kids in the back and younger ones in the front. Then I looked at the teacher's desk and there, sitting at it, was a teacher. Her skin was ghostly white. She sat frozen in the teacher's chair looking out over the empty room. I screamed and Dennis gasped and we both started running away from the schoolhouse. I never ran so fast in my life. We ran, laughing hysterically, until we were in the middle of the empty field behind the schoolhouse.

We crashed down on the grass, laughing so hard I thought I was going to die.

"Was that a ghost?" I asked, trying to breathe.

"That was the creepiest thing I've ever seen in my life," Dennis said. We were lying flat on our backs, still holding hands.

He rolled on top of me and we kissed that way for a long time. He made a groaning sound.

"I need you," he said.

"You have me." I put my hand on him like the Black woman had done to her boyfriend.

"We can't do that here. Someone could drive by. Come on." Dennis stood and helped me up. We started to walk back toward the schoolhouse.

"What if we look again and she's not there?" I said.

He went to the window and tried to open it. "You're from New York. You know how to jimmie a lock?"

"I'll need a credit card," I said.

He took out a credit card from his wallet and a jackknife from his back pocket. "Let's see what we can do."

In a minute the window slid open and we crawled inside. And we did something in there I was sure Laura Ingalls Wilder had never done.

"I'm going to teach you something new," he whispered. "This is called doggy style."

He went to the teacher's chair and turned her around so she wasn't facing us.

Then he made me lean over one of the desks.

27

"I have an idea," Dennis said.

"We already did your idea," I said.

"This is different."

"As long as your idea involves lunch," I said.

Dennis looked at his black digital watch. "We'll have lunch after. I want to catch my friend at his office before he leaves."

"You're introducing me to a friend?"

"It's risky but it's worth it. I'll say you're my niece or something."

He turned the teacher mannequin around so she was facing the front of the class again. It was a vey authentic schoolhouse. I put my jeans back on. I hadn't taken off my T-shirt. I looked around for a few minutes, at the old photographs of children staring out with warning looks.

There was a guest registry lying open on a table in the corner and I signed it. I signed my friend's name instead of my own. He had died the year before, and looking at the dead children in the pictures had made me think of him. He would have been very impressed that I had broken into a schoolhouse and had sex over a desk.

Next to the guest book was a small stack of note cards

with a drawing of the schoolhouse on the front and a sign saying they were twenty-five cents each. I took a card and envelope and put a quarter on the table.

Dennis put a chair in front of the open window and I climbed out. Then he put the chair back and climbed out without it, and shut the window behind us.

We got into his car.

"That was the most fun I've ever had in my life," Dennis said. "I'm not sure what that says about me, but it's true."

"Me too," I said, but in my mind I thought *so far* and I thought about how my friend who died didn't have any more chances for fun times. Whatever he'd had was it.

I wanted to stop somewhere and write a letter to my father on the note card. I thought about writing to him because the last letter I had written to him from camp had been all about how waterskiing was the most fun thing I had ever done in my whole life. I'm pretty sure I'd written those exact words. I'd written about being scared to death, but swimming out anyway, and grabbing the rope behind the motorboat, and staying up for a full nine seconds before plunging into the water again. Because I had written it, I had an extremely distinct memory of doing it. I could hear myself screaming over the sound of the motor, see my concentrated expression, feel the spray of the water on the backs of my thighs.

In reality, I had stayed on the sliver of sand by the lake with a book open on my lap, watching the other kids water-skiing, refusing to try it, but I would still always remember having done it. I wondered if I could prove philosophically that one could have a great time doing something one hadn't even done.

Once when I was a kid, I went to a birthday party all the way in the suburbs and the mother of the birthday girl called my mother and apologized that I'd had a terrible time. "What do you mean?" my mother had said. "She told me she had a wonderful time."

"But she just sat in a chair and read while the other kids played," the woman said.

My mother listed all the things I'd told her we'd done, and the woman said, "No. The other girls did those things."

We drove until we got to an office building. It was the kind of office building they had in the country, small and square, no more than six or seven floors, with a parking lot in front. A sign said, *Reston Optics.*

"What is this?" I asked.

"It's one of the perks of being a doctor. A doctor friend of mine is involved in a study. Trust me on this one. And say you're eighteen."

He got out of the car and I followed him into the building, into an elevator, and up to a doctor's office. Dennis spoke to a receptionist and she buzzed someone and a man in a white lab coat came out and shook Dennis's hand. I shook his hand too. "I was hoping you could get Swanna into the study," Dennis said. "She's a student at UVM."

"Is she wearing contacts right now?"

"Yes," Dennis said.

"Yes," I said. I did not want to be part of a study and I did not want to go to UVM, whatever that was. The whole thing was incredibly creepy and didn't involve lunch.

"Is she over sixteen?" the man said insultingly.

"Yup, eighteen," Dennis said.

"Okay, young lady, you're going to get to try out a new invention that hasn't been put on the market yet."

I was about to break it to them that no one was going to do anything to me that hadn't been put on the market yet, when the doctor said, "Has Dr. Whitman told you about disposable contact lenses?"

He explained I was going to get weekly-wear disposable contact lenses. Instead of sterilizing my contact lenses in a machine every single night and using an enzyme tablet once a week which I never did anyway, I was going to get to sleep in them for a whole week, then throw them out and put in a new pair.

I followed Dennis's friend into a room and rested my chin on his eye machine and looked at one of his ears and then the other. I gave him my name and address and phone number and a fake date of birth. He gave me a shopping bag with twelve boxes of contact lenses—fifty-two pairs.

"What do I owe you?" Dennis said to the doctor.

"Get outta here," he said. "Nice kid. We'll see her back here in six weeks so we can check on her."

"Thank you," I said. I didn't know what I had done that was charming, except act very suspicious and say, "I hope you know what you're doing," a few times.

"This is amazing," I said when we got back into his car. "What else can you do?"

"What else do you want me to do?"

"Take me to McDonald's." I could see one coming up on our left.

That had been one of the worst things about not getting to take the bus home. The bus stopped at McDonald's and

everyone got to get out and get food and use the bathroom.
I hadn't had McDonald's since June.

"Okay," he said.

I couldn't believe I was also going to get McDonald's.

28

We sat at an orange table eating Big Macs, large fries, and chocolate shakes.

I was getting used to eating in front of him. My body felt good from the sex and his comfortable bed and I felt beautiful because of the way he looked at me. I was laughing a lot and touching him. The place was over-air-conditioned and I wanted him next to me on the plastic bench, but he stayed planted on a round yellow stool that was attached to the table across from me.

"Sit next to me," I said.

"I like looking at you," he whispered. There were two old men playing gin at a table on the other side of the restaurant.

He had wanted to do something called a drive-through where you ordered your food through your car window and then ate it right in your car. I had talked him into going inside. He looked so uncomfortable I was starting to regret being that pushy.

"You know when you said I was a great dad?" he said.

"You *are* a great dad," I said.

He smiled. "That's the best compliment you could give me."

"I can think of other compliments too," I said, sucking on my straw and looking up at him.

"Those are good too. But being a good dad is the most important thing to me."

"More important than your big cock," I whispered.

"Shhhh," he said. "Yes, more important than that. My kids are the most important people in the world to me. You and my kids."

I wondered if right at that moment my father was telling his girlfriend Amanda that his kids and she were the most important things in the world to him. Maybe they were having disgusting fried oysters under the green plexiglass awning at the Dairy Queen or eating foot-longs standing up at the marina in Provincetown or lobsters and clam chowder at the Lobster Pot. We were done with our Big Macs but we still had a few French fries left. My mother didn't believe in McDonald's so I didn't get to do this too often.

An elegant man sat down near us with a family of four—a mom, a dad, and two kids, girls who both looked like boys, even though one of them had long hair.

"I'm sorry, William, it's what she wanted," the mom said. "Don't be silly," the man said in a proper English accent.

"When one gets off the plane in the States, the first thing one craves is a Big Mac and those delicious chips. We have them in London now too but I'm sure they're more authentic here." That was actually true. When I lived in London for a year, I was a strict vegetarian to get out of eating the meat in the school lunches, but as soon as I got back to America I ate a Big Mac before I even left the airport.

"Do you want your birthday present, Eloise?" the Englishman said to the girl with long hair. He handed her a book wrapped in brown paper. "This is a very special book. Do you know what a signed first edition is? It's quite valuable. You have to take care of it."

"It's the book *Eloise*," I whispered to Dennis.

The girl opened the brown paper while the man lit a cigarette. She held up the copy of *Eloise*. Dennis looked at me, amazed.

"Say thank you, Eloise," the mom said.

"Thank you," she said insincerely.

It was wasted on that girl. This man had come all the way from England and was sitting in a McDonald's in the middle of nowhere with the wrong family. I was sitting in the middle of nowhere with another woman's husband and she was in London where he should be. My father was in my childhood vacation home with some slut and my mother was in a nuthouse with a moron who liked to shit in the woods and for some reason my high school guidance counselor had been there too. Everyone in the whole world was in the wrong place, all fish out of water. I felt like a speck of meteor flying through space. I could crash anywhere. I could just as well sit with the Englishman and the family, or the two old guys playing gin, or put on a paper hat and stand behind the counter and lower the basket of fries into boiling oil. But that would be awful.

I smiled approvingly at the Englishman and he raised an eyebrow at me. I wanted to say something to him, but I wasn't sure what, and I didn't want to be the Ugly American.

"You're going to be a great mom one day," Dennis said.

I nodded. That seemed almost too obvious to bother mentioning. "Maybe one day I'll be pregnant and I'll go to the hospital when it's time to have my baby and you'll be the doctor."

He smiled at me with a little sadness or uncertainty, like he didn't know where I was going with this. "Maybe I'll also be the father," he said. "This is all madness. But seriously, Swanna. I don't want to lose you."

"Do you love me?" I whispered teasingly.

"I knew I was in trouble when I was sitting in my car in the middle of the night trying to figure out how to give you chocolates."

"What do you mean *in trouble*?"

"Head over heels," he whispered.

I loved when we talked like this. Reminisced. That had only been three days ago but it felt more like it was our anniversary.

"So, it's not madness. It's love," I said.

"You're not wrong."

That sounded like a double negative. I started to scrunch up all the foil wrappers and put them on the tray, trying to decide if not being wrong was the same thing as being exactly right.

"I meant what I said. I don't want to lose you. You have to promise me."

"Promise you what?" I said, laughing.

"Shhhh. That we'll be together for a decade."

"That's a long time," I said. I stood up and fed the cups and containers on the tray into the mouth of the garbage can.

"I'm not leaving this restaurant until you promise me a decade."

I always thought it was weird when people called McDonald's a restaurant. "I promise you a decade," I said.

We drove to the home of Rudyard Kipling, who was the guy who wrote *The Jungle Book*. I had seen the animated movie at the Wellfleet drive-in movie theater with Madding. Rudyard Kipling's house was called Naulakha and was in a town with the dumb name of Dummerston, Vermont.

"How did you know I would want to do this?" I asked Dennis.

"I don't know. I always kind of wanted to come here but no one wanted to do it with me. I want to show you there's cultural things in Vermont."

"I like Vermont," I said magnanimously, even though I absolutely didn't and never would.

"That's quite a statement coming from you."

"No it isn't," I said, pleased that he recognized that it was. I sat at Rudyard Kipling's actual desk.

It was the second historic desk I'd sat at that day, but this time my pants were on.

I had been to the homes of John Keats, William Shakespeare, Charles Dickens, Sigmund Freud, Herman Melville (gift shop), and now Rudyard Kipling.

"I need another iced coffee," Dennis said. It was interesting that adults could always announce what they needed, like *I need an iced coffee* or *I need a cigarette*, and get it instantly, but if a kid announced something they needed it was considered spoiled behavior. I couldn't just go around saying *I need a Hershey bar* or *I need a pair of Sasson jeans*. Kids had to wait until Christmas or their birthdays to get practically anything. Adults always had more needs than kids.

"Do you think I could stay here for a little while and look around?" I said. I liked this room. At all the other famous people's houses I'd been to, everything was roped off, but here you could just make yourself comfortable apparently. I didn't want to leave.

"Why?" he asked.

"I don't know. I like to take in the feeling of a place and get into my imagination." I wanted to tell him how I had the ability to transport myself back in time, but it seemed too complicated. "You're very cool," he said. "Maybe you can work on your novel."

"I think I can," I said.

"I'll get out of your hair, but only for a half hour, okay?"

I remembered that was what he had said at the pay phone at the bowling alley, that he was getting out of his wife's hair.

"Okay," I said. I kissed him and he pulled away, looking nervous. "There's no one here."

"I know, but we should be careful." Sometimes he wanted to be careful and sometimes he didn't want to be careful. He could kiss me anytime he wanted, but if I kissed him practically had a heart attack. I pretended to be absorbed in a glass case of artifacts—some letters and round spectacles. "Hey, are you mad at me?"

"No," I said. "Soon I'll be back in New York and you won't have to worry."

"I don't want that," he said. "I just want to be careful. Going to McDonald's probably wasn't the best idea. We have to really be smart about this."

"You should have said no then."

When Dennis left, I sat at Rudyard Kipling's desk, in his spindly wooden chair. The first thing I did was sort of pray. Dear God, I thought, please let some of this famous writer's talent sink into me. That was literally what I did. Praying was a weird thing for an atheist to do, but I was pretty sure all atheists prayed all the time. We probably prayed more than people who believed in God.

I opened my army-navy bag, noticing that the button that said *UNIQUE* in rainbow letters had fallen off, and took out the note card I had gotten at the old schoolhouse and my erasable pen.

Dear Dad,

You're not going to believe where I'm sitting right now. I am actually at the desk of Rudyard Kipling in the middle of Nowheresville, Vermont. There are many artifacts like notebooks and paperweights and letters and a pair of cross-country skis given to him by his friend Arthur Conan Doyle so that he could make his way to Brattleboro in a snowstorm and drink beer with him. I thought you'd like to know that Rudyard was a beer drinker like someone else I know (you). How is Cape Cod? Are there 1,000 rabbits? Please bring home a sand dollar. This house is called Naulakha which means "a jewel beyond price" but it actually does seem to have a price because you can pay a lot of money to stay here because it's also a B&B (bed and breakfast). I am having a wonderful summer. See you soon in NYC.

Love,
Swanna the Great

I put the card in the envelope and wrote my father's name on it, but I realized I didn't know his address. I'd been writing to him all summer at his temporary apartment and that seemed silly to do now that I knew he'd moved. I had forgotten to ask him the exact address of his new place. I wrote my name and address in the top left corner, almost writing my camp address instead of my real one, and I put the letter in my bag. I didn't have a stamp anyway because my stationery set was in the truck. Buying stationery was one of the most exciting things about getting ready for camp. Mine had Venetian Harlequin dancers surrounded by hearts on it, which was the nicest stationery in my bunk.

I wished I had written to Madding instead of my dad. Then I could address it to him in New York and it would probably be in the mailbox when he got home and he would be excited. Or *dex-cited*, as he used to say when he was a kid.

I felt terrible that I had deserted him but I couldn't take care of him forever. That thought made me incredibly sad.

I thought of when my dad took us to Great Adventure in New Jersey and Madding wanted to go on all the big rides like El Toro the roller coaster, but I wouldn't go on them with him because I was too scared, so he couldn't go on them either. I would only go on the Skyway, which was sort of like a ski lift. You just went very slowly on a cable high up in the sky. Then I saw a spinning teacup ride and I said we could do that one. I asked the woman who took the tickets if it was scary and she said from a scale of one to ten, ten being the scariest and one being the least scary, it was a one. So we got into our own teacup and it began to spin. It spun in a circle and it spun around the other teacups too. It was horrible. I couldn't handle it. I was really beginning to panic. Madding knew I'd made a mistake. Instead of just enjoying the ride, he used all his strength to hold the steering wheel in the middle still and he just looked into my eyes and said, "*Al*-most over, *al*-most over," again and again in a very soothing way, until finally it was. I was supposed to take care of him but he had taken care of me.

"Well hello, young lady," a man said behind me.

I thought it might be Dennis talking in a strange accent, but it was a guy dressed up in a weird suit with a waistcoat, holding a pipe. He had a bushy mustache and little spectacles like the ones in the glass case.

"My name is Mr. Rudyard Kipling, and what pray tell is your name, fair lady?"

"Laura Ingalls Wilder," I said sarcastically.

"Now, I know Mrs. Wilder and I believe you are not her."

You are not *she*, I thought.

"Alas, you are pulling my leg, young lady."

"Alas, 'tis true," I said, laughing. I knew this guy was probably making about five bucks an hour and it wasn't nice of me to give him a hard time. He was only doing his job. "Thank you for letting me sit at your desk."

"Well, that is my great pleasure," he said.

"No, it's mine, fair sir," I said. "I'm a big fan." I was giggling a little bit and he was smiling at me. He was young and I thought he might be pretty good-looking without the fake 'stache.

"Oh? May I ask which of my works has caught your fancy?"

"Well, I haven't read any of them yet, but I saw your movie,"

I said. "Which do you recommend I start with?"

"I don't know of this thing you call a *movie*, but perhaps my poems would be of interest? You look like you have the soul of a poet."

"I'll start with those then," I said, but I knew they would not be of interest. My mother dragged me to a lot of poetry readings and I had met a lot of poets. I definitely did not have the soul of one. "You have a nice place."

"Are you staying here tonight?" He dropped the accent and looked at me, smiling.

I shook my head.

"That's too bad," he said.

"I'm just waiting for my dad." I hadn't meant to say *dad*. I had meant to say *boyfriend*. I felt myself blushing.

"Oh, I just thought if you were staying here or in town somewhere, we could get a drink later. I get off at seven."

Dennis walked in.

"Hello, good sir, I was just making the acquaintance of your lovely daughter."

Dennis looked annoyed. "My daughter," he said.

"Yes, my name is Rudyard Kipling, sir." He put out his hand and Dennis shook it in a very pissed-off way. This guy had the worst possible job.

"Okay," Dennis said. "Swanna, you ready?"

"Bye," I said to Rudyard, following after Dennis who was already out the door.

"*Father*?" Dennis said. "I wouldn't say I look like your father."

"You're the one who wanted to be careful," I said.

"I don't want to be careful. Okay? I just want to stay on this planet."

"I don't know what that means," I said.

"We have to stay in reality here. I'm married. It's 1982, not 1882."

"1892," I corrected.

"Okay, 1892. I'm still married."

"You said that. And I know."

"I have two kids. Believe me, I wish things were different. I wish I could live in my imagination. But I have to be realistic. And it's hard. This is hard. I wish things were different."

A wishbone for a spine. "What's hard?" I said.

"Thinking that I'm going to drive you back to New York and have to leave you there and come back here."

I smiled because he said he was going to drive me back. "Maybe I could stay here and you could hire me as your live-in au pair." This was actually a fantasy I had been working on the last few days, but in my fantasy he didn't live in Vermont, he lived in a huge penthouse on Fifth Avenue overlooking Central Park.

"I'm not joking around here, Swanna."

"I'm just trying to amuse you," I said.

"I'm sorry I'm being paranoid. You don't deserve that."

"Then kiss me," I said.

We were standing next to his car in the parking lot. I put my arms around his waist and he bent down and kissed me. I touched the back of his soft hair. I loved his face. He leaned against his car and I leaned into him and we kissed. Maybe I could be his au pair in Vermont. I couldn't imagine leaving him now. But I couldn't take care of his kids for the rest of my life. I had Madding to take care of and my own future kids and I had to go to school. It was 1982.

He stopped kissing me and looked at me. "Should we go home or have dinner in Brattleboro? Maybe catch a band?"

"Let's go home," I said. I had actually been thinking about that lasagna in the refrigerator that the lady had made. My mother never made lasagna because she didn't believe in it.

He kissed me again, opened the car door for me, and I got in. I didn't tell him that Rudyard Kipling had been standing in the doorway watching us making out the whole time.

29

A*Seventeen* magazine on a rack at the counter when we stopped for a quart of milk made me panic a little because it said *Special Back-to-School Issue*. The model was wearing a tweed blazer with a white shirt and a polka-dotted man's tie open under her collar, and tortoiseshell glasses to make her look smart. It was the September issue which I'd read at camp, and the October issue was already next to it with a model in a high ruffle-collared white blouse with a blue bow around it. The school year was starting.

"Do you want to get that?" Dennis asked, counting five quarters in his palm.

"Oh, no, thanks," I said. I was curious to see the clip-out *Getting into College Guide* because the girl whose magazine it was had clipped it out before I got to see it. "It's still summer. I don't want to think about sweaters." I said that because it said *Fabulous Sweaters* in big letters over *What You MUST Know About Herpes*.

"Or herpes," Dennis agreed. "Or handling sticky dating situations. Hmmm, I'm actually curious about that one."

I laughed thinking about Dennis being interested in reading a *Seventeen* magazine.

In the car I thought about what I was facing when I got

home. Dennis was telling me about some sticky situation he'd had when he'd studied abroad one year, but I just kept thinking about the fact that my parents didn't live in the same house anymore. I thought about the kids I knew who I felt sorry for. Number one was anyone who was an only child. Everyone I knew who was an only child was anorexic or insane. Number two were kids who had to share a room with a sibling, or even worse, sleep in a bunk bed. But divorce was actually the worst of all. Going to sleep at night with your father in another house was like going to sleep without one of your legs attached to your body. You were literally broken. That's why they called it a broken home. We had no spine. We had a wishbone where a spine should be. We were a turkey of a family. We were just a wisp of a family now blowing in the wind, like a blown-apart gray fuzzy dandelion. We weren't even a family. We would never go to the Bronx Zoo or Coney Island or the Cherry Hungarian restaurant together again. How could a family end like that? I was a smart girl. I knew what divorce was. I didn't know why I had never thought about all this before. I hadn't realized that my zoo days were over.

When we got to Dennis's house, his phone rang and he answered it. It was his wife.

"Is everything okay?" Dennis asked. "It's the middle of the night there . . . He did? That's hilarious . . . I'm sleeping very well."

He winked at me and I listened to his side of the conversation for a few minutes.

I went into the living room and turned on *Eight Is Enough* on ABC, but it wasn't channel 7 here. At nine I could watch *The Love Boat*.

"What was hilarious?" I asked when Dennis came into the living room.

"My son was very excited to take the lift. All he wanted to do was take the lift up and down. He's never been on an elevator before."

"How is that possible? Hasn't he ever been to the hospital?"

"No kids are allowed on my floor. I never thought about it," Dennis said.

"I live on the fifteenth floor," I said.

We were from two different worlds. This was madness. He was married and I was divorced. I had more in common with Santiago or maybe Rudyard Kipling. Or maybe I had nothing in common with anyone.

"Do you want to watch *The Love Boat*?" I asked him.

"I think I'm going to heat up the lasagna and swim some laps," he said.

When he went out to the pool, I called my friend Julie Lender. She didn't have her own phone because her parents weren't divorced. Her father answered. The only thing weird about him was he had a collection of African masks. He was a psychiatrist. "Hello, Dr. Lender, this is Swanna Swain calling, may I please speak to Julie?" The only thing weird about Julie was she kept a running list of anyone who borrowed anything from her. She kept it on her desk. It said, *Jenny S. 25¢, Zoe W 75¢, Leslie K The Witch of Blackbird Pond*, etc. It had the date the person borrowed it and the date it was returned, all in perfect columns. She was dead serious about it. It was especially strange because her last name was Lender. I was always very curious to look at it whenever I was at her house.

"Swanna!" she said when she got on the phone.

"Hi!" It was actually extremely exciting because we hadn't talked to each other in so long. "Do you happen to know when school starts?" I asked her.

She laughed. "What do you mean?"

"What day do we go back?"

"Tuesday. Labor Day is the day after tomorrow and we start the next day, September 7. I thought you were kidding," she said. "Where are you?"

"I'm still on summer vacation so I was just confused for a minute." My heart was pounding. "We're coming back tomorrow. I'm actually at my camp counselor's house, so I should go."

"Okay, see you Tuesday," she said.

"See you Tuesday," I said, and hung up.

30

"Y ou've got to admit, Vermont has something going for it," Dennis said. He was looking up at a flaming-red tree. The leaves were starting to change and this clearly impressed him. "With the exception of those two evergreens, soon every leaf you see here will be all kinds of incredible shades of orange or yellow or red."

I nodded. "I know how trees work," I assured him. Every time I came to the country, people were always pointing this kind of thing out to me. We had trees in New York. What Dennis didn't understand is that fall meant one thing to me and one thing only, and that was school. School wasn't some kind of joke. Where he saw beautiful leaves on the trees, I saw sheets of loose-leaf paper blowing around with all kinds of assignments on them. I saw tests and studying and homework and notes and report cards. I saw misery and I saw exhaustion. People like Dennis loved school, but I hated it.

There were two kinds of people—people who could study on the subway and people who could not. I could not. In a couple of days I'd be sitting on the subway watching Ben Edelman and Simon Hess studying and already getting a leg up on me while I made eye contact with crazies.

Dennis didn't understand that one red leaf caused me huge anxiety, let alone a billion of them. And he didn't seem to realize that I wouldn't be there soon. No reminder of time passing was beautiful to me. Not all the leaves in Vermont, or sunsets, or even a Cartier watch.

"What's wrong?" he asked. "Not much of a leaf-peeper?"

If he had said the words *leaf-peeper* on the first day I met him, I never would have been able to let him kiss me. But now I was in love with him, so he could say it.

I was feeling something familiar but I couldn't put my finger on it. It was this incredible loneliness, but I didn't know what I was lonely for. I was homesick, I realized, but it was a homesickness that could never be cured because what I missed was the way things used to be. I missed having parents and a little brother. I missed something that didn't exist and maybe never had.

For some reason I thought of my mother's bed. It had sheets that were blue with big butterflies all over them. The butterflies had long terrifying antennae that curled around all over the sheets. I always wondered why you'd pick those sheets over all the other sheets in Bloomingdale's. But now I really wanted to lie on those sheets with Madding and watch game shows. I knew we must have all snuggled in that bed at some point—my mother and father and Madding and me—but now I couldn't remember ever having done that.

"What are we going to do when you're in New York?" he said.

I thought about how a guy had called me once. It was a wrong number. He asked to speak to Nicole and I said I wish I was Nicole in a really sexy voice and we laughed. I did it to entertain my friend who was over at my house, but she didn't think it was funny at all. The guy started calling every day and he gave me his number and I called him. He was in Los Angeles. He said he was thirty-five and I said I was twenty-two. I based the character of myself on my friend Liza Jacobs's older cousin who was staying with her in their guest room while she was doing a semester at NYU. I had only caught a glimpse of her once, because she was never home. She was beautiful and very intriguing and she had the exact hair I wanted, long and silky and parted in the middle with wings that blew back perfectly. In real life my hair was long, but it was puffy and wavy and very thick and Italian looking. Everyone complimented it but it was not the hair I wanted.

So pretty much every day after school I talked to him. He said he was a television cameraman. He told me things about his childhood and his job and I told him about made-up things that were happening at NYU. He was shooting a new TV show that was going to air in September called *Cheers*. He said I'd be able to see his name in the credits, but I didn't totally believe him. It seemed convenient that it was a future show that hadn't aired yet, and I didn't think they'd call a sitcom something stupid like *Cheers*, and I gave him a hard time about that. I also gave him a hard time about whoever that girl Nicole was who he had originally been trying to call, and he said he had no interest in calling her anymore.

I had a really clear picture of him in my mind from his voice. He said he wanted to come to New York to meet me, or I should fly to LA to meet him and he could introduce me to the stars of *Cheers*. He said he would send me a ticket.

Then one day I asked him what he looked like and he told me a totally different description from what I had pictured. He said he was medium height, and medium build, and he had reddish-brown hair and a reddish-brown beard and a mustache and glasses. I had been so busy describing Liza Jacobs's cousin's perfect looks that I hadn't even bothered to find out about his. I told him that sounded very attractive, although it didn't sound attractive at all. I didn't want him to come to New York to meet me and I didn't want to fly to LA and I didn't want him to call me anymore. I told him I was getting back together with my old boyfriend and our phone calls had to stop, and he said he had fallen in love with me and talking to me was the best part of his day and it was all he had to look forward to, and he said we should at least meet. Then I stopped answering the phone and then it was time to go to camp.

I didn't want to tell Dennis this story.

"I don't know what we'll do," I said. "Talk on the phone?"

Dennis kissed me. "We'll talk on the phone. And I'll come see you. We always go to my wife's parents' house for Christmas. I've been thinking I can make an excuse again and we could spend Christmas together."

"You mean Christmas day?" I said.

"The whole week."

"I have to be with my brother on Christmas," I said.

"Right, and I have to be with my kids. I just want us to have a plan. The day after."

"That's my brother's birthday," I said.

"You're being quite difficult. I can come to New York a lot. You know my feelings for you are very far from just sexual." I hated that word. He looked into my eyes and ran his hand through his hair. He seemed so young and boyish at that moment. I put my arms around him and hugged him. I wobbled on my feet like a drunk. I felt a drunk, in-love feeling. He shifted from side to side and put his fists up. "You want to box?"

I put my fists up. My father had taught me to put my thumbs on the outside of my fists and always guard my face.

"Not bad," he said.

"*Not bad?* I could beat you."

"I should give you a spanking," he said. "It's probably been awhile since you've been properly spanked."

"I've never had a spanking," I said, laughing. It was the most ridiculous thing I'd ever heard.

"Well, you need one," he said.

He looked at me seriously and a really sexy feeling came over me. I didn't know why, since I hated pain of any kind.

"I think you've been teasing me," he said.

"I think you want to be teased," I said.

"What I want is for you to go upstairs and put on the skirt you wore yesterday."

I didn't know if he was kidding, but he didn't look like he was. "Fine," I said sort of ridiculously. I wasn't sure if I should do it.

I went upstairs and changed into the skirt, which was piled on the green velvet chair with my other clothes. I had already made a total mess of his bedroom. My room at home was always messy and I was the worst slob in my bunk. I felt a little awkward and annoyed. I didn't know if he was going to come upstairs or if I was supposed to go back down.

Finally, I headed to the top of the stairs and he called my name.

I went into the living room. "What?"

He was looking at me and smiling. "I didn't think you'd do it," he said. He looked very pleased with himself. "Come here." I went over to where he was sitting on the couch and faced him. He reached up under my skirt and pulled my underwear down to my knees. Then he made me lie across his lap.

After he spanked me and we had both come, I lay on top of him on the couch and he gave me a million compliments, all of which I loved except when he called my ass plump.

My back was itching and I asked him to scratch it. He turned me around and lifted up my shirt. "What's this?" he said. "You have hives." I looked down at my arm, which was covered with raised splotches. "Did you eat anything you're allergic to?"

I shook my head. I knew it was from thinking about school.

I always got hives when I thought about school. "I get very tense," I said.

"It's okay, baby." He left and came back with a tube of ointment and slathered it all over my back and arms. "You seem so together and with it," he said. "I'm surprised. You seem like such a cool customer."

"I guess I'm not," I said.

"Everything is going to be okay. We're going to figure it out."

I didn't want him to put the ointment on my arms because they were very hairy. I had gotten good at shaving my legs at camp. I could do it standing up in the shower. Jacquie

Beller had outlawed Nair in our bunk because it smelled too disgusting.

"Don't put it on my arms."

"I have to. You're covered in hives. Otherwise I have to give you something orally, but that will knock you out. I want to see if the ointment will work first."

I knew I probably needed a Compazine suppository because I was probably also going to throw up. "I'll do my arms."

"Why can't I touch your arms?"

"I don't like my arms. I have a lot of hair on them." I had written a story for school called "October Octopus" about an octopus who is self-conscious about his hairy arms. It was very good.

"It's because you're young and you have a lot of estrogen." I had no idea what estrogen was but I knew I didn't want to have it. "Estrogen is the female hormone, and testosterone is the male hormone."

"I know what estrogen is," I said.

"You're perfect," he said. "Your skin is like velvet. I've never seen such perfect skin."

I looked down at my skin, erupting in raised white welts ringed in red, through a forest of black hair, mosquito-bite scars, and railway tracks of scratch marks. On my upper arm was the most giant inoculation scar in the history of the world and my father's freckles. It didn't look too perfect. I wondered what his wife's skin must look like if he thought mine was so great, and all those pregnant patients, all bloody with placenta everywhere and stretch marks. It must suck to be married to a doctor and have to hear about things like estrogen all the time. "Estrogen is what makes you sexy, and silky, and fertile, and voluptuous. I'm serious. I could get hard just looking at your arms. Try not to scratch."

I really wished he would stop talking. I just wanted to eat an ice cream sandwich. I had seen them in the freezer but there was only one left in the box, so I didn't think I should take it. What if he didn't eat ice cream sandwiches, and his wife came home and noticed they were gone? My skin was on fire and I wanted to sit in a cold tub.

"Have you ever read the Yeats poem about swans? 'The Wild Swans of Coole.'" He went to the bookshelf and pulled out a book. I wondered how I had managed to avoid it all these years, but I was going to have to hear it now.

I have looked upon those brilliant creatures,
And now my heart is sore.
All's changed since I, hearing at twilight,
The first time on this shore,
The bell-beat of their wings above my head,
Trod with a lighter tread . . .

But now they drift on the still water,
Mysterious, beautiful;
Among what rushes will they build,
By what lake's edge or pool
Delight men's eyes when I awake some day
To find they have flown away?

"I like it," I said. "That was very romantic." I wondered why he was reading a poem about a swan flying away and building a nest around another pool. Or maybe he thought *I* was building a nest by his pool?

"You make *me* feel romantic, Swanna. I don't think I've ever read a poem to a girl before. Tell me what you're tense about. Are you thinking about going home?" He looked at me so sincerely that I kissed him.

"No," I said.

"That's good. I get very tense too. I get depressed. Tell me what will relax you."

"Do you have any ice cream?"

He laughed. "I'll look. If I don't have any, I'll drive to Dairy Queen and get you some." Now I was no different from his wife, making him drive to the store to get me things. Maybe that's all that love was. He went into the kitchen and came back with the ice cream sandwich.

"Can I use the phone?" I asked.

"Of course, baby."

I went into his bedroom and sat on his side of the bed, licking the vanilla ice cream from the sides of the sandwich. I dialed the pay phone at the artist colony. A woman answered.

"Can I please speak to Madding Swain?" I said.

"I don't know who that is. Sculptor?" she said.

"No, he's a kid."

"Oh, the little kid who was here? With the couple with the dog?"

The people there were so stupid. "No, they don't have a dog."

"Yes they do," she said. "The couple with the truck?"

"Yes," I said miserably, "But they don't have a dog."

"They do. They have a dog. I think they found it."

This was crazy. My mother hated dogs. We weren't allowed to have a dog. All I'd wanted my whole life was to have a bulldog named Spike. "Can I speak to the kid?"

"He's gone," she said.

"What?" My heart started pounding. I tried to think how many days I had been with Dennis. "Are you sure?"

"Pretty sure. Yes. His mom and dad took him."

"His dad?" I wondered if my dad had come and gotten him. "The fox with the truck."

"Oh." It wasn't like a cast change in a movie. Family members were not actors who could be replaced. You couldn't just cast another man in the part of the dad, the way they had cast another guy in the role of Darren, the husband on *Bewitched*. Dadislav wasn't our dad. You only got one mom and one dad. *And now, playing the part of Swanna Swain, is . . . a dog.* "That's not his dad. That's just a loser our mother is dating," I clarified.

"I'm sort of waiting for an important call," she said.

I said, "Thank you," and hung up. I wished I hadn't left Madding. He had to drive home alone in the back of the truck with a stray vicious dog. I dialed our phone number in New York and let the phone ring and ring but there was no answer. I didn't know where my brother was.

After my father moved out of our apartment, I had a lot of trouble concentrating in school. I will admit that. I was also stuck in the back of a couple of my classes and I couldn't see the board that well. I had to go up to the board to copy down the assignments after class, which made me late for my next class. I loved Shakespeare but for some reason I couldn't read *Henry IV, Part I*. I kept thinking I was reading it and really enjoying it, but when I took the midterm I didn't know the actual answers to any of the questions. Usually for me the opposite was true. I could not know anything at all about the subject but I was so good at taking tests that I would just know the answers. It was kind of like a miracle. I would see the question, and the answer would appear in my mind by magic. I had even seen *Henry IV, Part I* at the Delacorte Theater in Central Park, so I was not worried about the test at all, but when I saw the test in front of me, to my incredible shock, I couldn't answer a single question. I had no idea who the hell Hotspur was and I thought Northumberland was a place and Shrewsbury was a person. I got a zero on the test. I told the teacher I had a concussion but he wouldn't change the grade.

Another teacher asked me why I hadn't done my homework and I told him very honestly that my father had moved out the night before. I was very surprised hearing myself say that. He hadn't moved out the night before, but he had moved out. Saying it, I started inexplicably crying right in front of the teacher, right there in room 211. I don't remember anything that he said, but I don't think it was too nice and understanding, and I was very angry at myself for crying in front of him like a baby.

I had decided to take Latin instead of French, which was the biggest mistake of my entire life. I think I had been trying to impress my father, who had said that Latin was a good foundation for being a lawyer. But in French, which I practically already knew, they spent half the semester going to French restaurants like La Bonne Soupe. You had to get money from your parents and you preordered either the quiche Lorraine, soupe à l'oignon, or coq au vin. It was a three-course meal with salade maison, your main dish, and pot de crème for dessert. You had to write a thank you note in French to the restaurant afterward OR draw them a picture. Every single person drew a picture. The teacher also made everyone bring lemons and sugar from home and she put an electric crepe maker on her desk and constantly made everyone in the class crepes. I had chosen to give up all that for the privilege of taking an incomprehensible dead language with the hugest nerds in the whole school. Meanwhile, we could literally hear the music and laughter coming from the Spanish class next door because they were learning to tango.

I very quickly fell behind. In English and history and science, I could make a fresh start with each new topic they introduced, but in math and Latin, everything was built on the topic before it. If you didn't understand one thing, it was impossible to understand the next. Without telling my parents, I went to another school and explained to the principal what had happened. I had gotten a concussion and my father had moved out of my apartment and I wanted to come to his school. "But you're at the best school in the city," he said. I convinced him to let me in.

What I hadn't counted on was losing my friends. We went to see a movie and then a guy on the street was selling cowboy hats and they encouraged me to buy a purple one, which looked really good on me and I felt so happy and relieved. I told them I was changing schools and I didn't notice how judgmental they were becoming. They were worried about me, but I didn't realize it at the time. Or maybe they felt sorry for me, even worse. But they didn't talk to me after that. Every day they made excuses for why they couldn't hang out.

Sometimes, when I was feeling really bad, I even wondered if their parents had told them they couldn't be friends with me anymore.

My new school was only seventeen blocks away from my old one, but I was on another planet and they wouldn't see me anymore. I remember watching them walk away from me that day. I stood there in my long black trench coat from Antique Boutique and my purple cowboy hat, like the bad guy in an old Western, literally watching them walk into the sunset.

At my new school I was in the accelerated program. I took French, I was the drummer in the school orchestra because it was too late in the year for me to learn a real instrument, and I got 100 on every test because I already knew everything from the previous year at my other school. I was the director of the filmmaking club, I won the creative writing award for my story "Snake Eyes" after the original winner was caught plagiarizing Hemingway, and we went on a very cool trip to Salem, Massachusetts, and Mystic Seaport. I literally got 100 in every class except for gym, which I didn't even have to take because the principal believed me about the concussion.

The thing was, when I thought about going back to school, I kept thinking I was going back to my old school. When I thought about seeing my friends, I kept thinking I would be with my old friends again. My mind somehow couldn't take in that I wasn't going back there. It was like I had talked myself into really having a concussion after all. I had amnesia. I couldn't remember anything.

I hadn't told Dennis any of this. I felt strangled, like my neck was being pulled into the long, thin, curved neck of a swan. I couldn't speak and I was having trouble breathing. I felt like I was in the Roald Dahl novel, watching wings grow where my arms had been. There was even a kind of a swan called a mute swan. And that mute swan was me.

"You ready to hit the hay?" Dennis asked.

"Hit the hay? It's only eleven thirty," I said.

"If I'm going to drive you home tomorrow, we should get an early start."

"It's too early for bed," I said.

"What did you have in mind? This is Vermont. It's not like we can head over to Times Square."

No one in New York went to Times Square. "We could go skinny-dipping," I said. "In the pool."

"I was looking forward to hitting the sheets with you."

"I can't sleep with all those crickets." I took off my spanking skirt and put it on the green velvet chair. It was my last night there. I got into bed naked and listened to him brush his teeth and blow his nose, which he did very loudly. He got into bed next to me.

"I'm tired, baby," Dennis said.

I was looking at a picture of a group of girls in prep school uniforms, framed on my bedside table. They were holding some kind of long polo sticks with nets on the ends.

"What is this?" I asked.

"My wife's high school lacrosse team," he said.

I looked at the girls' faces. They were all really pretty and confident and happy and rich. It didn't really matter which one his wife was because they were all the same. They had on extremely short gray skirts that went to the middle of their thighs, long blue knee socks, and white shirts. They were on a field with leafless trees in the background and it seemed pretty cold out. I was always very interested in how these kinds of girls didn't get cold when I saw them on the Upper East Side.

No one particularly stood out, or seemed to be trying to stand out. I always noticed that if you saw Marilyn Monroe in a group photo of Hollywood studio starlets or something, she always stood out.

The craziest thing was, even though I had never seen those girls in my life and had never worn an outfit like that, had never stood on that field or any field like it, and didn't even know what those sticks were, I still looked for a second to see if I was in the picture. I knew it was crazy, but whenever I saw a group photo, I always half expected to see myself in it, like maybe I had been there and didn't remember.

"My wife says boarding school was the happiest time of her life," Dennis said.

"That's not very flattering."

"No, it's not." I thought he would laugh but he sounded angry.

"She was probably kidding," I said.

"No. She wasn't."

"She must have been happy when you asked her to marry you."

"We used to have some fun," he said. "Yeah, we had a good time."

"What did you do?"

"I don't know, Swanna. We should get some sleep. The normal stuff. Went to hear some music, went dancing a lot.

In a way she was like a kid. Even though she was thirty when we met, she didn't know how to do a lot of stuff. She was more book smart. I had to teach her everything, but I kind of liked that."

"What do you mean?"

"I taught her how to roast a chicken." He laughed remembering the stupid chicken. I wished I hadn't brought up any of this. "I taught her everything. Finances, how to eat a lobster, how to change a diaper. She was very childlike in a lot of respects. She's a good skier."

"Did she know how to give a blow job?"

"As a matter of fact, no," he said. "And she still doesn't." He smiled at me but I just gave him an annoyed look back. I had to remember never to bring up his wife again. I realized I didn't know how to do any of the things he had taught his wife, except the blow job. "One thing I couldn't teach her to do was love books like you do. She's not much of a reader. She hasn't read a book since I've met her."

"I thought you said she was book smart." His wife sounded like a horrible monster. It was hard to imagine that one of the girls in that picture, whichever one she was, could turn out to not know how to do a single thing and not even know how to read, which is something all people learn how to do pretty much right away.

"You're right, I did say that. Hmmm. She's smart, but you're right, not really book smart either."

"She sounds like a real winner," I said. This night was not going how I wanted it to.

"What's your favorite book?" he asked, sounding sleepy. I wasn't tired at all.

"*Catcher in the Rye.*"

"If you really want to know about it . . ." he began, and then proceeded to recite the whole first page and a half in a weird monotone.

I really wanted him to stop. I loved Dennis, but not as much as I loved Holden Caulfield. I would never love anyone as much as that, and Dennis didn't sound anything like him. He sounded like a rich grown-up pretending to be Holden, the exact kind of person Holden would have hated.

I knew I was being stupid to get myself in a bad mood about Dennis's wife and Holden Caulfield, who weren't even real people as far as I was concerned.

"I might go swimming," I said.

"I have to sleep," he said. "I'm used to a pretty early schedule."

"I know. But I'm not tired at all. Don't you want to watch *Saturday Night Live*?"

"Isn't it a rerun?"

"That makes it even better."

"Maybe I should have given you the Benadryl," he said.

Fuck you, I thought. I had no idea why I had gotten so angry.

After he fell asleep, I got up and found my Vivitar camera in my bag. I had three shots left. I waited for the red light to come on, letting me know the flash was working, and took a picture of him and then two more, until I just heard the clicking sound when I turned the wheel.

* * *

I decided to try calling Madding again. I went downstairs to the living room and dialed our number.

"Hello," my brother said.

"Madding?" I almost couldn't believe I was hearing his voice. "It's late. You should be asleep. You have to get on a good school schedule."

"We only got home a little while ago. Where are you?"

"I'll be home tomorrow," I said.

"We have a dog! We have a dog! He's the whole family's dog but he sleeps with *me*."

"What's that noise?" It sounded like there was banging in the background.

"Boring Slob is throwing out all our stuff," Madding said.

"What do you mean?"

"He threw out our couch and the chairs and the coffee table."

"What do you mean, threw out our couch?" I said.

"The living room is going to be his art studio. He's putting that black-tar road thing he made on the wall."

"What? How do we sit down?" I was shaking with fury. "Tell him to stop!"

"I don't think I can stop him. He already did it." He sounded like he was going to start crying.

"It's okay," I said. "It's not your fault."

"We can't make forts anymore and we can't have sleepovers in the living room."

"Yes we can, and we can have sleepovers in my room. We can have a sleepover in my room tomorrow night."

"With the dog," Madding said.

"I thought you were scared of dogs since Pierrette. What's his name?"

"I forget. It's from a Russian writer but we can give him our own name."

"I like Spike," I said.

"I like that too."

"How's Big Bird?" I asked.

"Weeellll . . . Big Bird died actually. But he's still green. But his leaves are lying all the way down."

"Okay, well, see you tomorrow," I said, and hung up. I hung up because I was starting to cry. I cried so hard that my whole face and chest got wet. No wonder no one wanted to be friends with me anymore. I didn't even have a couch. Even though none of this had happened yet, on that day we went to the movies and I bought the cowboy hat, it was going to. All these things had been about to happen, and somehow, somehow, my old friends must have known that. I was sure their parents knew and had told them not to be friends with me. I had thought Liza Jacobs's parents loved me, and Holly Polsky's, and Izzy Rothstein's, but they all knew what would happen to me the way they all somehow knew what would happen to Holden. The last straw before I had changed schools was an assignment we had. We had to write an essay about what would happen to Holden Caulfield in the future, and have a class discussion about it. "Holden Caulfield will not be successful," Liza Jacobs had argued to the class, and everyone but me had wholeheartedly agreed. He wouldn't be in any shining group photos on anyone's bedside table. He was finished. Not one person in the class thought he had a chance.

I couldn't stand to listen to them talk about him like that. His future wasn't any of our business and it wasn't for us to decide. Nobody saw the irony in how much Holden would have hated these phony essays. I thought I was protecting him, but by refusing to write the essay, I had actually betrayed us both.

I went upstairs and put all my clothes back in my duffel. I took the play garage I had bought at the yard sale and put it in the kids' room. Dennis's kids would like it. Then I went down to the kitchen and packed a couple of individually wrapped American cheese slices and three Tabs. I took the candle that was shaped like an ice cream sundae from the windowsill and put that in my bag too.

31

I stood in the kitchen, deciding what to do. Sometimes if it was late at night and I couldn't sleep, if I made an ambitious plan of what I could do, like getting out of bed and doing all my homework, or cleaning my room or something, just thinking about it would make me so tired that I would just instantly fall asleep. I waited to see if the thought of leaving and hitchhiking to the bus station would make me tired enough to go back up to Dennis's bed. I could climb back in next to him and in the morning he would bring me hot chocolate. I waited to see if all that thinking made me sleepy, but it didn't.

I decided I would go through the back door, because if Dennis woke up and heard the back door open, he would just think I was going out for a swim. He wouldn't come after me.

I unlocked the door and opened it as quietly as I could and shut it behind me. I already missed him so much I felt like my face was caving in, like a carved pumpkin you see on someone's brownstone steps a couple of weeks after Halloween. I was collapsing in on myself. I felt like I was going to throw up.

I was doing this crazy, silent, crying-open-mouthed, shaking thing I did when I was really upset. The shaking was the worst part. I was gasping for breath and sort of squeaking.

I had an intense desire to hit the ground, which was what always happened when I felt like this. As if the ground would somehow help. It was cold and I was also shivering.

I couldn't walk until I calmed down. I wanted to lie down on the slabs of cement around the pool and pull out the weeds growing between the cracks, but I had no feeling in my fingertips. I didn't want Dennis to look out the window and see me lying on the ground, or come out and find me.

I went into the kids' playhouse and crouched in the corner and cried. It was pitch dark inside. I was really shaking hard. You are so stupid, I tried to whisper to myself, but no sound came out.

I wished I could call Jacquie Beller and tell her all about Dennis and ask her what she thought I should do, and tell her about my father being "PhD" the whole time, but the thought I hadn't let myself think finally hit me—I didn't have her number and she didn't have mine. We were going to write them down on the bus. I might never get to talk to Jacquie Beller again.

I could go back inside and get into bed. I only had myself to blame for this. If the door had locked behind me, I could ring the doorbell. I could say I got locked out. Dennis wouldn't mind.

Oh no, I thought, as I started to retch. I threw up on the wooden floor of the playhouse, next to the little table and chairs. I wished I had a flashlight, the number one most important thing to bring to camp.

I said to myself what my mother always said to me after I threw up—"Good, now you'll feel better." I hadn't told Dennis my address or my phone number. I didn't know his address. I didn't know what road we were on or even the name of this town. I couldn't have even called a cab if I had wanted to. Unless I looked for a piece of mail, but it was too late now.

I was going to throw up again and I crouched down and then said to myself, "Good, now you'll feel better," when I was done. I left the playhouse, got one of Dennis's wife's stupid rolled-up towels in the stupid basket, wiped my mouth, and then wiped off the floor so his kids wouldn't come home to dried-up vomit. I threw the towel on the ground near the basket and I pushed one of the chairs over to the fence, climbed up, threw my bag over, and then climbed over myself. I had a feeling this was one of the stupidest things I had ever done.

I could have just unlatched the gate and walked around to the front of the house and up the driveway to the road, but now I was on someone else's property. It was bigger than Dennis's. There was a bigger house that was dark and a smaller house that was also dark and a giant pool that wasn't lit up, but I could see the water in the moonlight.

I walked across the property to another fence, spraining my ankle about a hundred times. I wasn't cold anymore, I was hot, which meant I was probably going to throw up again. This was so stupid. Dennis wasn't going to look for me. He was sleeping peacefully in his bed. I could have walked out the front door and made it to the Black Swan Motel.

The next fence wasn't wood. It was just a stone wall of some kind, layers and layers of flat stone. It was easy to climb over, like the stone pyramids at the playground next to the Metropolitan Museum of Art. On the other side there was just woods. I couldn't see a house. I followed along the stone wall, toward where I thought the road would be. It was very dark and I really couldn't see much.

I could go back over the stone wall, and over the wooden fence, and into Dennis's house.

I heard barking and my whole body stiffened.

The barking stopped and I started to walk again, very carefully.

You either love me or you don't, I thought. I realized I'd been saying that in my head the whole time.

And then something hit me in the back. I screamed and fell down and just kept telling myself to get up in case there were mice or snakes or all the vermin of Vermont. Then I saw a flashlight coming toward me.

"Oh my God, it's a child. Oh my God, oh my God," a woman said.

"I'm fine," I said. I was wet from the ground but I couldn't get up. I was lying in some kind of warm water. "I'm trying to get to the road. I need a taxi."

32

When I woke up I was in a hospital bed. "The doctor will be right in," a nurse said.

"Dennis?" I said, but she just looked at me. I was hooked up to an IV and there was sunshine coming in through the window.

A doctor walked in but it wasn't Dennis. "Do you know your name?" he asked.

I laughed because I thought that was hilarious. "My name is Swanna, but you don't know my name, so neither of us will know if I'm right," I said.

"Swanna Swain," he said.

"How do you—"

"The police told us. They looked through your bag."

I remembered my laminated A-Division swim test card.

"You took quite a hit," he said. "You'll need a lot of therapy."

"I don't think my parents will go for that. My father hates all shrinks."

The doctor looked at me strangely. "Physical therapy. For your arm. You'll need quite a bit of it."

"What happened to my arm?" I said.

"You were shot."

I looked down at my arm which was completely bandaged. I had no feeling in it. I thought about how my father hated Ronald Reagan but admired him for making jokes when he was shot. To my father, making a joke when you were shot was the best thing a person could do. "I forgot to duck," I said.

"If you had ducked, she might have shot you in the head."

"She?"

"The woman whose property you were on. She's in the waiting room, I can send her in. What were you doing there?"

"I'm really thirsty," I said. "And hungry." I had to think of what to say. I turned to look at the tray by my bed. There was a plastic cup with something in it. I couldn't move my arm to reach for it. "What's that?"

"The bullet," he said. "I saved it for you."

"Thank you." Madding was going to *love* that.

I thought about Dennis waking up. He would see my things missing from the green velvet chair. Maybe he would think I had just gotten up and packed everything and brought it downstairs so we could get an early start. Or maybe he would know right away. He would see that my side—his wife's side—of the bed was unslept in. He would run downstairs to try to catch me. He would open up the front door, then the back, and see the patio chair pulled up to the fence.

Or maybe he had been awakened by a gunshot in the middle of the night.

Maybe he would ask the neighbors, *Did you see a girl with long black hair?* Maybe he would jump in his car and go to the bus station, go to the artist colony to see if the truck was there, or ask if anyone had seen me at the Cumberland Farms.

You either love me or you don't, I thought.

I picked up the phone next to my bed and dialed Dennis's number. "May I please speak to Dr. Dennis Whitson?" I said.

"Who's calling?" the woman said.

"I'm a patient."

"Please hold."

Then the woman's voice rang out in the hall over the PA system—"*Paging Dr. Whitson. Paging Dr. Dennis Whitson. Please pick up line seven.*"

After a few seconds she came back on the phone. "He's not answering. Can I leave a message?"

"No," I said, and hung up as two cops came into my room, the same two cops who had come to the artist colony.

"How are you feeling?" the woman cop said. I wasn't sure if she remembered me.

"Not bad, considering I was shot," I said.

She laughed. Even when I was shot, people laughed at what I said.

"Are you up to answering a few questions?"

"Okay," I said.

"Your name and age?" the woman said.

"Swanna Swain. Fourteen."

"Can you tell us what you were doing on a stranger's property?" the man asked.

"I was staying with my friend's family," I said. "They were going back to New York, and I decided I should go back to the artist colony, you know, where you came before, and go back to New York with my mom and brother. I thought I could find my way back, but I got lost and it got dark."

"What is the name of your friend?" the man said. He was writing my answers on a pad.

Dennis, I thought, his name filling up my whole mind. "Debbie," I said.

"Debbie what?"

"I actually don't know her last name. We met at camp."

"Is she an outtastata?"

"Yes," I said. "They were only renting."

"Do you understand trespassing is a serious crime? Running away, sneaking around . . ."

"Yes, I'm sorry. I understand. But I didn't run away. I'm trying to get back to New York. If you had listened to me . . ."

"We've contacted your family," the man said.

"How?"

"We contacted the place you called us from the last time. We had your father's phone number. He's coming to get you."

"You talked to my dad?"

I heard the woman's voice on the PA system again— "*Paging Dr. Whitson. Paging Dr. Dennis Whitson. Pick up line four.*"

"Are you okay?" the woman cop said.

"I'm fine." I wondered if they had talked to my dad or to Freakislav. I hoped they knew that idiot was not my father.

"I'd like to talk to her alone for a minute," the woman cop said.

The male cop nodded and left the room.

"Is there anything you want to tell me?" she asked. "Female to female?"

"I'm not sure what you mean," I said. My shoulder was starting to hurt very badly.

"Paging Dr. Whitson. Pick up line four."

"Who's this?" She took out a photo envelope from her back pocket, opened it, and pulled out the three photos of Dennis I had taken. "We found your camera in your bag and had these developed."

She handed them to me. There were twenty-four black-andwhite photos. I started to look through them, using my good arm. There were all my photos from theater camp. There were a few of Nestor Perez at the hockey rink. Then Dennis asleep in bed. He looked so cute sleeping. The side of his face was strong and masculine. I wanted to kiss the photo.

"Who's this?" she said again. "Who's the man?"

"That's my friend's dad," I said. "She must have taken these pictures."

"I want you to be very honest with me, honey. Did this man touch you?"

"What? No!" I said. "That's gross. I'm not answering any more questions. I didn't know it was against the law to get lost."

"You're not in trouble," the woman said.

"I know I'm not in trouble," I said angrily. I tried to lift my arm to put the photos on the table, but it was impossible. "Can you put those there?"

"Just to be safe, I'm going to ask a nurse to examine you, if that's okay with you," the cop said.

"No, it is not okay with me. None of this is okay with me. No one will be examining anything."

After a while they left and I finally got some ginger ale. I was starting to think getting a cup of ginger ale in that place was the hardest thing I had ever accomplished.

33

"The woman who shot you wants to see you," the nurse said. "Send her in," I said. I tried to sit up and look regal like Anne Boleyn pardoning her executioner, but I couldn't use my arms and ended up just wriggling a little. I loved Anne Boleyn and actually spent a lot of time thinking about her.

"Are you okay? I'm so sorry," a woman said, coming into my room.

"I'm fine," I said.

She didn't exactly look like a cold-blooded killer. She was wearing sweatpants and a University of Vermont sweatshirt and she looked like she had been up all night. She had red hair and she was pretty and for a minute I wondered if she was Sandy, the neighbor with the lasagna.

"What's your name?" I asked.

"Laura," she said. "I'm so sorry I did this to you."

"I'm fine," I said. "My dad's coming."

As soon as I said that, I had the terrible thought that he might not be alone. He might have Mistress Amber with him. I might have to sit in the backseat and not even go to McDonald's or anything. I realized I had been wondering if we might stop somewhere really fun on the way home, like the Danbury County Fair or Mystic Seaport or an apple orchard. At Mystic Seaport you could have a rope bracelet made right on your wrist. It stayed on your wrist permanently. You wore it in the bath. I'd had one once from my school trip and I wore it for a long time and now I couldn't remember why or how it was gone. I looked down at my wrist expecting to see it, although I knew it hadn't been there in months. My father probably wouldn't have gotten me one anyway. He was actually pretty cheap about stuff like that. Plus, I kept forgetting I couldn't move my arm.

"I'm so, so, so, so, so, so sorry," she gushed.

"If only you had said one more *so*," I said. That was something I always did with Madding. He'd ask for something and say a million "pleases" and at the end I'd say, "I would have done it if you had just said one more *please*."

"What?" she said.

"It wasn't your fault. I shouldn't have been in your yard."

"I heard someone and I was so scared. There have been robberies in the area. I was home alone. I'd had a couple of drinks. Anyway, that's no excuse."

"I'm really sorry," I said.

"No, no, I'm the one who's sorry. Just the other day a friend of mine said, 'Sandy, you should not have a gun in the house.'"

"Sandy? I thought your name was Laura."

"Laura Sandretti. Everyone calls me Sandy. I just want you to know I'm sorry. I'm here if you need anything. I'll stay until your parents come."

It was her, but this time she wasn't holding a lasagna.

I remembered her flirting with Dennis. *How's your game these days?*

I wished he could see her now, looking terrible, but I probably didn't look too good myself.

I saw the stack of photos on the bedside tray facing up with the top photo showing. It was one of the pictures of Dennis.

"Do you think you could get me a Tab?" I asked.

"Yes, of course," she said. "I've never been so scared in my life. Thank God you're okay."

I smiled at her to show her I really was.

"Oh my God, I'm so relieved." She started to cry. "Yesterday was a bad day for me. I brought my daughter to her boarding school and my ex-husband called with some news."

"What was the news?" I asked, suddenly dying to hear. I wondered if her daughter was the one who had babysat for Dennis's kids. I wondered if the daughter was older than me and if Dennis thought she was pretty, or if this woman, Sandy, was older than Dennis. Her lasagna was still in my stomach. I felt like the wolf with Little Red Riding Hood inside, still whole, like my secret.

"How old are you?" I asked her.

She stopped crying. "Thirty-eight. Why?"

"What was the news?"

"It's pretty ridiculous. He called to tell me something very personal he had done. It's nothing I care to repeat."

"Something personal he had done?" I wanted the Tab but I wanted to hear this more.

"He's a jerk," she said.

I nodded. "How so?"

"He called to tell me he had gotten a vasectomy, if you really want to know."

"That's a good thing," I said. "My mom made my dad have that. Maybe he thought you'd like it."

She laughed angrily. "He's so full of himself that he thinks some young woman is going to want to have his baby, or maybe try to trap him and then he can say, 'Ah ha, I had a vasectomy! I can't be the father!' He really hates women."

"And children, it sounds like." I could see why she liked Dennis. I wished more than anything I could tell Dennis that his crazy neighbor had shot me. That was the worst thing about breaking up with someone—the story was over. He wouldn't know that I got shot by Sandy and I wouldn't know what his wife would say when she saw the sundae candle missing. He wouldn't know how I got home or how my school year went or anything that would happen to me. I wouldn't know if he ever thought of me again. My heart filled with a pain so bad I almost wondered if I had been shot there too. My heart hurt a million times worse than my arm. It took my breath away.

That's what Dennis had said about me—*You take my breath away.*

"I would love to cut off his balls," crazy Sandy said.

"Huh?"

"I'm sorry. I should be praying for your recovery, not burdening you with grown-up problems. Dear Jesus, Lord, help this child! I need a cup of coffee badly and you need a Diet Coke."

"Tab, if possible," I said.

"Right. I'll go get it. I'm just saying, that misogynistic bastard was always so worried about a woman castrating him, what does he do? He goes and castrates himself. He marches in to a doctor's office and says, 'Cut them off, Doc.' In fact, then he told me about a family wedding he had just gone to that of course I wasn't invited to, which is fine with me, and do you know what he said? About his own niece? He said when he talks to her, he might as well just put his testicles in a jar of formaldehyde and hand them to her. That's his way of saying she's a feminist."

"Have you ever been to an astrologer?" I asked.

The woman's voice came on the loudspeaker—"*Paging Dr. Dennis Whitson. Line four.*"

"I know him!" Sandy said. "He's my neighbor. He's the one I called."

"When?"

"I called him before I called 911."

I waited to hear his name again but the loudspeaker stayed silent. I wondered if he was here and had picked up line four. I looked at the IV taped to the top of my hand. My heart was throbbing and the room started to spin. Suddenly it was too much.

"Did he answer?" I asked.

"Who?"

"The doctor you called."

"Yes. He was there in minutes. Wearing nothing but underwear and his coat. He stopped the bleeding and told me to call 911. I had been too scared to do it, but he said I had to. He said you were in shock and he held you in his arms. Then he told me to wait in front for the ambulance."

"He held me in his arms?"

"He's such a good dad. I never saw a doctor be so kind and caring. He was crying. He was holding you and crying. I would kill for a man like that."

You almost did, I thought.

I closed my eyes and imagined him holding me in his arms on the grass the way he had outside the schoolhouse. Even though my eyes were closed, tears squeezed out of them.

Once, I was on a whale-watching boat in Cape Cod and the person on the loudspeaker giving us information about the whales said they branded them with a mark so they could track them in the wild, for scientific purposes. I felt like that whale. I was imprinted with Dennis, covered in his fingerprints. I thought I was free but I really wasn't. I had been branded and I could be tracked.

"That's his coat," she said. I had wondered whose coat that was on the chair in the corner. It was brown, shearling. "You were shaking and he put it over you. I guess he sent it with you in the ambulance. He must have gone home half naked."

"Maybe he's here? Maybe he went home and put his clothes on and came to the hospital."

She shook her head. "He said he was catching an early flight to London. His wife and kids are there."

I put my hand up to my throat to feel my star necklace, but it was gone.

Could Dennis have taken it? I wondered. He had said buying it for me had been a risky thing to do. I tried to shake the terrible thought from my mind.

It was funny. When you walked around New York, a little part of you was always on guard. You kept your eyes open and your hand on your wallet. You didn't exactly expect to get shot and killed in the middle of Vermont and have the necklace ripped from you neck. Vermont really was a terrible place.

"Could you bring me that coat?" I asked.

"Why?"

"I'm a little cold."

"Sure, honey," she said. She laid it over me in the bed. It smelled like him. Like Vermont and Ivory Snow.

"Could you please do me a favor?"

"Of course, anything."

"Could you give that doctor, your neighbor, my phone number? I want to thank him."

"Sure, but I don't have anything to write on," she said, helplessly looking around. Some people didn't have an ounce of problem-solving abilities. It was a miracle I was still alive and she hadn't let me bleed to death on her lawn.

"I have a piece of paper and a pen in my purse."

"Sure." She unzipped my army-navy bag and found the list of kid-friendly places to eat in London that I had taken from the refrigerator, and my erasable pen. "What is it?"

I told her my phone number in New York and she promised she would give it to Dennis when he came back from London, but who really knew if she would or not?

34

The crazy thing was, when I thought of myself on that hill at camp, waiting for my mother to pick me up, after they made me get off the bus, it was almost as if I was still there. I was like the girl in the Andrew Wyeth painting *Christina's World*, an invalid splayed out on the grass. I could see myself there in my Hawaiian skirt, my body twisted, holding my upper body up with my arms, and my mosquito-bitten legs bent behind me. In my mind, it was like I was frozen there. And I always would be.

I just kept wondering over and over if Dennis was angry at me. I could stand anything, I thought, but I couldn't stand that. I'd read in *Seventeen* magazine that the number one "relationship killer" was asking a guy the question: *Are you mad at me?* Basically, according to this article, you could do or say anything— probably cheat on him and murder his best friend—and the relationship would be just fine as long as you didn't say those words. The article called it a "fatal mistake."

But the trouble with those articles is they never knew your particular situation. They didn't know the terrible thing you had done by leaving him in the middle of the night. They didn't know he was married and that he loved you and you had gotten shot and hurt him.

There was a phone by my bed. I picked up the receiver, laid it on my chest, and started to dial my mother. I couldn't dial with my hurt arm.

My brother answered. "Hi, Madding," I said in an upbeat voice. I didn't want him to be scared.

"Swanna!"

I started to say something, but suddenly it was my mother on the phone. She was crying. I wondered if Tarzan the Stupid had broken up with her.

"Swanna," she cried.

"Hi, Mom," I said.

"This was very naughty of you," she said in a weird pouty voice like a child. "I have a splitting headache."

"I'm fine. Can I talk to Madding?"

"We're selling the apartment," she said.

"What apartment?"

"*Our* apartment. This one. The actress Tuesday Weld made an offer."

"I don't want to sell our apartment," I said.

I had seen the actress Tuesday Weld in the movie *Author! Author!* starring Al Pacino, and I actually considered it one of my favorite movies of all time until this moment.

"Don't do it," I said. "Tell her the deal's off."

"We're in contract. I'll lose too much money if I back out now. This is your father's fault."

"How is it Dad's fault?"

"Talk to your brother."

Madding got back on the phone.

"Do you know if Dad is coming to get me?" I asked.

"Yes, he is," my brother said. "Did he tell you that he's moving?"

"No, but that's good. He probably wanted to be closer to us." But closer to us where? I thought. If my mother was selling the apartment, where were we going to live?

"He's moving to Japan."

"You mean Chinatown?"

"No." Madding started to cry. I could barely understand him. "The place with cherry blossoms."

"Gramercy Park?"

"No. Kytoko."

"Tokyo?"

"No."

"Kyoto?"

"Yes."

When you're a kid, your whole world is your classic six on the Upper West Side of Manhattan. Then you grow up and make the mistake of going to sleepaway camp and then you find out there's terrible places out there and the whole world opens and swallows you up. It was like that *New Yorker* cover that was supposed to show how people from New York see the map of the world. You see Ninth Avenue and Tenth Avenue and the Hudson River, then a few random Vermont-like states scattered around, and then the ocean and China, Russia, and Japan. The fatal mistake wasn't asking your crush if he was mad at you—*Seventeen* magazine was wrong about that. The fatal mistake was leaving. None of this would have happened if I had just stayed put.

I soothed Madding for a while and then we got off the phone because it was long distance.

Before I left, I had looked at that picture again. The one of Dennis's wife when she was a kid with all the girls on the lacrosse team.

"I've never worn an outfit like this," I had said to him. "I don't believe in all-girls schools and I would never wear a uniform."

"Why not?" Dennis had asked, smiling. He was being slightly condescending. He probably thought I wouldn't be accepted at a school like that, even though I would.

"Because boys are 50 percent of the world and you have to learn how to deal with them. And I believe in personal expression, so I wouldn't go to a school where I can't wear whatever I want."

"So you defend your right to wear an Elton John T-shirt whenever you want."

"That's correct," I had said. "I'm not going to wear some slutty uniform."

"My wife still has hers." He had opened his wife's closet, which was bigger than my bedroom, and came out with a hanger wrapped in dry cleaner's plastic. He carefully removed the short gray skirt and white blouse with a blue embroidered crest on the pocket.

"Does she wear this for you?" I asked, starting to feel annoyed.

"No," he said, still smiling.

"How did you know she still has it?"

"I don't know," he said. "I guess I knew it was in the closet."

"Do you want me to put it on?"

He nodded. "That's the sexiest thing I could imagine."

I had slipped on the itchy wool skirt, zipped it up, and buttoned the waist band. Then I put on the white shirt without putting on a bra first. It was too tight so I left some of the buttons undone and tucked it in.

"Oh my God," Dennis said.

"I wish I had knee socks," I said.

Dennis was looking at me strangely, sort of like he was in a state of shock. "I love you," he had said. "You make me incredibly happy."

"Why don't you just tell your wife to put this outfit on?" I asked.

"Swanna, my wife doesn't have sex with me."

I had looked at him in disbelief. "Yes she does."

"No, she really doesn't."

If that was true, she was even more stupid than I thought. Sex was the easiest thing in the world to do.

"Why not?" I asked.

"I don't know the answer to that," he had said. "I think it's just marriage."

I thought about kissing Dennis. Sitting on his lap in the car, facing him, straddling him, after we had done it in the Black Swan Motel. I saw him smiling at me. I closed my eyes so I could see it better. But then I saw something else. He had cringed a little. I had kissed him and he had cringed. Now I cringed, suddenly realizing I had made him uncomfortable.

The uncomfortable look in his eyes. The shrug of his shoulders and the slight wince when I kissed him. He had moved his head away from me and I was left sort of kissing his jacket. He had pulled away, wincing again.

I had forced him to do it. I had molested him. I was an adult molester.

I was no better than Mistress Amber, or Amanda, or whatever her name was. In fact, I was worse.

I had seduced Dennis into doing something he didn't want to do. My whole life, I always thought seducing someone was a good thing, but now I realized it wasn't.

Now he was running away from me to go back to his wife. He wouldn't visit me in New York. He wouldn't take me to the museum to see the painting I reminded him of, or Café des Artistes, or a Broadway show. Or anywhere.

He wasn't Poseidon and I wasn't a muse. I was a siren. I was Medusa who could turn men into stone. He was Leda and I was Zeus dressed as a swan.

I was a big dirty bird.

I was a monster.

I wished the bullet had shot me in the heart instead of the arm. I felt like it had anyway. I wished so much it had killed me. "Is there a chance I could still die?" I asked the nurse when she came into the room.

She laughed as if I had said something funny. "No, you're a very lucky young lady. Let me see." She looked at my chart. "They say you have nerve damage? You won't never use that arm no more. But you ain't gonna die, thank Jesus."

"What?" I said.

"What, they didn't tell you nothing yet? The doctor's probably waiting for your parents to come."

She squeezed the bags floating above me like small balloons

and wrote in my chart. The curtain around my bed had polka dots that were suddenly blurry, making it look like the circus.

"Can you confirm your name, address, date of birth?" she said.

"I am Eloise, I am six, I am a city child, I live at the Plaza," I said.

"What?"

"Oooohhh, I absolutely love the Plaza."

"I'll get the doctor," she said, and left.

The clock on the wall between the windows said five o'clock. I picked up the phone and dialed Julie Lender's number. She answered right away and I could tell she was in her beanbag chair.

"Jacquie?" I said when she answered.

"What? This is Julie."

"Julie, sorry. That's what I meant. I don't think I'm going to be at school the day after tomorrow," I said. My eyes were filling up with tears.

"Who is this?" she said.

I am Eloise. I am six. I am a city child. I live at . . .

"Hello?" she said.

"It's Swanna," I said.

"Swanna! Where are you?"

"Do you happen to have a copy of the *Weekly Wag* lying around your apartment?"

"Are you okay?" she asked.

"I'm fine."

"There's one in my mom's room." She didn't say *Hold on* or anything, I could tell she had just put me down in the beanbag chair or on the floor, probably next to her glasses.

She had John Lennon glasses like I did, but she wore hers. I thought of her parents' room with the African masks over the bed. Her parents went to the symphony a lot. My parents never did that when they were married. It was taking her a long time and my dad was going to be angry when they gave him the long-distance bill. "I found it," she said when she got back on the phone.

I had almost fallen asleep. It felt so normal talking to Julie Lender on the phone like that. I felt like I was sleeping over at her house.

"What date is on the front page?" I asked.

"Wednesday, September first," she said.

"Can you read me the Mistress Amber column?"

"Sure." She flipped around for a while and then found it. "Ew, this is so gross."

She read the whole thing. They were going to our Cape Cod house with the crossed oars over the doorway. She couldn't wait to sit on the porch with him and see whales and planets. He had bought her a stuffed animal. He was moving to Kyoto for a year and had asked her to go with him. She was sure he was going to propose as soon as his divorce was final.

"These people sound like idiots," Julie said. "I can't believe you're missing the first day of school. Maybe your parents want to avoid Labor Day traffic. Will you be there Wednesday?"

I was crying too hard to talk. "Maybe not Wednesday," I said finally. "But soon."

I thought of this dance performance I had seen on the last night of camp. Two kids played a bride and groom and two kids played the mother and father of the bride. Two counselors played an old grandma and grandpa, with talcum powder in their hair and brown lines drawn down from the corners of their mouths to look like jowls. Some younger campers played the grandchildren. They were arranged in a giant wooden picture frame, frozen to look like they were in a family portrait, wearing old-fashioned wedding clothes.

It had a Yiddish title, *The Ngendl,* or something like that, and the band was playing klezmer music I could have done without.

The bride and groom came to life, stepping out of the frame, and danced together. Then they stepped back into the frame and froze, and the grandmother and grandfather limped together in a gentle dance and returned to their frozen positions in the portrait. The bride danced with the father, and the groom danced with the mother, and then the children danced together, each pair always returning to their place in the frame. One dance after another, painfully slow and mesmerizing, and always returning back.

Finally, when it was over and the music stopped, I felt like I had watched an entire life pass by.

Each one of us had a frame we always returned to, no matter how many times we ventured out of it.

I had to get home to my brother.

If my father was at the Cape Cod house, he might not even be coming for me. I didn't know the number there. I could see the phone on the kitchen counter next to the radio. I could hear Ringo Starr playing, "*You walked out of my dreams, and into my car.*" And, although I did obviously get home eventually, I really don't remember how I got there. I don't remember anything about it.

ACKNOWLEDGEMENTS

For someone who has practiced her Academy Awards acceptance speech as often as I have, this should be easy. As you read this, please imagine me in a Norma Kamali gown, instead of weeping at my desk in the Writers Room.

I want to thank my most wonderful agent, Doug Stewart, who changed my life one summer by making this happen. Thank you also to Maria Bell at Sterling Lord, for wise guidance.

Thank you to my publisher Johnny Temple, whom I have admired with good reason from the early days of Akashic, and to Johanna Ingalls, Aaron Petrovich, and Holly Watson, for the love, care, and work you put into this book. Thank you for publishing bold books in these times. I could not be more honored or grateful to be in your company.

I am enormously grateful to my UK publisher Harriet Hirshman for bringing Swanna to England and making her feel at home, and everyone at Dead Ink Books, especially Nathan Connolly, Nathaniel Ashley, Bekkii Paley, and Emma Ewbank.

Thank you to the members of the Belle's Hell writing workshop: Kristina Libby, for my controversial US cover; Marilyn Simon Rothstein, for emergency editing, advice, and begging me not to go with that cover; Sam Garonzik, for giving me True Grit; Donna Brodie, for vast knowledge on all subjects and too many Friendsgivings to count; Andy Delaney, for talking to me about guns and cars; Leslie Ross, for teaching me the ways of the great state of Vermont; Maria Pramaggiore, for your powers of persuasion; Barbara Miller, Nicola Harrison, Meryl Branch-McTiernan, Joanie Leinwoll, Stephen Reynolds, and Stephanie Krikorian, for giving me courage by believing so much in this book; and Amy Lorowitz, Joi Brozek, Melanie Jennings, Matthew Ochs-Kaplan, Angela Dorn, Brandie Knox, Helen McNeil-Ashton, Sherri Rifkin, Suki Weston, and Lisa Smith, for your work and support. I love you all and I hope we will write together for decades.

Thank you to the brilliant playwright Lanie Robertson, for editing, encouragement, and treating me to fancy dinners. For camaraderie and a beautiful place to work, my thanks to everyone at the Writers Room. If you are a writer in New York, there is nowhere better.

I'd like to thank my trusted advisors, friends, and family—Kathleen Carter, Nicky Weinstock, Jeanine Cummins, Penny Arcade, Jen Cohn, Rob Siegel, Aaron Zimmerman, Arthur Nersesian, Jocelyn Anker, Tim Huggins, Craig Burke, Stefanie Teitelbaum, Liz Sherman, Anne Landsman, Laren Stover, Anne Ortelee, Robert Cook, Alan Rothstein, Chuck and Dee Clayman, Danny Hellman, Jeff Chenault, David Khinda, Ken Howe, Barbara Gaines, Denise Mullin, Gary Terracino, Rossella Galli, Liz Gibbons, Sandra Schwartz, Bebe Kranze, Karen Krents, Ruth Robinson, Eileen Abrahams, Lewis Schwartz, and Matthew Schwartz. My sons, Jasper Krents (who really does think I'll win an Oscar) and Shepherd Krents (who gave me most of Madding's lines), and my husband, Andrew Krents—every day and every minute I thank you.

BIOGRAPHY

Jennifer Belle is the best-selling author of four novels, *Going Down* (named best debut novel by *Entertainment Weekly*), *High Maintenance*, *Little Stalker*, and *The Seven Year Bitch*; and *Animal Stackers*, a picture book for children (illustrated by David McPhail). Her stories and essays have appeared in the *New York Times Magazine*, the *Wall Street Journal*, the *Independent*, *Harper's Bazaar*, *Cosmopolitan*, *Ms.*, *BlackBook*, the *New York Observer*, *Post Road*, *The Mirror*, and many anthologies.

About Dead Ink

Dead Ink is a publisher of bold new fiction based in Liverpool. We're an Arts Council England National Portfolio Organisation.

If you would like to keep up to date with what we're up to, check out our website and join our mailing list.

www.deadinkbooks.com | @deadinkbooks